Corey is a writer and student living in Australia. He grew up moving between states Queensland and Victoria constantly shifting. He would always be taking inspiration from the world around him. He began writing from a young age always creating short stories and other projects. He has a love of fantasy books that can be seen on his bookshelves filling his room which motivated to finish a book of his own. When he isn't writing he is studying and working toward universities. He is currently working on a multitude of other projects such as a sequel to *The Great Prophecy,* a collection of short stories and a murder mystery novel.

For Barak,

A home away from home that holds true to my heart.

Corey Tusak

HYLENIA: THE GREAT PROPHECY

AUSTIN MACAULEY PUBLISHERS®

LONDON * CAMBRIDGE * NEW YORK * SHARJAH

A CIP catalogue record for this title is available from the British Library.

ISBN 9781035816330 (Paperback)
ISBN 9781035816354 (ePub e-book)

www.austinmacauley.com

First Published 2024
Austin Macauley Publishers Ltd®
1 Canada Square
Canary Wharf
London
E14 5AA

When I first started writing this book all I had was an idea and an end goal. Juggling school, work and writing was challenging but the people around me made it all the easier. When I first pitched my idea Shaonika you encouraged me to pursue and would always motivate me to continue writing even if I had writers block and felt drained. Yishai, when we first wrote *'Adventures of Naribu'* in year one (a horribly written and illustrated book, may I add) was when I knew I wanted to become a writer. This story couldn't have been possible without you by my side, you were often my inspiration when I was writing Austin into some adventurous plot. Sofia, Trecia and Prayusi, my three musketeers, thanks for being great friends. You guys are such motivated hard workers, and your influence made me able to write something like this. Without you three I don't know where I would be right now, certainly not here. Once I had created the base of my story, after many long nights and hot chocolate breaks, Dina and Nathan, you two helped me structure my book and gave it direction. Your criticism was so important as it was influential in triggering my second draft.

A massive thank you to Andrew, for all your guidance in the industry, because without it, none of this would be possible. You helped me land a contract and your advice gave me the confidence to get this book published otherwise this would just be another long-forgotten story on my laptop.

Austin Macauley Publishers, I am beyond words that you saw my book and saw potential in it. I cannot even put to words how grateful I am that you guys took a chance on this book. Some kid from Melbourne, Australia with a dream that your team made possible. I can only thank everyone that helped behind the scenes to make this book a reality.

A huge thank you to my family. All four of my sisters Esmee, Tifferet, Samara and Zahara Kesem Tusak, you guys are my mini army supporting me and helping me by just being yourselves. There are so many ways that this book wouldn't have come to fruition but without my parents, Ada and Paul, there would be no book at all. You guys never had any doubt and put all your faith in me that this would be the next big hit. You supported all my dreams and accomplishments and stood by me every step of the way.

There have been so many versions of *Hylenia; The Great Prophecy* but I am proud to present this version to all of you. Thank you to every one of you who has picked up this book and fallen in love with the hidden world of Hylenia and read long enough to get to this point. Without you guys I wouldn't be able to do what I love most in this world, write.

Table of Contents

MAP TO HYLENIA
Fortune Lake
Grobs
West Brook
Louive
Golden Oak Tree
Brook
Mortamic
Troll Village
Cliffsmout
School
Little Grob
N
W
E
S

Prologue

It was just my mum and me Everything seemed normal; life was so uncomplicated up until six months ago. My family lived in a small town called Mertamic. It was peaceful. It was one of those towns where everyone knew each other. The town was perfect, and everything was cheerful. You could always hear birds chirping, no matter what part of town you were in. It was very secluded from the rest of Hylenia; it was a riverside town surrounded by the deep ancient forest. Our house was along the Mertamica River, so we got the best view of the waters and even Fortune Lake if you had binoculars. Our two-storey white and blue-coloured house had a basic red-tiled roof that Ethan, my friend, and I would always climb on, even though it was dangerous. The tiles would always fall, but we didn't care. The inside of the house was messy but still felt cosy; it always smelt of some kind of natural incense. My dad, for as long as I can remember, had always been a soldier. He wasn't at home much. He missed most of my birthdays, but he never forgot to write a birthday card. They mean the most to me, I still have each one of them displayed in my room. He worked for the AOS, an organisation founded under the army umbrella as a special operation to keep tabs on an internal terrorist organisation. That was until his disappearance six months ago. He left without any warning, and no one has any idea where he might have gone. We were used to this sort of behaviour; it came with the job, but it had never extended to this length of time. I often saw my mum fidgeting with her wedding ring. Although she didn't show it much, she missed him, but she always kept a brave face on. She had this determination that soon he would send a card and that everything was all still under control. I did not. I was often doubtful; I heard all the rumours that spread around town about my dad. There wasn't much I could do except listen. When I was younger and my dad was more involved, my life seemed happier. I always had my friends over, but lately, all my friends were transferring out and leaving for high school. There wasn't any high school in Mertamic; it was too small, and the closest school was a forty-minute drive away. So eventually, most kids my age transferred out and left for boarding schools across the island; it was very common. I had tried home-schooling for my freshman year, but it was lonely. The town felt empty except for Irora, who had also chosen to home-school the past year. This school year was just about to begin, and she had even chosen to transfer to one of the most prestigious schools in the country. She had begged me to join her, but I was scared to leave the only home I had ever known and leave my mum. I'm just your average guy: brown eyes, blonde hair, 5'8"; my mum named me Austin because she said I reminded her of some TV show she watched as a kid. The kid from Mertamic, alone and lost. The world is still sort of a mystery to me; so much uncharted territory that maybe my dad is still out there somewhere I lay awake at night thinking about it. The island that I live on is in the middle of the Bermuda Triangle; it's the only safe space for anyone who isn't completely 'normal'. It is unknown to the human species, but for the few that randomly chart their way onto the island never go back. Usually, there are powerful barriers separating the two worlds apart, but sometimes creatures seem to slip through the weak spots and can get in or out. I have never gone out of Mertamic, not to even think about crossing the boundaries of Hylenia. It was forbidden unless you had permission from the Council of Justice, but they hardly ever let anyone out. It kept the peace and made everything run smoothly, so the myths stayed myths.

Chapter 1
Escape

"Ten years have passed, Mum!" screamed a boy. "I deserve answers!" The newly 16-year-old boy paid no attention to the doorbell. His mum, Natalie, seemed buried in sorrow.

"I'm sorry, but what's done is done. You will leave tomorrow for Westbrook Academy of the Arts," Austin heard his mum say. 'Arts', as if it had a mysterious meaning. "It's not up for negotiation, you will leave and have a better life in the new world. You WON'T stay here!" Austin never heard his mum this sure of anything. Natalie, her brown eyes emotional much like her son's, got up and turned to answer the door, her long dark hair following her like a cape.

"Hi!" exclaimed a man who Austin had never seen before. This was unusual since Austin lived in a really small town excluded from the main world. "I have a letter for a Mr Bolden," the man continued. Austin took the letter from the man and realised it came from the one and only Westbrook Academy of the Arts. Why did this place keep on coming up everywhere Austin went? "Well, I've got many letters to deliver, the busiest time of year; after all, it is the beginning of the school year." The man was fully dressed in a blue jumpsuit with the name Mike stitched on to his chest. "I hope to see you soon," the man said as he left for his delivery bike. He felt so angry, something seemed to take over. He couldn't go to this school, not this one. Austin left his mom standing in the corridor and left for his room. As he leapt up the stairs, two at a time he paused feeling her eyes on his back. He knew that she wanted the best for him but he couldn't tell her the real reason he couldn't go. He entered his room it was the same as how he left it. This has been his room for as long as he could remember. The minimal features the wooden desk, the unpolished furnishings. He had been contemplating leaving home to go to Hylenia, to start fresh with his girlfriend but now that seemed like the furthest thing from possible.

The boy glanced at the birthday cards displayed on a shelf; his 16th birthday card was missing. Austin loved his mum, but he couldn't go to that school; it would feel like a betrayal. He didn't even want to go to a magic-oriented school. Ninety-five percent of schools in Hylenia taught general subjects like math and English, much like the rest of the world, but for those who chose to, there was another option: schools designed to teach about the history and uses of magic as well as how to use it. These sorts of schools only opened up from grade nine, and Austin was going to start grade ten; he would already be so far behind in the curriculum. He knew his dad would've wanted him to go to this school; he was an old collegian. Since his dad had gone missing, his mother had become more secretive, like she knew something. With all the rumours going around, Austin just wanted an explanation. His mum knocked on his door, then a moment later, she entered without an invitation. Natalie joined Austin, sitting on his plain bed next to him. They shared a moment of sympathetic silence between themselves. "Tell me the rumours aren't true, Mum. Tell me he wasn't really a spy," the boy pleaded.

"I don't know, Austin." She left the room for a second and returned with a gift-wrapped box in her hand. "A late birthday gift." She handed it to Austin; it wasn't too heavy. He unwrapped the box methodically, and underneath was the newest model of the 'magician's compass'. He always saw his favourite local explorers use them on TV; it was a must-have for the outdoors. It worked like a regular compass but also measured the weather, calculated coordinates and could identify samples of elements and plants. Austin loved the outdoors since he was a kid and always planned camping trips with his father, but they never went; there was always something stopping them. Nonetheless, Austin loved to dream; he would play outside and mimic the explorers on TV.

"Thanks, Mum," he said as he gave her a hug.

"You're welcome, darlin'. Please think it over. The school, I mean; we have to leave tomorrow morning if we are going to make it," she said. There was a plan already forming in Austin's head; he had to escape. He started to pack up his room, one thing at a time. He stopped when he got to the birthday cards.

"I will make you proud," Austin said to himself. He stared at some of the only family photos they had. It showed a young Austin, no older than six, trying to get away while his father had caught up to him. Austin wore a huge smile with chocolate smeared all over his face. A second photo, more tame, he was about eight in this one and in between both his parents on some hill; they both held

Austin's hands while they faced away from the sunset. A flash of regret struck Austin, but he hurriedly finished packing up and jump-starting his new magic GPS.

* * * * * * * * * * *

Austin felt like he had been running forever, his blonde hair all muddy in this foggy forest. He couldn't see further than a few feet in front of him; everything just seemed to blur. Was he going crazy, or did he hear something following him? Every now and then, a branch cracked, which Austin knew he didn't step on. Was this the right thing to do, runaway, at least till the school year started. Stay with his uncle. Live off the grid for a bit so he could avoid going to that school. His nerves were already at an all-time high before he thought he was being followed. Austin had started the hike about an hour ago at 11:00 pm. It was roughly midnight now. The weather had changed to an ominous murky haze about half an hour ago; that's when he had initially heard the voices. They were approaching him fast, but Austin managed to outrun them. *Damn it, this was such a stupid decision,* Austin thought to himself. He knew about the recent kidnappings in Hylenia, but he always thought that crime was always so far away from Mertamic; nothing ever happened near this area. Every so often, just as Austin started to slow down, he saw a black figure from the corner of his eye. Was he hallucinating and just imagining things, or was he really in danger? Austin's mind started to race. *My mum is going to find the note I left on my bed in the morning. She is going to think I am just being stupid, but she won't think to send anyone out to search for me if I actually go missing.* Austin recalled the note he left on the bed:

Sorry, Mum, but you left me no choice. I can't go to Westbrook Academy. It's where Irora wanted to go, and I feel like a traitor if I go there when she can't. I just want a normal life at a normal school, and I don't want to be far away from you. I want to just go to the school in the next town over. At least I already know some people there. I have left for a week-long camping trip. I have all the supplies I need and know what to do in case of an emergency. I will be fine. I just need to clear my head. We can talk things over once I get back; don't worry about me.

I love you.

Most kidnapping cases are solved within the first 72 hours. I won't have that chance to be found. Austin started to panic. Everything seemed to pause. Austin stopped running. *No, I'm not going to let it happen again. I just won't.* The night turned silent except for the occasional owl and the chirping of insects. Austin couldn't continue for that much longer; his back ached under the weight of the bag. Austin stumbled into a clearing. He began to feel a sudden heat come on and a blurry blaze through the fog. He could smell it before he could see it clearly. He crept closer towards the heat; it was a pyre. The vicious crackling of the fire pierced through the silent night. Who had set it up? He thought of that too late as he felt something jab into his neck, then he was pushed to the ground, and his vision went dark.

****

He was barraged with dreams that showed him and Irora at a carnival. Wait, this wasn't a vision; it was a flashback. He continued to watch. He couldn't move. Both Austin and Irora were on a Ferris wheel, where they shared cotton candy while the ride spun around and around as the sun set into the distance. Austin finally felt relaxed, but then the vision changed to him and his dad playing together in the backyard. Life was so simple back then. The grass was as green as can be, and the house was in perfect shape; it almost looked like something out of a magazine. All his thoughts blurred into the darkness…

Chapter 2
Rediscovered

Think, Austin, the student thought to himself. He had binds on his arms, which held him upright against a tree. All he could see was a seemingly endless forest now that the fog had cleared up. *This stuff only happens in movies,* Austin thought to himself, *being tied up to a tree in the middle of a forest.* He searched his surroundings for immediate danger or anything he could use to escape, but there was nothing. His neck throbbed from where he was injected, and he had a massive headache. Austin tried to wriggle his hands out of the ropes, but the knots were tight. He felt like a guinea pig, forced to watch the sun set. *How long was I out?* The day already had passed. He thought about how if he had stuck with his mum, he would've already been at Westbrook Academy of the Arts by now. It was officially the first day of the year. His consciousness seemed to be slipping in and out of focus.

"Austin," whispered a mysterious girl. Austin found himself in some sort of laboratory, trapped by three walls around him.

"This can't be real! This already happened!" screamed Austin. He was lying down on a plain bed, looking towards a glass window when he saw a girl. "Irora?" *But that's impossible,* he thought to himself. "You're dead!" Austin's hallucination ceased for a brief moment. He was slapped into focus and yet again punctured by some mysterious injection. He finally saw his kidnapper's face: a troll. Austin thought he would never live to see one in person. The troll was short and blue; he wasn't ugly like in all the movies that Austin had seen. The man seemed well dressed and proper; the way he presented himself gave off some sort of authority figure.

"The serum is still working, huh? Strong stuff," the troll said, but not to Austin. Was he talking to himself?

"Do you care to tell me who you are and why you have come here?" questioned the troll. Austin was too stunned to answer.

"Uhhh," he mumbled, "I'm just out on a camping trip."

"Your name," the troll stated sternly.

"Austin Bolden." Austin had obviously said something right because the troll's eyes lit up.

"As in the son of Tony Bolden?" The troll couldn't keep his excitement a secret.

"Yeah, that's my old man," Austin said, obviously not thrilled to be recognised in his father's shadow usually that came with a lot of disapproval. The troll quickly untied Austin and turned him around to show him the wondrous city of trolls. *So I was given the view of endless trees when right behind me was a small city of trolls. Great.* Austin was on the edge of a cliff, looking down on the multiple caves and caverns that housed many families of trolls. Austin could see the colourful and vibrant centre of the village, which was filled with markets of all kinds and stretched out for miles. The place was so beautiful, and the scene was so unique. The houses all looked like oversized ceramics with large domed roofs. Flags were strung from house to house. The path was made out of dusty gravel. Austin was in awe taking it all in.

"I am so sorry about the precaution; we have high security alert within these parts of the woods. With all the kidnappings going around, you can never be too careful. Plus, you really should have announced yourself at the forest border and can't just wander in like that." The troll had a disappointed look.

"I really didn't mean to wander in. Where exactly am I?"

"Well, Troll Village, of course! I am the troll to ask. After all, I am the mayor of this place," the troll said triumphantly.

"But wait, that's not possible. I couldn't have gotten that far since Mertamic. I wasn't even meant to be going in this direction," Austin said with confusion showing on his face. The drugs still in his system were making his brain all fuzzy. He went to check on his new GPS device, and sure enough, it proved the troll's story. The troll gave him a concerned look. The boy's look of confusion did not cease, he was hiking toward his uncle's house out in the woods in the opposite direction. How did he end up here? Austin's mind had been playing overdrive ever since he thought he was hearing people following him. Maybe it was paranoia but then being kidnapped and held prisoner even if it was briefly now playing too much on Austin's mind. He needed space, he felt a heaviness in his chest.

"With the fog, it must be very easy to get lost, son." Eager to change the topic, the troll continued, "You know, your father had a big part in creating this. He and I worked together to unite both of our worlds, but…long story short, your father was not in the good graces of 'The Other Side', or as the youngsters say, OS."

"What's that supposed to mean?" Austin was now more curious than ever to understand his family's history.

"Your mother would not want me to tell you." He paused. "There are plenty of other adventure-packed stories I could tell you about what I and your father went through. Like how we fought together to stop the Kraken from awakening." The troll seemed very proud of himself. "I am Mr Trolt; your father and I were very close associates." *Maybe my father wasn't what everyone claimed him to be,* he thought to himself. The troll went on to explain how he and Tony were a part of the same squadron that belonged to the A.O.S.S., the Anti Other Side Society, but the rumour that Austin had heard around was now confirmed. His father was blamed for being a spy among the ranks.

"I was one of the only people that continued to stand by him until he was discharged. Your father said he was being framed and that the rat was actually Hammond Hurt, our squad leader at the time. Dark unsocial fellow that man was, but since last year, he has retired from the force. Sorry if I am rambling on a bit."

What Mr Trolt said had only brought up a dozen more questions. *How have I never heard of this before? Why hasn't anyone mentioned Mr Trolt before if he was so close to my dad? Who else have my parents never told me about? If my dad is not in the A.O.S.S. anymore, where is he?*

"You aren't actually; it is actually the most insight I have ever heard about my father."

"Your father was a good man, dedicated to his work," Mr Trolt said. "You know you look exactly like him." Austin didn't respond.

"This land owes your father a great debt. He was the one who saved this land from just being another vantage point for 'The Other Side'. He redeemed himself in his own rediscovery; he went on a path to self-righteousness to show the AOSS that he was not the bad guy." Mr Trolt scourged through his pockets to take out something that looked like a photograph. The photograph showed Mr Trolt and Tony together right where Austin and Mr Trolt were standing, on the edge of the cliff with the whole troll city at their backs. His dad almost looked like an explorer with the outfit that he had on: beige baggy pants, a button-up shirt, one of those floppy hats and his round glasses. *I didn't know my dad needed glasses.* Austin's thoughts drifted off; there was still so much that Austin didn't know. "I want you to remember your father in a more positive light. He deserves that. Please keep this photo. It's one of the latest photos before he went"—Mr Trolt thought about his next words carefully—"missing."

"Thank you." Although Austin was grateful for all the new information, he had still not quite forgiven the troll for drugging and kidnapping them, even if it was partly his fault. Austin just felt uneasy; he needed to get going. He suddenly felt extremely homesick, just a kid wanting to stay home. This experience has been completely random and dangerous. He hated himself for even leaving he should've just accepted going to a new school. Like his mom said it was most likely for the best.

"I really must leave now. Do you have my backpack?"

"Julian!" A troll appeared from behind a tree with all of Austin's belongings. *How had I not noticed the young troll?* Mr Trolt answered as if he knew what Austin was thinking.

"Trolls are masters of disguise." Austin obviously looked puzzled. He took his belongings and packed up ready to leave. Only problem he had no idea how to get back to the main road. "Before I leave do you know the easiest way to get to Westbrook?" Austin said.

The troll gave him a slight smile, "It's about a one days hike in that direction to get you to the main road. No roads in or out of our village. Do be careful." He sensed the confused fear in Austin's eyes. "This area is very dangerous at night with all the nocturnal animals roaming around, so you should be careful." Austin waited for the troll to break character as if that was some joke but the punchline never came. The boy thanked the troll and left in the direction he was instructed too.

∗∗∗∗∗∗∗∗∗∗∗

His father was not only a special operative army personnel but a secret agent who managed to save a whole city without Austin knowing. He felt as if he was always kept in the dark about who his family really was. He really was living under a rock, just one called Mertamic. No, Mertamic was more like a prison cut off from the rest of the world. The sky was now dark, and he remembered something that Mr Trolt had said: "This area is very dangerous at night with all the nocturnal animals roaming around." Austin decided to set up camp and would continue his journey in the morning. The trees seemed restless around him as if they were about to come to life and crush his small campsite. His little orange tent would be nothing against an actual tree deity. He had read a lot about mythological creatures as a kid. He used to have a whole book with all the creatures and wonders in the universe called 'The Hidden Wonders of Creation'. In that book, there was a section on living trees, although most of the tales are conflicted on the details. Some say that the trees are only connected to a tree spirit, while others say that they are a race of creatures without a human form. Whatever the case, the book stated many warnings about some of these creatures. They could be very dangerous to outsiders because they are very territorial about where their roots are planted. Austin had had enough of being kidnapped for one day though. Austin felt restless, like he would never fall asleep, but slowly, he drifted into another reality where all the stars faded while his dream came into focus; it showed his mother back at his family house. "Where is he?" she said as she paced the halls of their family home. She was talking to a man who Austin vaguely recognised. *Why does he look so familiar?*

"He could be going to the academy," the man said bluntly. Austin hated to see his mum act this frantic.

"No, he wouldn't; that is the last place he would go," his mum spat out.

"Just in case, I will check it out; you know, that is where it all started." The man spoke with no tone. Austin's mum paced the halls so quickly that she tipped over a vase and it crashed. That vase was a family relic, an heirloom; his mum cherished that vase. Austin felt tinged with guilt knowing he was the cause of all this. The scene changed; now it was Julian, the troll he had just met. Julian seemed scared; he was surrounded by darkness with a single red flashing light in the corner of a cold concrete room.

"Julian!" a voice boomed over an intercom. The poor troll was so scared; he had some papers in his hand. It read 'confidential' in a red stand. *What has the troll got himself into?* Austin woke up to crickets and sunlight, lots and lots of sunlight. *What just happened? Was that all fantasy, or was that real? Did I just dream of what was happening in real life?* He pushed his thoughts aside while he packed up the campsite. He slipped out his phone, no service. He needed to call his mom once he got back to civilisation. He yet again cursed this dumb idea of running away though in theory it did sound good.

The landscape was very mountainous; it made for a strategic placement for the troll's village. Although it was just as secluded, much like Mertamic. It had one dust path leading down, which Austin followed; not an easy hike, but it was a magical morning with amazing weather. Austin could see the city of Westbrook in the vast distance; it seemed impossible that Austin would ever get there. Subconsciously, Austin knew he had made a decision and convinced himself he was just going to tour the school. Still, he felt guilty as he made his way down the mountain. He had been travelling for a few hours and took the route that Mr Trolt suggested. Once down from the mountain, there was a hiker's path through an open part of the forest. Austin was glad he could knock going on a survival hike off his bucket list, but he was still weary of the forest. Mr Trolt warned him of the dangerous creatures in the forest; it was all getting into Austin's head. *How have I even made it this far?* It still bothered Austin, it was a day's hike at best to Troll Village, and he had made it in a mere six hours. Austin's mind was still racing with questions, but he pushed everything aside trying to get over this whole crazy experience and decided to daydream. He travelled back to the night when everything went wrong. The port of Mertamic was a serene place full of music and character. With the sun setting, it was only Irora and Austin at the port. Mertamic seemed silent, except for the waves crashing down on the jagged rocks as the smooth Italian music came from a distant café. There was a soft breeze coming in from the sea. Irora's platinum blonde hair flew into her face, and the couple laughed. Austin leaned towards Irora since she felt cold, so cold that the colour drained from her face as she collapsed. Austin noticed a dart in her neck. "What?" But his question was answered as soon as he said it. Two men approached the port, and they did not look friendly. The first man was a tall, bald man with bushy eyebrows, which only drew more attention to his death-filled eyes. Both he and the other man were dressed completely in black, but the other man was completely covered like an executioner. The second looked more Austin's size and held a gun and pointed it towards Austin, but the first man shook his head. Austin felt helpless on his knees grasping Irora, but it was no use, the men were stronger than him and carried Irora away. Austin closed his eyes and waited for a gunshot, which never came. Austin opened his eyes, only to see Irora being carried out of sight. The last thing Austin saw before completely losing consciousness was the symbol on the men's backs; it was a circle divided into three different sectors: red, black and blue.

Austin remembered that night clearly; it was his last memory of her. He knew she had been one to cause trouble with the police but never thought it would ever endanger her. He once visited her in the Mertamic cells; she was there for shoplifting and only for a few days. She ultimately got community service instead. Still, she looked so guilty; it was a side to her that Austin almost never saw. Austin never really knew what happened to her; the police investigation concluded their investigation saying it was gang violence and that she had got in with the wrong crowd, but Austin knew that wasn't true; there was more to it. She wasn't the type of girl who would risk it all and be involved with gangs; she had too many hopes and aspirations. She wanted to go to Westbrook Academy and after that study to be a veterinarian. She had a big dream of saving all the animals in the world and was deeply concerned about endangered species. Although she wasn't too popular in middle school, she always had a few friends and was a passionate learner. She was really going somewhere. Now Austin was fulfilling her dreams by going to her preferred school. Going hiking in forests, he wished she was here to join him. Everything reminded him of her. His past few months have been full of controversy and grief. He knew it wasn't just him. People all over the island were going missing and here he was walking in the forest alone. Even the trolls seemed a bit hostile, usually a species known to be very welcoming. It felt wrong. Austin had heard many stories coming from that school: abductions and recent break-ins. In spite of all that, it was where Irora wanted to go. It had the best resources for her to get into a foreign country's university. Austin's instincts told him that that was where he needed to go. Maybe the reason she was abducted was connected to that school. Austin was convinced it was and now more than ever was determined to go. The hiking trail came to an end after a few hours, and Austin was again at the same dusty road. Apparently, the hike trail was a shortcut, but it felt like Austin hadn't made any progress. Everything looked the same. The road looked like it hadn't been used in a decade. Austin checked his GPS and continued Eastbound to Westbrook, ironic. His phone still had no service and the guilt kept creeping in on him about leaving on his own to Westbrook. The day progressively got more and more hot, the sun beating down on Austin's back, heavy with all his possessions. To keep himself entertained, Austin made a mental note of all the different species of birds, animals, insects and even plants he came across. As a kid, Austin was a nerd about all things nature; that was one thing he had in common with Irora but also his old best friend Ethan. They would always camp out in tents in their backyards and study some of Austin's dad's nature encyclopaedia set. He could pretty much identify every species of plants, animals and birds. So far, on his list was a forest of redwood trees, a couple of different types of fern, a desert horned lizard, a pair of antelopes, woodpeckers, various types of chickadee birds and some ibis. Nothing too special that was until he saw it, a unicorn-like creature except about three times the size of a horse. It was multicoloured almost like an opal colour scheme with one rough horn jutting out from its head. It was a majestic creature but definitely not harmless. It had rows of sharp teeth and was so big. The creature also had two massive wings tucked into its side almost blending in. *Can it really support its own weight on those wings?* Austin wondered. It hadn't noticed Austin yet; it was grazing on some grass. Austin genuinely thought that the creature was fictional or at least extinct; that was how rare they were. All sorts of cultures had their own version of the creature, but this one most resembled a Tachash from Jewish mythology. Austin slowly walked towards it, not meaning to cause any alarm. It probably wasn't too smart to go near the deadly creature, but it was impossible not to. Austin acted on his spontaneous tendency. There was a section on them in 'The Hidden Wonders of Creation', the book Austin received as a gift from his father. Austin tried to recall any details. He crept closer to the area the creature lay in. *Rumoured to be extinct, opal-coloured coat of fur, huge wings, razor-sharp teeth, large frame, four-legged mammal, natural horn extending out of their foreheads. They are herbivores. Am I missing anything?* Austin thought to himself. As Austin approached, he stepped on a branch, which cracked immediately giving his position away. The animal turned its head quickly and as a response blew smoke out of its nose. *Damn, they are territorial and definitely not friendly when approached.* It jumped to its feet with incredible balance and ran through the trees towards the hills with poise and elegance. It was incredibly quick for a creature of its size. Austin ran after the one-horned wonder and finally saw it by a waterfall, which led to a small pond. It laid down on a boulder on the edge of the pond. Fish swam inside the water, which was so clear, all the fish made the pond look like a kaleidoscope. 'Wow' was the only word Austin could manage as he took in the scene. He crept closer to the Tachash until it noticed him again. He put his hands up in the air as if he were surrendering. Apparently, the creature saw that as a sign of attack. *Aren't unicorns supposed to be peaceful and stuff?*

Austin thought to himself as the creature charged at him. He fled the scene, but the Tachash was still on his tail. He ran all the way to the side of a very steep hill. *No way I can climb down that,* Austin thought, but the horned creature gave him no choice; it pushed him down the hill with its giant head. Austin was just grateful he wasn't skewered on the horn. Austin sat up groggily; his vision was in doubles. No, wait, there was a second beast closing in on him. He had nothing to protect himself; his machete was stuck in his backpack, which was lost somewhere on his fall. He had to resort to his voice. "Look, I don't mean any harm. I am just trying to get to Westbrook." Surprisingly, the Tachashes seemed like they understood. Austin reached into his pocket, and the unicorn-like creatures whined incredibly loudly. It was terrifying. Austin was half a metre from the sharp teeth. The second one was a bit smaller than the first, but not by much. Austin pulled his hand out and held some leftover trail mix he had in his pocket. The original creature sniffed his hand and then got bored of Austin and flew off. The second one, a bit smaller in size, inched forward, intrigued. The food Austin held in his hands wasn't much compared to the size of the creature. The creature's glossy opal-coloured coat shined in the sunlight streaming in from between the trees. This one didn't seem so aggressive or scared; it actually calmed Austin down. The creature ate all the food gently from Austin's hand, a tickly feeling for Austin, but he didn't dare flinch, not while the creature had upward of 100 razor-sharp teeth. Once it was done eating, the creature put its head down, and Austin took that as a sign to get on its back. "One minute," he said. It was probably rude to leave a Tachash waiting, but he left to find his backpack. He found it, and thankfully, all the items were still intact. When he returned, the creature was still there waiting for him. When it saw him, it whined as if to say, "Took ya long enough." The creature once again laid down to let Austin on. This was all so surreal for Austin. He felt he had some sort of connection to the creature like two bodies one mind. Looking at every feature of the Tachash it really was something to take in. Austin thought about his dad and how much he would freak if he was what Austin was seeing now. He managed to get on top. Even once the creature was lying down, it was still quite tall. As soon as Austin was on, it immediately took off. "I think I'm going to call you, Bob," Austin laughed, but the creature didn't seem to be impressed. The creature had so much speed and force in its flight, but it was still very balanced. Austin didn't feel like he would fall, but he still had so much adrenaline rushing through him. They flew above the clouds for what seemed like hours. He wished he could stay up there; he was riding a real unicorn. How the creature understood him or let him ride was still beyond him. Austin dug his hands deep into the fur gripping for dear life. His hands going slightly numb. The wind felt like numerous slaps to the face. Yet Austin was enjoying every second of it. Bob was going in the exact direction Austin needed and for once in the past twenty-four hours things were finally starting to look up.

The unicorn navigated himself and took Austin to the boundaries of the city. Austin saw the city of Westbrook out in front of him; it was so big that you could probably fit about 100 Mertamics in it. They landed on the ground, just outside the outer walls. The creature whined in protest. Austin fished through his bag and gave the rest of the trail mix to his newfound friend. Before you could say 'unicorn', the creature took off out and shot into the sky. Austin was still so shocked that he gazed up into the sky to see if it would return, but it didn't.

Chapter 3
The New World

Austin stood at the Westbrook city border, one of the most secure borders in the world; the city was built like a fortress, protecting its citizens, especially the high-ranking government officials. Westbrook was the capital of Hylenia and had the unofficial title 'capital of magic'. From what Austin knew from school, the city was split into two parts: the ancient coastal side, 'Brook', as the locals called it and was originally known for its massive ports and explorations and the new side, designed like a hexagon with skyscrapers, parks and all sorts of revolutionary architecture. The city pretty much had a clear divide between the two, but both were within the city walls, which towered over him. It was at least six storeys high. The walls were thick and made completely of cement. Although all that was just a show, there was an entire forcefield like a bubble that surrounded the city and prevented unwanted flights and people trying to get over the wall. There were five checkpoints to enter, but for that you needed a student visa or some other credentials to enter, and unfortunately, Austin left that at home and was out of time. The boy needed to make it to the school and register today because at the end of the day registration would be closed till semester two. He didn't want to have to stay back. He felt so stupid; he should have just listened to his mum. Austin pulled out his phone and texted an old friend who might just have a way around it.

****

It took 15 minutes for Ethan to respond and another 30 for Ethan to finally reach Austin at the destination that he had sent. It was a service gate; not another person was in sight till Ethan emerged from the automatic cement door. There was a keypad on one side, but apart from that, if you didn't know that the door was here, you would walk right past it as it was so camouflaged into the rest of the structure. "Ethan!" Austin started walking towards his old friend. Ethan was 16 years old; they grew up together in Mertamic. He was a short, pale kid, but he seemed a lot older than 16. He had this persona of an older, more mature person; he too had been raising himself since his parents' disappearance. Ethan's parents mysteriously went missing a year ago. He had lived with Austin for a bit and then was taken into childcare, but he said it didn't suit him and ran away a few months ago. He had moved to Westbrook and lived off the grid and under the radar of the government. Until he was 18 he wasn't legally allowed to live on his own. Austin missed the kid that Ethan used to be. Austin helped him through everything, he knew what Ethan was going through, he knew why Ethan chose to run away. The childcare system was no pretty place. Austin used to visit him in the 'care facilities' which is what they called them. It was the opposite of that. Filled with rough kids and people who only cared about their next paycheck. Each time Austin visited he saw how much Ethan had adapted, changed, becoming more resilient. Crafty even, so when he ran away, there was strategy behind it, planning. Avoiding cameras or anyone that might ask questions. So he knew how to get in and out without being detected. Ethan looked very different from the last time Austin had seen him. The boy wore a plain black t-shirt with a black leather jacket on top and a pair of black jeans. Ethan looked very scruffy, like he had just woken up; his dark hair was very shaggy. The boy fidgeted with one of his many rings. He had been living in a small apartment; his parents left him with quite a bit of money, but most of it was tied up until Ethan turned 18, so he had been fending for himself for quite a while. Austin always felt so sympathetic, like he should have helped Ethan more, but he and his mum did what they could. Ethan was the sort of person who never wanted to accept help, even when he needed it. The pair could really relate to each other. Austin's dad went missing at the same time as Ethan's parents. It had brought them closer together. Looking at Ethan now it brought back all these memories. It also felt strange feeling how different they were now.

"Hey, sorry I'm late," Ethan said with a weak smile. "Irora finally got you to go with her to that school, huh?" Ethan elbowed Austin playfully. Austin was silent, completely forgetting that Ethan didn't know. Why would he? Irora used to be Ethan's friend as well, not that Ethan had many; he had never quite fit in with the Mertamic crowd. He was always a bit shy and socially awkward and more the smart type. Not many people talked to him, but Irora was always nice to everyone, no matter what, and that's what Austin really loved about her. She was a good person. Who saw the good in everyone. Even oblivious to the bad.

"Hi." Austin paused for a second. He looked at the ground. Ethan could already tell something was wrong, but he was patient with Austin. "Irora…" Austin started, but he didn't know how to finish; he himself didn't really know what happened. "She went missing six months ago. I should have told you."

"Oh." Ethan hugged Austin. "I'm so sorry."

"I am too."

The two held the embrace for a few seconds, and then Ethan broke it off, there was this awkward tension. The two didn't know what to say to each other. They hadn't seen one another in so long it was weird to be in person. They both stood there awkwardly without saying a word for a few moments until Ethan nodded his head and led Austin into the security tunnel. Ethan scanned a security card and typed something into the keypad, and they shut the door behind them.

****

The corridor was very eerie, much like what Austin had expected—a bit claustrophobic and poorly lit by flickering fluorescent LED lights hanging from the ceiling. The tunnel clearly doubled as a fire escape route from the city, with emergency and fire signs everywhere. The one good thing about fire safety exits is that the doors can't be locked. A minute into the walk Austin spoke trying to break the silence. "So, what have you been up to recently?"

"You know, life." Ethan's voice faltered; he looked as if he wanted to say something but chose against it. Austin felt as if everyone these days was just more held back after all the recent attacks.

"How's Aimee?" Austin asked. Aimee was Ethan's younger sister; she was three years younger than him, and she was placed in a children's refuge centre in Westbrook, which was why Ethan decided to move here. Into the apartment to stay closer to her.

"Don't talk?" Ethan said, but for some reason, Austin didn't think it was because of his question but something else. The sound of footsteps was quiet in the distance, but they were approaching. The escape route was only a one-way tunnel, how could they get through without being spotted? Ethan gestured towards the ceiling.

31

"I'm not Spider-Man. I can't just crawl up to the ceiling." But as soon as Austin whispered that, he realised what Ethan was trying to communicate—the air vents.

"Hoist me up," Ethan said in a very eager tone. Ethan was unscrewing the first few screws before they were within earshot of the two men. Finally, all the screws were undone, and Ethan pulled himself through right before pulling up Austin and replacing the screen. It was some heavy duty pumps that must've been part of the underground system that circulates around the city.

"Do you always carry a screwdriver?" Austin questioned, only to be shushed. Austin felt as if he were back at the Mertamic Library, with the local librarian hushing them to be quiet. *Why did you always have to be so quiet in a library anyway?* That memory was cut short when the two men were right under the air vents, with Ethan and Austin right above them; they were two janitors wearing grease-stained blue jumpsuits. The first man spoke.

"Did you hear what happened at Westbrook College?" the first man asked; he was a lot more tanner than the other janitor.

"What, John?" the second man said, obviously exhausted by the first man.

"They let out that guy from prison. You know, the one that was in the news all the time? He almost pulled off the biggest school robbery Westbrook has ever seen! Well, here's the twist: they are employing that same guy as the new science teacher to replace that old crone, Professor Tentable. What was his name again, the vigilante?" John asked.

"Phillip?" the second man answered, unsure of himself. Both men stopped right under the air vents and didn't seem to be going anywhere in a hurry. *Oh no. They're not going to check up here, are they?* Austin thought to himself.

"Yes, that was it, JOHN," the first John claimed. "Anyway, I hear Philip is now supposedly working for the OS," John gossiped. At that moment, a few things happened at once: a pipe burst about a kilometre away from them, the way Austin and his old friend had come from, an alarm shook the cavern, which then caused the screen to fall down, but apparently, the janitors hadn't noticed. Whilst more voices came rushing down the dark corridor, they came at a run, their metal boots making loud thuds and echoing through the hall. Ethan silently cursed to himself, but it was in a language Austin had never heard of before, but the way Ethan said it, Austin knew it was a curse.

"Intruders!" screamed a security guard.

"We have had a breach in the exterior walls; you two come with us." A second security guard pointed to the janitors.

"But we're just the janitors," stated the first John.

"You can't do this!" screamed the second one. "Even we janitors have rights, you know!" Both men were outraged, but the cool, collected voice of the security guard eased them.

"Be calm; all we are going to do is take you in for questioning. You're coming with us." The security guard made it obvious that there was no room for a rebuttal. All four men walked away, the burst pipe still audible from the distance. Soon it was just Ethan and Austin left, but they waited 10 minutes just to be sure they were alone before they got down.

"I must've forgotten to disable the alarm. I'm sorry." Ethan was clearly distraught.

"It's not all that bad. We didn't get caught; you have nothing to be sorry for." Even Austin didn't believe himself.

"No, it's not. I put both our lives in jeopardy," Ethan said.

"Look, we're getting out of here together; we could even both go to Westbrook Academy of the Arts together." Austin made it a show by putting on a proper British voice when he said the school's name. Ethan smiled in response. They walked a bit faster, now hoping not to get caught. On the way out, Austin noticed a crumpled pamphlet on the floor that had been walked all over, but he still picked it up. It read, 'Westbrook, the land where all your dreams come true'. "I sure hope so," Austin whispered to himself.

"What was that?" Ethan asked, his voice still a little shaky.

"Aha, nothing."

Chapter 4
The Golden Oak

Austin and Ethan breached the surface of the massive city of Westbrook. The underground network of tunnels led into a park that seemed to stretch on for miles. The grass was as green as could be, and it felt like autumn, although it was only summer. The maple trees were in full bloom all around them; there could've been hundreds. Austin never thought he would be so happy to see the sun, especially after their run-in with the janitors and the security guards. After all the chaos that Ethan and Austin caused, they decided to be extra cautious about the route they took. With every crossroad they met, Ethan took the longest and apparently the most 'safe route' they could have taken. Every single detour that the friends took delayed them even more from reaching Westbrook. The underground network stretched on for hours; it would've been a big project to construct. "I wonder what happened to those janitors?" Austin asked sympathetically.

"You mean John and John," Ethan said with a smirk. "They probably just got questioned; there is no way they can have proof of those janitors actually breaching the city limits. I disabled all the cameras." Ethan sounded so proud of himself, as if to say, "Wow, at least I did one thing right."

"You should come to the academy with me; I can help you enrol," Austin said. "They have just about everything you could think of in 'the world of magic'. Did you know that Westbrook is the most renowned school in all of Hylenia? The school is supposed to be the safest place on Earth; you'll be safe there." Ethan stopped walking and turned to Austin; his black leather jacket must've made him very hot, but if he was, Ethan didn't show it.

"The schooling system is a joke. I have all the necessary tools to survive out in the real world. School is really about popularity contests and learning a curriculum structured to make middle-class citizens not independent thinkers. I have had my experience with schools, the teachers and worst of all the students; it's a toxic environment for me at least."

"Westbrook is different. It will teach you other things besides the regular school subjects, and I don't know about the students, but I will be there, and I'm sure at least the teachers will be supportive; they aren't some Mertamic school."

"I don't want to go, and I don't want to hear any more about it." Ethan hissed with an undertone of a threat still on his tongue. The boy stormed off, with a thunder cloud seeming to follow him. It gave a whole new meaning to storming off. Austin just watched as Ethan slowly walked out of sight. "Okay, I'm lost in the middle of the biggest city in the world," Austin talked to himself, "yet there isn't a person in sight." Austin continued sarcastically to himself. He chose a random direction and walked for a kilometre until he met a path. Walking on the tamed grass like it was some normal day. He thought about his fight with Ethan. *We will work through it,* Austin reassured himself. Finally, some signage pointed Austin in the right direction through the park. It was a ten minute walk before he saw it. The academy was huge. The school was the size of 10 football fields and was at least six storeys high. Definitely bigger than any school in Mertamic, with terraces full of students and their pets or 'familiars', that's what it said on the pamphlet; every student of magic had one, and it was connected to their souls. He saw about 50 different species of animals: owls, lorikeets, a duck-sized leopard, snakes, pugs, pandas and a dozen different animals Austin didn't recognise, but they all looked so free. The closer Austin got to the school, the more details he could see; it looked as if the castle was made out of, was that ivory? There was a white pillar every half a kilometre, encasing the whole school, and in between every two pillars was a blue-tinted force field that stretched above the whole school. The scene seemed perfect; the grass was green, and the birds chirped. Separating Austin from the school (besides for the giant forcefield and amazing security system) was a stream that was a shade of ocean blue.

"The Little Grobs," Austin said aloud; he had read about the stream in the pamphlet he picked up on the walk here. There were symmetrical trees on either side of the massive entrance; unlike the rest of the castle, the doors seemed to be made out of golden oak, not ivory. From what Austin knew, the city was founded by four different houses: Destiny, Killian, Venus and Terra. Those houses all came together and planted the unique golden oak tree, which was later partially made into the doors of the castle, although the tree was still an important monument in the city. The four were all siblings but grew bitter against each other, their power splitting them against each other. Each family member had their own unique character traits. Destiny was always magically oriented and focused on fortune and the future; Killian used dark magic and summoned the spirits of the world to give him power; Venus was the favourite child, the pretty one who chooses her own vanity and fame above even her own siblings; and Terra was more down to earth and used the powers of medicinal magic and earthen magic to manipulate everyone into giving her rights over the land. One day, Terra grew jealous of all her siblings and decided to plot against them and planned on using various nature spirits and monsters to give back to the Earth. She took the clay from the earth and announced a powerful incantation from her mother's spell book and raised a golem from the Earth. She had also managed to obtain a powerful relic, Sigon, a magical amulet. For that, she went where the wind met the ocean and where the Earth split open to encase a pit of fire: the wiccan coven's sacred ritual grounds. She consulted the head wiccan and stated that she wanted to give power back to the source nature. The wiccan gave her the amulet of the prophecy: Sigon. With that, she had to undergo three trials, all of which she passed. She then took the amulet and summoned the nature spirits and went back to the golden oak tree. The power it radiated was so strong that it sent a signal throughout Hylenia. All four siblings had returned to the golden oak they had all planted together, which had grown 10 times its original size with the strength of Sigon.

"Sigon," said Destiny in awe. "How dare you!" She rushed at Terra, only to be stopped by the golem Terra had summoned.

"You performed the incantation from our mother's spell book!" screamed Killian in outrage.

A dark mist rose from the Earth and circled his feet.

"And what do you plan on doing with Sigon?" questioned Venus in a cold tone.

"I will take control now. I will rule the earth in my image, including Westbrook; it is going to be my city," Terra announced with a cruel smile.

"How dare you! You will never be able to stop us all." The mist grew thicker around Killian's feet.

"Oh, but that's where you are wrong. I can." Terra summoned the spirits of nature while her golem protected her. "I actually kind of think that it's funny that you didn't see any of this coming, Destiny."

Destiny looked flustered for a second but then counteracted the spirits with an evil-warding chant; golden symbols circled all around her, making a purple barrier. Destiny then sent a beam of magic forward towards Terra. Killian had the same idea and took a magical chain he had around his neck and flashed it into a staff and summoned the dead to join the fight. Venus was also quick to take her wand and drain the colour of her surroundings and focus it into powerful energy beams and aim them at her sibling. All the energy combined at the one place brought down a massive thunderbolt into the Earth, which swallowed up all the siblings. The ground was now just a battlefield, with no one left to fight on it. The siblings were never seen again, but legend says that Terra survived the fight and is gathering her energy to bring the fight to the new world. It was one of Austin's favourite stories; his father used to have a book on it, and his mother read it to him as a child after his father left. Now Austin was walking into the real-life version of the story.

Austin had finally got to the river where he had found a bridge with surprising ease. He walked over, and something felt different from that point on. *That wasn't hard. What's so magical about it, anyway?* Austin needed to pass through the barrier as well; it was about 100 metres from the stream. If you didn't focus, you could barely see the barrier, but Austin went to touch it, and it was as solid as bricks. The only way to get through must be at a security point. He found an entrance between two pillars. It was called 'Killian's Entrance', the western side of the barrier. There were security guards in Westbrook Security uniforms positioned there. He walked up to the main booth that was open; the man inside was behind a solid sheet of glass and had a slip at the bottom to slide things through like a bank. "Student ID?" the man grunted; he seemed a bit disgruntled. He took a sip of very strong coffee from a mug that said, 'Put it where the sun doesn't shine,' classy.

"Actually, I am new here."

"Student admissions paperwork and city border pass?"

"About that, I don't have that." Austin made an innocent face. "I do, however, have my general Hylenia ID." He slid it under the glass. It got the right reaction Austin had hoped for.

"Well, looks here that your preadmission has already been accepted and you aren't on any wanted lists." The guard must've cross-checked Austin's ID with a database. "Have a lovely day," the man said, with zero note of anything lovely. He took another sip of his coffee and went back to his computer. Austin stood there for an awkward five seconds, waiting for his ID back, but the man seemed to not care.

"Isn't it like 11:30? Why are you drinking coffee?"

"What else do you want, kid?" The man said it like he had a million and one more important things to do. Austin gestured towards the ID still on the other side of the glass. The man made it look like a whole effort to push it back to the other side, then went quickly back to his screen. Austin made that fake smile that you do with customer service people and left on his way. The path was a brick-coloured cement pavement, with random stones every now and then. The walk seemed a lot longer than it looked but guided Austin right to the front entrance. The overly big golden wood doors loomed down on Austin. On either side of Austin were ultra-sized statues of the four siblings and the founders of Westbrook. The features on their faces were so cold, it was as if they were looking down on him. The most powerful people to have ever existed were represented here stuck in time.

"Wonder if Destiny foresaw this," slurred Austin.

"Hey, I heard that!" screamed a woman. Austin thought the statue had spoken to him until someone tapped him on the shoulder.

"You know, she was the most powerful sorceress. It is rude to talk about her like that," the girl said sternly. She couldn't have been older than Austin. She had long brown hair and wore the Westbrook uniform; she had a wand on the right side of her skirt. Austin always thought wands were silly.

"What's your wand for? Turning rude pigeons that land on the statues to worms?" Austin said with a smirk.

"Actually, it's used for concentrating all my magic into kicking your ass!" She unsheathed her wand and sent a blast of energy at Austin, which hit him into the nearest tree and kept him bound there. Hadn't he had enough of this for one day?

"Well, that was rude. I'm sure they do not condone swearing here at Westbrook," said Austin. But the student ignored him.

"Who even are you? I know everybody in this school, and you're not one of them." She analysed him like an assignment.

"I'm actually new here. I came from Mertamic. I just transferred here, and my greeting was amazing," said Austin sarcastically.

"Your name?" the girl asked more sternly now.

"Austin, Austin Bolden." There was a silence between them for 10 seconds until Austin spoke. "Did I say something wrong or…" The girl continued to examine him as if he were a science experiment. "What?" Austin asked.

"Nothing. I'm Wendy. It's just that your father is sort of a big deal around here. Your father is Tony Bolden?" Wendy questioned.

"Yeah," Austin said, clearly unimpressed that he was being recognised for his father again. Wherever Austin went, he would still be in his father's shadow. *Now everybody had some sort of opinion about me and my family.*

"He's a good man, unlike yourself." Wendy looked him up and down.

"I got past the river, so that means that I'm good or something, no?" the boy questioned.

"Firstly, the Little Grobs is a stream, not a river, and if you actually knew anything about the school, you would know that the stream is enchanted and can sense your intentions, but if you are a talented wizard, you could simply put a strong casting spell so there are ways around it," Wendy explained.

"You mentioned something about my dad being here; when did he visit last?" Something still bugged Austin.

"Around a year ago."

So his father found the time to meet this random girl but didn't have the time to come visit him. "No one has heard from him in months. Do you know where he is?" asked Wendy.

"No!" screamed Austin; he snapped out of the magical bonds that kept him up to the tree. "I know a little magic myself," Austin lied; he didn't know how he got out.

"Where is your familiar? I saw kids on the terrace had theirs." Austin said the word 'familiar' as if it were another language. Wendy looked him up and down and looked like she was about to laugh.

"Close, he always is. But familiars only come out when needed or summoned, and it takes powerful magic to summon one. They're free creatures."

"Then how come I saw around 50 of them on the roof?" Austin said.

"Like I said, they were probably summoned for a class with a teacher who probably has some sorta device to attract them all. They won't all be there for long, though. I'm guessing you've never even met your familiar."

"No." Austin looked down. "But sometimes I see my mum's. Hers is a red fox."

"I didn't ask." Wendy rolled her eyes as she walked off. Apparently, Austin had a talent for getting people mad. Austin followed the girl he'd just met inside the building. The interior of the building was so amazing; the room had a checkered marble floor and half a dozen golden chandeliers hanging from a dome-shaped glass roof. The room was full of portraits of pristine men and women, all of which were unknown to Austin except one; he recognised his father on the far wall. Austin found his way to the reception to administer himself in.

"Hello," greeted the receptionist. "What's your name?" *Here we go again,* Austin thought to himself.

"Austin Bolden, and I'm here to enrol." He smiled.

"I'm Alana. It is very nice to have you here, dear. Do you have your enrolment ticket? It should have come in the mail." The receptionist was a nice elderly lady, dressed in a long floral dress and had pearls around her neck. She had that receptionist smell, like washing detergent and apple pie scent. Austin panicked for a quick second but reassured himself.

Uhhh, actually, mine never came in the mail, but it should be in the system. Austin quickly thought.

"That's quite strange; the mailing system is all W.A.A. staff, that's what the youngsters call out school, by the way. You know what? That's fine, Mr Bolden, I'll just have you quickly sign this form here while I call up another student to give you a tour around the school. Seeing as the preadmissions all seem to be aligned." Alana handed him a sign-up sheet. Wow, Austin had never been called Mr Bolden before; that was always his father's title. Austin was just glad that Alana didn't recognise him because of his father. "Are you, by any chance, related to"—*Here it is;* Austin braced himself—"Natalie Bolden?" asked the receptionist. Wow, Austin had never been recognised because of his mother before; it just occurred to him that his mother must've also been cast in his father's shadow.

"Yes, she is my mum." Austin smiled as he handed in the form.

"You know, your mum and my daughter were in the same grade; they were best friends here," Alana explained. *Wait, my mum really went to this school? Why have I never known about this? That is why she must've been so persistent for me to come here.* "Your guide should be here any minute now," said Alana. Austin was so lost in his train of thought that he didn't even realise when the guide student had arrived. "This has to be a joke," said the girl he had just met, Wendy. Out of all the students, it had to be Wendy.

The girl let out a sigh, then explained herself. "It's for my extracurricular points. Well, come on then," she said hastily. Austin got a closer look at her; she had light-coloured skin and had her brown hair up in a tight bun. She had clear, perfect skin and had this country club-entitled aura about her. He followed her down what seemed like a never-ending corridor. Classroom after classroom, full of students practising magic. "This is the Venus wing," Wendy said, starting to explain the origin story of Westbrook, all of which Austin knew already. Austin spaced out for most of the story. "That is when Terra went to the—" Wendy paused mid-sentence. "Hello! Who is there?" Austin didn't notice anyone. They stood there for a solid minute before Austin completely thought Wendy had lost all the sanity she had.

"I don't think that—" Austin attempted to speak before Wendy shushed him.

"Come out!" she screamed, but no one responded. "Last warning, or you're going to the principal's office." Another student of Austin's age joined them in the halls.

"Hey, I'm Fred, or how she likes to call me, 'stop staring at me, creep'." The guy was tall and tanned, with a shaved head. He looked like he could've been from a Latin country, maybe Mexico. His jumper read Westbrook Academy in purple and green, but it wasn't like all the other uniforms that everyone else had. He couldn't keep still; he was very energetic and excited. The usual uniform Austin saw was a plain white button-up shirt and black shorts or skirts for girls. Everyone also wore blazers or woollen jumpers, with some students even wearing ties.

"His uniform is for the technology club, also known as the dork club," Wendy said as if she could read Austin's mind.

"Hey, you're one to talk, Miss 'last warning or you're going to the principal's office'." He did his best to imitate her. All Austin needed was popcorn; this was first-class entertainment watching them go at each other's throats.

"Hey…how did we not see you?" asked Austin to break the tension.

"Ohh, it's an invisibility incantation."

"Cool, you have to show me," Austin said.

"No, what he has to do is go to class. Plus, those are forbidden unless you are under the supervision of a qualified teacher." Wendy frowned.

"Let me properly introduce myself at least." He didn't wait for permission. "So as you know, my name is actually Frederico, but most people just call me Fred or Rico, whatever you prefer. My parents brought me here from Mexico, where I was born, because they wanted me to have a more magical life and to utilise all my talents. And I am not just part of the technology club as Wendy already said. I am the head of that club." The boy beamed; he also dropped an imaginary microphone. The boy spoke with a slight accent. He seemed really friendly and had a very upbeat persona to him. If Austin hadn't actually talked to him, he would seem very intimidating. He was at least half a head taller than Austin, not that Austin was short for his age; he was just average. "I'm Austin," he held out his hand. "I just transferred here from Mertamic."

"Okay, now go to class." The girl rolled her eyes.

"Whatever. Later, guys," Fred said as he walked away.

"He is not going to class, is he?" asked Wendy; she gripped her hands together tightly, her back to Frederico as he walked away.

"Not a chance," replied Austin.

Wendy continued the tour; she went through the elemental wing, fortune and future wing, sports facilities, general studies wing and other basic school classes. "What about the dark magic wing?" asked Austin.

"That wing is forbidden to any students, except for me, of course. I have the key, you know? Now no more talking about that, let's continue with the tour, and you know what? No more interrupting," exclaimed Wendy. The tour continued...

Chapter 5
Tested

The bell finally rang. Austin thought the tour would never end. "Now it's lunch, and everyone will be at the cafeteria," announced Wendy.

"So you mean the tour isn't even over yet?" Austin sighed; he really had to get Wendy as his tour guide out of all people. She was insufferable and talked like a pre-recorded lecture. She was thorough, that was for sure; she talked about everything and anything, no detail left unnoticed. While they walked towards the cafeteria, Wendy talked about the ivory walls of the academy and how when the school was founded the land was an elephant sanctuary, one of the original native animals of Hylenia. They harvested the ivory cruelty-free to build the school, and it was quite impressive. She also talked about trading with India during the Renaissance period, but Austin zoned out for that portion of the conversation; all he could think about was *FOOD*.

"You know that our cafeteria is purely plant-based and designed for a healthy and nutritional diet?" They walked into the hall, but Wendy continued explaining. "Like I said, Westbrook was founded in 1889 and Westbrook Academy shortly after that. Interestingly enough, the cafeteria was only made in 1999 to properly attend to the health of all students, even ones like him." She pointed to the boy they had met earlier. *What was his name again? Fred!* Austin remembered. His brain was on overload right now; he could probably navigate his way blindfolded around the whole school after his tour. Fred came over and joined them.

"Hey, you're a tough one, huh? Most people who go on this tour don't last till lunch. Usually, they dropped dead from boredom." Fred smirked.

"That was once," Wendy answered in reply, clearly unhappy.

"I'll take it from here, Your Highness, unless the young man wants to hear more about the rich history of Westbrook?" Fred questioned.

Austin was so glad that the tour was over. "Thank you, Wendy, for the—" Wendy had already walked off for lunch.

"Well, let's go get some food, then I'll introduce you to everyone." They proceeded to the self-serve islands with steaming hot containers of food. Austin took a tray and wanted to try everything; the smell was unlike anything he had smelt before. All the foods were so colourful, and the texture and variety of everything were almost overwhelming. Austin slapped an amazing smelling curry sort of food on his plate, although he didn't know quite what it was. Then he added some salad to be healthy. "So, Austin, what is your story?"

"Uh. A pretty boring one. I lived in Mertamic my whole life and decided it was time for a change, so I transferred here because both my parents are alumni of the school. It's my first time really in a big city and a big school."

"Trust me, I know the feeling. It's overwhelming. I came here mid last year, and I thought everyone already knew each other and that there wasn't a place for me, but that is the beauty; there is a place for everyone, Austin. So many students you will never even know them all. They come from all over the world, even Humaline families."

"Sorry, Humaline families?"

"Basically, the rich wizards who live in the outside who send their children here to learn magic. Although most people here are Hylenia born and raised." They started walking towards the nearest sets of tables and chairs. The cafeteria was already packed with students, table after table, chatting loudly across the room; everything was so busy. Frederico started introducing Austin to everyone. "This is Leslie and Jill," said Fred; they both wore school turtlenecks, coloured purple and green, similar to the uniform Fred wore. The one on the left, Jill, had a bowl cut and weird small cat ears on her head. The second girl had shoulder-length brown hair; she seemed like the textbook nerd type, but she had honey-coloured eyes that seemed so inviting and sweet, magnified by heavy-looking glasses. The second girl spoke. Jill had almost completely black-coloured pupils, which seemed to look right through your soul. "Hi, you look like shoemaker-levy 9 after it collided with Jupiter." Jill snorted. Austin got the gist of what she had tried to say, but her reference definitely wasn't common knowledge.

"Yeah, I know, long story, actually—" Austin tried to answer.

"It's a long story we don't have the time or patience for." Leslie turned towards Jill. "How are we going on Section 73b law and communication?" she asked as if Austin didn't even exist; maybe she was just introverted, but whatever the case, she was set on completing her work at the lunch table.

"Affirmative commander." Jill snorted. Austin noticed the emblem on their uniforms and everyone's uniform: the school symbol, a four-headed beast. The beast consisted of a bear head, a tiger head, a gazelle head and a gorilla head. Under the emblem was the school's name in red. *I wonder what all the animals represent?* Austin thought to himself. Just then, a lady came up to speak to Austin. He stood out like a thumb; everyone was in their uniforms and Austin in his mucky cargo pants and hiking shirt. No wonder she found him so easily.

"I am Mrs Rimesdome, the vice principal here at Westbrook. And I assume you are the new student here that Alana notified me about, Austin. All the paperwork checks out, and I am pleased to have you in our school! I see you're already making friends as well." The woman looked towards Fred. The woman was about in her late 40s; she wore a blue and white, striped, short-sleeved shirt, tucked into a long skirt. Austin noticed something different about her immediately; she had this aura of power that she radiated. But it was more than that; the air around her seemed to spark or crackle, almost like electricity. Her hair almost gave the appearance of metal spiral wire; her long black hair was plaited into tight locks.

"Yeah, I just moved here today; nice to meet you," he said.

"Well, I'm pleased to meet you too, Mr…" greeted the lady.

"Bolden," Austin finished her sentence. He supposed he would get some sort of recognition because of his father's name as the picture of him was in the building entrance.

"Bolden?" said the woman, clearly more intrigued. "Well, we have much to talk about, and I have set up a meeting for you after school today since you missed orientation." The woman paused. "So ask directions to my office later, and we will further discuss your admission. We will also have to get you into a uniform then too." Austin nodded in agreement as she walked away hastily, as if she had something important to get to. Austin turned his head back to the two girls, who were still deep in conversation about their work.

"Don't mind them; they're probably just doing some other students' homework," another girl said. The girl wore the usual uniform: a black skirt and a white short-sleeved top with the four-headed beast emblem on her chest. She had a rainbow pendant that hung loosely on a simplistic necklace she wore. The girl had long, auburn-coloured hair that was split between her two shoulders.

"Homework? We get that here?" Austin complained.

"Yeah." The girl laughed, which was very infectious and radiated to Austin. "I am Ena," the girl stated.

"Austin." He put his hand out for a handshake, which she turned into a high five.

Fred intervened. "Hey, Austin, while you meet these lovely ladies, I just need to talk to someone for a bit. Meet me at our table in a bit." The boy pointed at another group of teenagers a few tables down before he left. Austin shook his head.

"This is Lela," Ena talked again, punching the girl next to her, but it wasn't aggressive; it was playful just to get the other girl's attention. She also had parted long hair, but hers was black; she had peace pendant earrings on both of her ears.

"Hey." The girl rubbed her arm in response to Ena's punch, then her tone changed as she noticed Austin. "Hey," she said, much more low and embarrassed.

"Hey, weird question," Ena, the first girl, intervened in the awkward interaction, "would you want to join the leaders of the Pacifist Club in an attempt to bring peace to this gossip-filled school?" She gestured to herself and Lela.

"A what club?" asked Austin confused.

"Basically, it's just a group of us who hang out during the break; we mostly do whatever, but we are also into our mysteries. We are really just the glorified journalist club of this school. We would really love to have you there," Lela explained. Austin wasn't going to pass up an opportunity to meet new people in this overwhelming environment.

"You know what? I'll check it out as long as I don't have to wear a rainbow pendant anywhere." Austin surprised himself.

"Cool." Ena smiled.

Lela continued, "The next meeting will be tomorrow at 1:00 pm, if you can make it, new boy."

"AUSTIN!" someone called him from the other side of the cafeteria.

"I guess I'll see you there." He smiled and left for where Fred was sitting.

"You know, joining the Pacifist Club is basically social suicide?" said another student, who was wearing a sports uniform, which was baby blue shorts and a baby blue t-shirt with the school emblem in the centre.

"These are Riona, Carter and Jack," Fred introduced.

"Nice to meet you all. I'm Aus—" Austin began to introduce himself.

"—tin. Yeah, we know; news travels fast," a boy said. Jack, that's what Fred called him. The table was a weird mix of athletes. Carter was tall and built like a machine; he looked as if he were part of the football team, but Austin could see all the cliché popular footballers and cheerleaders at another table. Riona was in her sports uniform, and although Jack wasn't wearing any sporty uniform, he seemed very athletic like his friends. He was tall, a bit skinny, so maybe he did running Austin assumed. Jack had cropped, brownish reddish hair and intense brown eyes. Fred seemed almost out of place in his robotics uniform.

"Are you two siblings?" Austin directed the question towards Riona and Jack.

"Yeah," they both said in unison, but only Riona continued. "You obviously are some sort of psychic because we're twins, nearly no one ever guesses that…Oh, damn it. I'm late, nice meeting you, but I have got to go to soccer practice," she stated, just as the announcements started. Her brownish, reddish hair waved in the air, right behind her like a cape as she ran outside.

"Hello, for those of you who don't know me, I'm Mrs Rimesdome." The woman tapped the microphone.

I guess this was her important thing to get to. Austin gathered.

"I wanted to have a quick assembly to present to you our newest teacher here at Westbrook Academy. Please give a big welcome to Mr Rhike!" The students gave an unenthusiastic clap as Mrs Rimesdome left the stage and Mr Rhike came on. He wore a grey rock 'n' roll shirt and black jeans. He looked about 35 and was the most generic person Austin had ever seen.

"Wait, isn't he THE Phillip Rhike, like the one who allegedly pulled that heist a year back?"

"Wasn't he sent to jail?" whispered Carter to the table. Carter seemed a bit older than Fred and Jack; he was maybe a junior. The student was a blonde-haired, Caucasian boy; he was a bit on the larger size. He had a big build, almost like a wrestler and blue eyes that were sunken into his face.

"Yeah, I heard about that." Austin kept his voice low.

"Hello, everybody. I'm Mr Rhike. I will be your new scientific matter and magic teacher."

The crowd was silent until a student yelled, "THIEF!" All the students cracked up laughing. Mr Rhike then left the stage full of embarrassment and left the room red-faced. *Why would the school hire a teacher who tried to rob the school?* Austin had the question running through his head. Another person walked up on stage, but this was a student. A cheerleader actually.

"Hi, I'm Lilly, your future carnival queen, and I would just like to welcome a new student to our school. Austin." She acted way too positive and energetic. She looked like she was about to start a cheer; she had two multicoloured pom-poms in her hands and started to clap but struggled with the pom-poms blocking her hands. The cheerleader had blonde hair and blue eyes; she was quite short and thin. Fred told him to stand up, but he felt so anxious about standing up in front of the whole school. He wasn't used to big crowds and being the centre of attention; he was from Mertamic! The school cheered his name, 'AUSTIN! AUSTIN! AUSTIN!', until he walked up to the centre of the stage and joined the cheerleader.

"Hey, I'm Austin…I don't have a speech or anything." He chuckled nervously, "But this school seems really cool, and I am so excited to start here and meet all of you." More cheers went up for Austin. Both he and the cheerleader walked off the stage. "How did you know my name?" Austin asked inquisitively.

"Ohh, I know everything in this school. Come sit with us. I am Lilly, two 'l's by the way." She brought him to what he guessed was the popular table. "This is Tanner, Bobby, Scott, Billie, Mary, Brittany and Tracy." They all waved, most of them in sports uniforms. The girls wore cheerleader uniforms except for one: Billie, Lilly said her name was. The guys all wore football jerseys. "I'll give you the rundown of the students you want to stay clear of," Lilly continued without asking. "Obviously Fred is too much of a geek to do that. Do you see those guys over there?" She pointed to where Ena and Lela were sitting. "They are all a bunch of weirdos; don't talk to them again."

Billie introduced herself to Austin and went on to ask him, "Where are you from?" She wore the usual girl's uniform, which made her look like an outcast at the popular table. She had black hair and distracting blue eyes.

"I'm from Mertamic."

"Oh, a Hylenia country boy. I'm from Ibiza, Spain. I transferred to Hylenia back in freshman year, but I still go back every holidays. I take all of my friends."

"Humaline."

"Yeah, but that's so formal."

"How is the outside world?"

"It's fun. So many rules though and countries and people. But you haven't lived to you have been traveling there are so many amazing destinations and restaurants; you have to try food from a Michelin star restaurant." The girl went on passionately, playing with her food, poking at it with her fork. The conversation continued for a few minutes before the bell rang and everyone left the cafeteria, with Austin still standing there, not knowing what to do. All the cheerleaders and jocks had left the table not that he could even remember one of their names. He was still just a bit lost. Everyone else around him knew what to do and he was just standing there.

"Please tell me you're not one of those people," a familiar voice said. He turned to see Fred. "And did they just ditch you?" Fred asked.

"Definitely not, and yeah," answered Austin.

"Hey, you wanna join in my class? I have scientific matter and magic class," asked Fred.

"Isn't that the class with Mr Rhike?"

"Yeah." Fred seemed disappointed, but Austin saw this as an opportunity to find out more about this teacher. *Why had Mr Rhike enrolled as a teacher in Westbrook considering his history at the academy?* Both Austin and Fred walked to class talking for a bit. "Hey sorry, I did mean to warn you about the whole assembly thing, it's sort of a tradition when a new transfer comes to the school everyone chants out their name. Can be a bit intimidating. The school is so big." Fred said. Though as big as the school was Austin was already starting to recognise parts of the school from his tour. They entered the general science wing and shortly after, the scientific matter and magic class.

"You're late, Mr Diamond, and who is that with you? He isn't on the class roll," said Mr Rhike, who wore a grey coat on top of what he was already wearing at the assembly. It looked so out of place on top of his jeans and grey rock 'n' roll t-shirt. Austin recognised a few students in the class already. Leslie and Jill, the nerds and other familiar faces from the cafeteria were present in the class too. The room was very dark and secluded, with no windows, and the only light source coming from various candles spaced around the room.

"This is Austin; he is new," explained Fred. "I needed to show him around and stuff."

"Very well, sit down." They took the last two empty seats at the front of the classroom. They sat in individual seats connected to those singular loop around tables, and like everything else in the room, the chairs were black. "Today, first day of school, we will be learning about the power of light and how to harness its energy," Mr Rhike said in a low voice. He started his demonstration, waving around his wand, gathering all the light from the candles and pulling it all into one light orb at the centre of the room. Austin counted till the count of three until the orb exploded, spewing out light across the room and making it instantly warmer. The light spread across the classroom and continued to give out light. "The energy contained within the lights from the candle is very powerful, but like all things powerful, it has a weakness. Does anyone know what that weakness is for the light?" questioned Mr Rhike.

"It is unstable," answered Wendy. Austin hadn't even seen her in the classroom until now because it was so dark. She sat at the back of the classroom.

"Very good, Ms…"

"When the light is pulled into the orb, all the protons and neutrons are pulled in without having any electrons to balance it out, creating an unstable source of energy that can be harnessed into a powerful weapon," she continued to explain.

"Precisely, and today, we will be trying to do so but on a smaller scale. I know it's unorthodox to start the year heavy on with a practical, but we have a lot to get through in the syllabus, and it shows me where each of you pupils are at and how best I can teach you." Everyone was given a candle and a wand. "Focus on the flames and the power it gives off in heat or light control, whichever you choose. The fire relies on oxygen, so we will attempt to create a field of air around the fire to create the orb like my demonstration. Everything is made of matter, even if we can't see it with the naked eye. Next lesson, we will dive more into the theory side of things, but what I want each of you to do is pick up the wands. These wands are designed especially for fire properties, but if you would like to use your own, that's fine. Then put the tip of the wand near the fire, you will feel a sort of force push against almost like a magnet. You need to push it up, which will do one of the two things: separate it from the wick, leaving only light, not fire and separate the protons and neutrons from the electrons of the fire. We will explain why this happens when we do our practical reports." Everyone started attempting the experiment in their own zones, creating the balls of light.

Towards the end of the lesson, Austin himself, after a few tries, was able to capture the fire in a ball of air, which he held for a few seconds before it exploded in a more powerful explosion than the other balls of light. "What did you say your name was again?" Mr Rhike asked Austin.

"Austin, Austin Bolden." The teacher seemed unimpressed, which was a first, but everyone had an opinion on his family.

"Well"—Mr Rhike was interrupted by the bell—"that is the end of the class; you are all dismissed." Austin and Fred walked out of the class.

"How did you do that?" asked Fred.

"Do what?" asked Austin.

"Use fire to control the light, you made a freaking fireball. I just made a lame ball of light," said Fred, still amazed. Austin shrugged.

"Hey, do you know where Mrs Rimesdome's office is? She told me to meet her after school."

"Yeah, it's down the hall and on your right, but be warned, Mrs Rimesdome is almost as bad as Wendy."

Austin let out a chuckle. "See you tomorrow, bye," Fred said as he left, and Austin walked towards Mrs Rimesdome's office with the instructions he was told. The halls were empty; all the students had already left for their dormitories. He walked into the office and was immediately blinded by all the artificial lighting. The floors were sleek rubber-tiled floors and linoleum walls; the office was pretty normal besides the inbuilt electricity rods in the wall showing through translucent Perspex. Energy rushing through the rods around the room was pretty amazing to see, such loose energy like thunderbolts without the sound.

"Wow," Austin murmured to himself.

"Ahh, there you are." Austin almost didn't notice her with all the electricity in the walls. "Don't mind all that. I know it's strange, but it's the only way…" She gestured to her hair, and on closer inspection, her hair wasn't just black plaits but rather seemed to be exerting some kind of energy itself. "I put my hair in this slot right here," the woman described her actions, "and voila." The new energy pulsated the room. The lady took it out and returned it to normal, and her hair could've easily gone under the radar without anyone noticing if she wanted. Austin couldn't speak; he was just in awe. He had so many questions. *How does your hair do that? Why do you need to let it out? Can it power your phone?* But his mouth seemed to fail him. Being at Westbrook Academy of the Arts was only going to get more strange. "Here is a uniform for you, more will wait for you in your dorm and a gift…it is a specialised wand left here by your father to give to you."

How did my father know that I would come here, and why would he leave a wand here? Austin kept that thought to himself. "Top of the range wand here for you, and don't worry about the size of the uniform, it always fits the size of its user." Mrs Rimesdome smiled.

"Now onto a more serious matter: your father. Do you know where he is? He has been missing for a number of months now." Mrs Rimesdome's smile failed her.

"I don't know where he is, or who he is, or why he left," Austin said.

"I see. Well, we better get you to a room, shall we?" The cheer was back into her voice. Mrs Rimesdome got up from her seat and walked through the door, and Austin followed, but when they walked through, they were no longer in a hallway or even the same building; they were in a separate building. *Had they just teleported? Of course, We just teleported; we're in Westbrook Academy of the Arts!* Austin had a silent conversation in his head.

"Your room is at the end of the hallway on your left," Mrs Rimesdome announced.

Really, could she not have transported me there? Austin complained to himself. He turned to look at the hallway; it was so long and didn't look like it could fit in a building this size. When he turned back, Mrs Rimesdome had already left. He walked down the hallway in silence, but the corridor didn't seem to end. The longer he walked towards the end, the further away it seemed. *Really, in a school of magic, and they can't invent something to teleport you to your rooms? Wait, maybe this is some kind of test?* Westbrook Academy is the school of the arts. WAA is an exclusive school and he was just let in. I mean, of course, he was a legacy on both ends and the son of a prodigy, the MR Bolden. He had preadmissions and good grades, but there were no interviews or testing; maybe this was it. Even though he was accepted prior to the regular screening with early admissions, it was still unusual for zero testing. Just being let in bugged Austin; it couldn't have been that easy. "I know this is a test!" Austin screamed to no one in particular. *Now all I have to do is pass.* He started to knock on doors, but there was no answer; everything seemed too quiet. He stopped at room 657 and decided to break in. It looked like the least expensive door to break. It was a plain wood door with the number 657 on it in brass. Every door was unique; no door was alike, but the strange thing was that the doors weren't in order; a lot of doors were missing. Austin rammed the door with no avail; the door seemed indestructible. He tried the next door up, 789; it was a metal-studded door with a gold outline. Austin tried to break in, but it was just as indestructible as the first. Austin went back to 657 and took out his wand; he focused on all the lights surrounding him and pulled them all in front of him into a massive orb. He was so proud of himself that for a second he didn't realise that there was a reactive orb in front of him about to explode. Austin ran away at the last second, and the explosion blew him off his feet and onto the ground. His vision started to tunnel, and everything closed in until it all went black.

Chapter 6
The Nurse

Austin woke up in the nurse's office; four poster-filled walls surrounded him. The room seemed normal enough, although it had a very cold feel to it. Somehow, the clothes Austin was wearing had magically repaired themselves. The room was very bare, besides the human-sized skeleton in the corner of the room. Austin sat up on the plastic-lined bed and looked towards the whiteboard opposite him. It had two words written down in bold black font, followed by a question mark: 'Austin Bolden?'

"You only had a minor concussion, nothing to worry about," said a woman who had just walked in; she didn't look that much older than him. She had brown hair and a doctor's coat on, which was about two sizes too big. She had also had a custom nametag that presented the name Peggy.

The light shimmered. "What's with my name on the board?" He gestured towards the whiteboard.

"Well, it's something I do with all my patients when I start to build a portfolio. Speaking of which, do you have any medical background information I should know about? Allergies? Operations? Conditions? I need to finish this portfolio for Dr Tatson. He is your official doctor and head doctor on the campus," she said with a contagious smile.

"I don't think I have any allergies and don't have any conditions or anything of the sort. Although when I was ten, I ate a tiny magnet, and it's still inside my throat, but the doctor said it was no problem and could be ignored," he described. Peggy frowned and stretched out a mechanical mechanism attached to the wall and positioned it in front of Austin's neck. It scanned his neck, but it didn't hurt. It was some sort of X-ray machine.

"Don't move for just a moment while I get a clear read." The machine scanned once more, then she pushed it back to the wall into its original position then looked at the photos scanned on the laptop she had brought in. Sure enough, there it was, a tiny ball lodged in his throat.

"I mean I don't mind it. It makes for a cool party trick. I can put magnets on my throat, and they stick there like magic." Austin said motioning his hands like a magician.

"That was very irresponsible of your doctor; it could've become rusty or gotten dislodged and blocked your windpipe. That is a major choking hazard. Will you be okay if I take it out? You may feel a little discomfort," asked Peggy, already reaching for a surgical-looking wand. Austin nodded in response, and she tracked where exactly the metallic ball was and pointed the wand directly against Austin's skin.

"*Avidanen chatum*," she announced, and immediately, Austin felt it in his throat; it was a weird feeling. She controlled the magnet's course and dragged it out of his mouth with the levitation spell. Strangely, it didn't hurt that much. The nurse laid down the magnet on a side table.

"Wow, that's so awesome; you must've had a lot of training for that."

"I'm just a substitute nurse. I am actually a senior here at Westbrook, practising to be a magically trained nurse. I am Peggy." She took off her gloves and disposed of them in a hazard bin, together with the magnet and then put her hand out for a handshake. Austin accepted.

"Together with my magical knowledge and general health knowledge, I can identify and cure just about every common sickness or injury."

"What was the spell you just used?" asked Austin.

"It just helps to control magnetic fields. So I can channel the energy of the magnet onto the table," explained Peggy; she was always multitasking and jotting notes down into a leather-bound book.

"Cool," he said, more interested than amazed.

"I need to run through the symptom list of your concussion and see how you are feeling. So do you have feelings of nausea, headaches, cramps, vomiting, disorientation or fatigue?" She shined a flashlight into both of Austin's eyes to see the dilation.

"I guess I have a really bad headache, and I am feeling nauseous, but apart from that, nothing," Austin replied.

"Okay, take this pill; it will bring down the headaches and feelings of nausea, and you should feel better in about half an hour." She handed him a white capsule. "I just need to note down a few things, like height and weight, so when you can, just jump up on the scales."

Austin did as he was told; then after that, he went to get his height taken and lied down on his back against a wall as the nurse pulled down a measuring tape. She than took his photo and asked more background information. "That is all I need for now, so let's finish up. Do you have any questions?" she asked, still writing notes. Austin shook his head.

"Great. Let's take you to the rehabilitation centre then." She walked him out of the office and just down the hall filled with other nurses' offices, maybe a dozen in total, which all led to a vast chasm with a dome ceiling with patients of all kinds. The room was brightly lit, with a homely feel to it. He hopped on to a high chair and waited. "Mrs Rimesdome will be here soon to properly assess everything, just wait here. I have to finish your portfolio and upload it digitally." She smiled, then soon after walked back the way they had come. Austin noticed so many students, some in beds, some in a lounge area on low couches, while others were at a kitchenette area, talking, although everyone had some sort of injury. Most were common injuries, like a broken bone or a sprain, but there were others that looked like they had just exploded and burst into flames, much like himself. A student walked up to him and started to talk.

"How did you get here?" It was Tanner, one of the popular jocks; he was still in his sports uniform, but it was tattered and muddy.

"Ohh, I was in this hallway. I think it was a trial, and I had to enter a door, but they were all locked and had some sort of magical barrier around them, so I channelled the energy from the light into this flame to burst open the door, but I wasn't exactly clear of the blast zone. What about you?" Austin explained.

"Classic trial." He chuckled. "I was dared to levitate off the side of Killian Tower, that big tower on the southeast corner of the school," Tanner said, as if that explained everything.

"Okay," Austin said, still very confused.

"Ohh, I can't levitate, and I fell off the side through a tree and into a mud lake." He showed off his clothes as evidence.

"Excuse me, Mr Tanner," interrupted Mrs Rimesdome; he stood to the side a few feet away. Everyone stopped what they were doing and watched the vice principal as she gave her verdict on whether Austin was officially a student at Westbrook or not.

"Did I get in?" Austin asked in a soft tone; he was so nervous he could feel his heart beating 100 miles an hour. Austin wasn't sure whether all the nervous energy came from him or his vice principal.

"It is unorthodox." She hesitated. "But you passed the test in quicker time than most, but we will still be keeping an eye on you." She seemed very unimpressed, but she managed a smile. "You are officially a student at Westbrook Academy of the Arts." Everything else didn't matter. *I got in!* Austin forgot how to breathe; he was so excited; the whole room built up a cheer, even if it was a muffled scream from a few patients. Tanner slapped him on the back, congratulating him. The hall went silent as Mrs Rimesdome began to speak again. "Well, if you are feeling up to it, I expect that you will be heading off to class; tardiness is not accepted at Westbrook Academy. In the next period, you have a free; all the necessary school supplies will be left in your dorm for you to go and retrieve and clean up. And your mum, Natalie, has sent your suitcase here already and has asked you call her as soon as possible," she said in a stern voice. "Your timetable." She handed him a sheet with all his classes. He examined the sheet and immediately recognised where he needed to go and hurried off. It was already the next morning since Austin's accident, and he just realised he had slept through the night. He waved back at Tanner and left the room in a hurry. He recognised the hallways from his tour with Wendy and ran down the empty hallways towards the Terra wing, which was all the way up at the northernmost part of the castle. He entered the room with no hesitation and ran to the nearest empty seat on the side of the classroom, opposite the teacher's desk.

"Austin Bolden," the teacher said.

"Here." Austin realised he was doing the roll call.

"Ena Marigold," the teacher continued.

"Hey, what's up?" said Fred from behind him.

"I got in. Do you think the teacher noticed I'm late?"

"The teacher is a complete doofus; he didn't realise a thing," continued Fred.

Austin read his timetable while the teacher continued the roll call, so many classes that Austin had never ever heard of, but he was excited to try them.

"Welcome to the elemental magic class. I am your teacher, Mr Davon." He looked at his full class. The room was buzzing with energy; all the elements were present in the class at the back. There was a giant fish tank with many colourful fish swimming around arches and various corals. The floor wasn't tiled like the rest of the school, but it was left open to the solid ground, and the air was all around them soaring around at the top, even blowing off a few people's hats. The room had natural sunlight coming through the see-through glass ceiling. Last but not least, the fire burned in a fireplace at the heart of the room, spreading warmth to the earth.

"Who knows what order the class roll was called out in? Anyone?" The class was silent, so Mr Davon answered as he paced in front of the class. "Okay, it was in elemental connectedness. Each one of you is connected to the elements in some way, and you can harness at least one of their powers. Terra could harness all the elements and dedicated her life to understanding the workings of the elements. The elements have the most powerful magic within them; it is the source of all magic. When Terra realised this, she drew power from it to gain superiority over her siblings. Today, we are going to learn what your elements are." He gestured for a kid in the front row to come up in front of the class of about 30 students. He stood on some sort of makeshift altar. It was a black stone slab with markings engraved into its side, with symbols Austin couldn't read. For a count of five, nothing happened until a fire symbol blazed through the air. "Very good, boy. Who's next?" the professor said. One by one, all the students stepped onto the altar. Ena went up, and an earth symbol appeared; she seemed happy with that. It was Austin's turn; he walked up to the altar and stood there for a minute. *Is the altar broken? Do I even have an element?* His thoughts were cut short by the four symbols dancing in front of him. "I have never in my entire life…" Mr Davon was in awe of him. The whole class was in awe; all of them were speechless; the class was silent for a count of five. "What is your name, young man?" the professor asked.

"Austin Bolden." The professor excused him, and the next student went up.

"How did you do that now!" asked Fred, still amazed.

"I don't know." He was the first person to ever have the ability to control over all four elements since Terra. Fred went up and stood for only a second before a fire symbol appeared.

"That obvious, ehh?" He grinned. After all the students' elements were identified, the teacher asked the students to go near their assigned element. The water kids went to the tank, the fire kids went to the fireplace, the air kids went to the windows and the earth kids went towards the earth sculpture near the door. Was that Gaia, the Greek Mother Earth? Austin was left in the middle of the room with no specific element to go to. Everyone was staring at him. Which element would he choose to go to? Finally, he chose to be with the water kids.

"It'll be fun," said a student from behind him, Riona. She was Jack's twin, as Austin remembered from their brief interaction at the cafeteria. She now wore the regular uniform, not the baby blue one and had her dark reddish hair in a bun, ready for whatever task they were about to do. The teacher took Austin's place as the centre of attention and stood in the middle of the classroom. "Although usually we all have a specific element that we can control best with years of training, any wizard can take it upon themselves to control another element, like learning another language. But for today, we are going to stick with what we are used to. I want you all to think about a happy memory, something that involves your element specifically. The clearer the memory, the better the magic, so make sure you remember the details; as long as you do that, the magic should flow right through you. You need to accept the initial rush of the power and control it. Just say the words *entacio chatum*. Make sure to point your wands at the element you want to control, not just anywhere. I'm looking at you, Diamond."

Austin started to tune out and bring himself into his own zone. He closed his eyes and aimed his wand, the gift he had gotten from his dad, towards the open part of the fish tank. Many other students did much of the same thing, some already getting the hang of it. He concentrated on a memory and began to remember him and Irora looking out at the ocean, watching the waves crash against the jagged rocks; the waves sprayed him with water, but he didn't mind being wet, nor did Irora. He felt the current of the water running through his hands and then through his whole body. His hands felt numb; the memory was too strong. He felt the anger of his memory washing over him; Irora felt lifeless in his hands. He opened his eyes to see Riona holding a bowling ball-sized water sphere. He looked at his own water, which he wasn't controlling, but it was rather in control of him. It was shaped like Austin, a mirrored version of him made out of the water, but the water gave off emotions. It was as if all the worst parts of him took form to destroy anything that gave out a positive light. It took a step towards Riona, who only just took notice of the beast. She let out a scream, which was soon muffled by the water washing over her face. Austin punched the hybrid version of himself on the back of its water makeshift head, but his hand went right through. At least he got its attention; the water turned its head towards Austin, then its body. It completely lost interest in Riona and left her body limp on the floor. A few of the other water kids rushed to her aid. *Was she*—Austin couldn't finish the thought if she was her blood was on his hands. The water pushed him to the floor and rushed over him, slowly drowning him. He should be able to control it. What had he created? Austin saw the other water kids trying to use their water against the beast and control it, but it wasn't theirs to control; they weren't nearly strong enough. Austin had let out a beast. Mr Davon had a staff in his hand and started to harness the wind. The air pressure built up and ripped the water apart at an incredible speed. Austin saw the class in chaos: kids screaming, other elemental spirits running around untamed. He had caused a ripple effect; he closed his eyes and faded away from the chaos.

✶✶✶✶✶✶✶✶✶✶✶

He opened his eyes to see a room filled up with middle-aged people, all screaming at each other. *So much for getting away from the chaos.* He stood in a large room made of wood. It sort of looked like a courtroom with a large horseshoe table and a single person out in front on a podium, who started to address the room in a loud voice that shut out everyone else. "SILENCE!" The hall fell silent, "The boy is at Westbrook Academy, and we have reason to believe he is the one of the prophecies." The man emphasised on the word, as if it meant something. Everyone in the court wore the same uniform of a white shirt, black pants and a purple coat that went over it. Mrs Rimesdome was present in the crowd, looking strange with the purple coat.

"One of my professors witnessed the boy being able to control all four elements," she said dryly. *They are definitely talking about me, but can they see me?* He walked right through the horseshoe table like a ghost.

"Well, he is Tony's son; you have to take that into consideration what his father has done here. It is our duty to protect him against the Other Side and its partner branches." It was the same guy he saw in his dream at his mum's house.

"Caleb, sit down and do not speak; you know you are only here as an honorary personnel," the podium man said. Austin stood between the council and the spokesperson. One person from the council stood up and seemed to sense Austin's presence and spluttered out a spell that sent Austin back to reality.

✶✶✶✶✶✶✶✶✶✶✶

"You can't go one day without keeping yourself out of trouble, can you?" said Peggy. Austin sat up groggily, waking up from his nightmare. "You seem to be all fine, as if the 'water beast' as your friends called it only tried to knock you out. My analysis concluded that it sent a rush through your body to gain complete control over you. Your classmate, on the other hand, wasn't so lucky." She gestured towards Riona. They weren't in Peggy's office but rather in the rehabilitation centre with the large domed ceiling. They had made it into a temporary emergency room with beds everywhere. He saw many people from his class either resting or injured here. Riona was asleep with something attached to her arm, a sort of machine. A few nurses were crowding her while she was lying down blissfully.

"Is she alive?" Austin couldn't live with himself if her blood was on his hands.

"Yes, she is in a stable condition. She is very lucky," Peggy said. "Anyway, are you trying to break the record for most visited patient in the rehab centre in one day?" When he didn't respond she continued, "It's four; you are only halfway there." She joked around, trying to get Austin's mind off Riona; he appreciated that.

"You make my job very full-on, Austin, always keeping it interesting," she said, but Austin's mind was somewhere else; he looked at everyone he had indirectly hurt and about the ripple effect he had caused. "Looks like you have a visitor," continued Peggy.

Mr Davon approached him. *Why is he here? Has it got something to do with my dream?* Austin thought.

"I have made an effort to visit all my students," Mr Davon answered Austin as if he read his mind. "You know, it takes great skill to control an angry memory; it's not your fault." He saw most of his classmates also in the centre, but Fred was nowhere to be seen. "The spirits all have links within themselves; the emotions spread like wildfire." Mr Davon muttered something under his breath and took out the video surveillance with his wand and showed it to him mid-air, as if there was a projector showing the footage in the air. The video shimmered as it started with Austin's mirror version growing from the water, then it attacked Riona and then Austin himself; then everyone else started losing control, fear in their eyes. Little earth monsters rampaged the floors, fire caught onto the walls and anything remotely flammable; the air spirits turned into mini tornados, and absolute chaos erupted. "Never in all my years of teaching has anything like this occurred. These spirits are connected through emotions, and whatever set this off was pure regret, anger and sadness."

"That is why, Venus has some sort of power over Terra's creatures. That is the story they never tell; it's the only reason Terra didn't take complete control. Maybe try earth next time; it's a bit more passive." Mr Davon paused on the word 'passive', then walked away to see more students. Austin checked himself out of the med bay and walked towards the teleporting station. Wendy talked about the science behind it for around 30 minutes. He remembered her saying, "It is a wormhole in space that is contained within a machine, which will take you anywhere on the campus, but if you go off-campus, you will need to disable the school boundary that prevents creatures from getting in." Austin remembered totally zoning out while she explained it, but he did get the basics.

1. Westbrook is the only functional teleportation system in the world open to the public.

2. You needed some sort of ID to use them, for the school, a student ID or staff ID. In Westbrook, a city ID or visa.

3. You can only travel within the teleportation limitations. For the school, it only travelled to certain key locations, the dormitories, the science wing, sports wing and a few other that Austin couldn't quite remember, but there were eight stations in the school in total. It was a pretty cool system. The actual teleporter just looked like a door with a keypad on it. The area wasn't very busy because it was mid class time. There were ten of them, each with an empty queue in this little hall area, with four different hallways, all leading towards this station. Austin picked one at random and looked at the guide.

'Each teleportation centre has a code number. Central teleportation centre is 001. Science wing 002. Sports wing 003. Emergency exit (1) 004. Emergency exit (2) 005. Dormitories 006. Recreational centre 007. Library 008. Swipe ID card, then type in code for desired location, then open door and shut behind you once done.'

"Simple enough," Austin said to himself. Austin swiped his ID card that Ms Rimesdome gave him together with his timetable into a reader. The light turned green, and Austin jotted in 006 into the keypad and opened the door. He stepped through onto the red carpets and shut the door behind him. Two teleports here, one for entering and one for exiting. It didn't feel any different when he walked through the portals; it felt normal. Austin knew that wizards could also teleport at will from any location, but it took a grave amount of effort and skills. *All of this is so overwhelming: teleporting systems, element class, magic classes, new school, new city and these weird dreams I'm having.* Austin pushed his thoughts aside for the moment and walked down the wide hallway. Much like his trial, certain door numbers were missing, but less. The door number that were missing were the unoccupied rooms in the trial hallway. Austin figured that all the doors missing in that trial were rooms that were already taken. All the doors here were unique; he looked at each. It was quite cool to look; they were all customised. At regular intervals in the red carpeted hallways were red couches for just socialising. Austin continued walking, admiring the doors until he came across his room door number, 657. It wasn't burnt to smithereens like the last time Austin saw it but rather looked completely new. It was a modest door compared to some of the others, a plain wood door with brass finishings. Austin swiped his ID card and was gained access to his room. There was also a master key Austin noticed; he guessed the staff had the key if anyone lost the key cards or if they just needed access. His room was pretty much what he imagined, plain single bed, a few windows, a wooden desk, a few shelves, a large cupboard space and a bathroom with a toilet, a shower and a sink. It was nothing special, but he liked that it was simple. Austin saw his suitcase left for him, a bunch of books and utensils on the desk, a care package and welcome basket on his bed and a few pairs of uniforms with a note on top, all neatly folded. The note read:

'If you need any new equipment, school supplies, uniforms or repairs, don't hesitate to contact me.

Alana'

Austin went to the care package and opened some snacks while he got changed from all his damp clothes. He quickly called his mum and apologised for running away for four days without calling; there was some screaming from the other side of the phone, but Austin knew that she just was glad she didn't have to worry. After putting everything away and doing up his room with everything that his mum had sent, including some posters and photos, he looked around and saw a clock, 12:30. *Wow, it was already 12:30! What time did the pacifist meeting start? 1:00!* Austin hurried out of his room and saw the hallway buzzing with life; the school day was already over at 12:00 pm, and the crowds had already formed. Austin saw a poster for the Pacifist Club, together with the information of all the other clubs on the bulletin board. It was in fact at 1:00 pm, and he needed to hurry. *Maybe this pacifist class wouldn't be too bad for me. I do need to calm down for sure.* Austin was heading towards the portals, but it was incredibly busy; it would take forever for him to get to the front of the queue. Austin changed plans and decided to walk on foot to the recreational centre. He got out of the dormitories from a side exit and found himself in one of the ovals and started a run for the rec centre. It was the furthest possible building within the school grounds from the dorms.

He arrived just at 1:00 pm and entered the room.

"They said that they just invaded the school, but no one knows how they got in," said one of the club members as Austin walked in. There was about a group of 20 kids in the moderate-sized room. The room was furnished with random pieces of furniture. The back wall was set up with a desk and two computers that whirred in the background. There was a fridge in one corner, with a whiteboard/blackboard next to it, depending on which side you looked at it from. There was also a few cupboards with locks on them; Austin wondered what was in them. There were chairs set up everywhere and a few beanbags, which were already taken, all around a low, plastic, flimsy-looking table.

"Ohh, Austin, I'm glad that you could come. I wasn't sure after the whole elemental thing…erm," Ena said.

"I'm fine," Austin said; his face flushed bright red. "Continue what you guys were talking about. Don't let me interrupt." Austin smiled; he had had enough attention for one day.

"Ohh, I'll fill you in. I'm Jarred. Anyway, so ents were spotted in the school, and usually they're peaceful, but they completely destroyed the sports wing." Everyone seemed calm, understanding and in agreeance. Jarred was a short, light-skinned black kid, with curly short hair; he had this sparkle in his eye that was very energetic.

"Wait, what variation of ent are we talking about exactly?" asked Austin; he felt stupid asking; usually, he knew most things about magical creatures. He remembered his time in the forest and looking at all the tall trees and thinking if they were ents. They were tree spirits; mostly, they were dormant, but otherwise, they were active and could function like people. There are many stories about the magical creatures, all of which Austin couldn't tell the fake from the real.

"Tree spirits, the ancient kind, a nasty brood; they haven't been seen in the last five centuries until today. They are huge, not the regular type. These ones are like giants; they take the form of an actual tree but have arms and legs and eyes; you get the gist," Ena answered; she was the only person in the room besides Austin who seemed even in the slightest bit worried. *That's right, I read something about those in my book*, he thought to himself. Jarred continued.

"So the question is how did they get in? They must've been let in."

"So the real question is who let them in?" said Lela; it was the first time she talked since Austin got there. He had met her as well in the cafeteria; she was one of the leaders of this club. She was taking all the information in and looked like she was calculating something in her mind. She was obviously very worried because her familiar was in the room, a parrot that sat patiently on her shoulder. Everyone in the room had an expression of shock, but there was a general sense of curiosity about the mystery behind who let the ent in. They all huddled in around an oversized plastic table that looked like it belonged in a kindergarten somewhere.

"It would have to be someone that has access to the control room," responded Ena. Everyone was in agreement, but Lela took charge.

"We all need to investigate and contact everyone we know. Someone has to know something. Beatrice, you have a special mission: to examine the crime scene for clues." She directed the statement towards a young girl that looked about the age of 12, but she had to be a Year 7 student, but classes only started from grade 9. How was she even here? Although she seemed very intelligent, with ocean blue eyes and stormy blonde hair that was borderline silver. "And bring Charlie with you." That made the little girl laugh. Lela's parrot squawked at that too. Beatrice said goodbye and went to her job with another boy a few years older than Beatrice, who Austin could only guess was Charlie. He was also blonde and quite bulky, obviously the muscles of the mission.

"Hey, Austin, you can come with me to check the control room," Ena blurted out; she was a little red but recovered quickly.

"Sure." Austin smiled. The club meeting was not what Austin was expecting; this was an actual full-on investigation he had stumbled into. He thought that everyone would just be socialising and chilling; it definitely was a change.

✱✱✱✱✱✱✱✱✱✱✱

Everyone left in groups, slowly but surely, until it was just Ena and Austin, who locked up the room. A large wooden clock hung from the opposite wall to the now closed Pacifist Club.

Was it 2:30 already? After Beatrice and Charlie had left, everyone talked a little bit more before they left, and now it was 2:30. They left for the control room hastily. "All portals have been shut down in the last half an hour because of the attack. Just means we will have to take the old fashion route." Ena led the pair down multiple corridors that Austin hadn't gone through on his tour. *And I thought Wendy was thorough.* They ran down the hallways with glee. They slowed down as they got closer to the control room.

"Lela seemed really serious about the meeting. I didn't notice how tough of a leader she was," said Austin.

"A lot of people at first can't see past the rainbow pendant and long hair, but everyone in the Pacifist Club knows. She wasn't always like this; her twin used to be the pacifist leader, Delio. He was funny and powerful. Everyone respected him…" Ena's words shifted off track.

Austin noticed she had used past tense to describe him, and immediately something in Austin's stomach sunk. "The point is, he was killed by a wraith, a brain-sucking, human-looking monster. I saw when the creature slit out its claw-like spike from its wrist and jut it into the back of Delio's neck. Four students died that day last year. They call them the courageous four because they all saved someone else from dying by sacrificing themselves. Since then, Lela stood up as leader, but the Pacifist Club became the laughing stock of the school. You were our first recruit in months. But Lela has been very strict on rules since then. That includes any intrusions in the school's barriers. She doesn't want what happened to her brother to happen to anyone else that's why she takes these things so seriously. Even if it is a harmless hedgehog that wanders in." Ena turned to Austin. "Don't bring this up with Lela. Just promise me that." They stood in the middle of the dimly lit hallway, the ivory walls towering over them.

"I promise." They faced each other for five seconds until Ena turned, her head swinging her auburn hair and continued walking. They didn't speak for the rest of their journey.

Chapter 7
Missing

Ena and Austin had reached the control, only to see the door swung fully open. *Wow, it's really nothing like the control rooms in the movies*, Austin thought to himself. It was cool in the room, with very vibrant colours. It had a woollen rug that stretched across the whole room with a few sleek white desks strategically placed in front of the massive windows. The windows shone in lights and made the area feel very open for such a small room. Austin noticed that from three of the sleek desktops on the desks, one of them had not been switched off properly. Austin continued looking around the room for anything that seemed suspicious, although he didn't really know what he was looking for. The room was kept clean and tidy; a Venus flytrap sat on the desk, unmoving but thriving, taking in all the sunlight. Austin looked out the window, which had an incredible view of the green fields surrounding the school and the boundaries of the school and the Little Grobs. The water rushed on in this part of the stream quicker than other parts; it was quite a cool view.

"Why is the door wide open?" Ena practically screamed. Her face was completely worried and frazzled; she got onto her knees on the verge of tears, unable to stand up.

"Hey, erm…It's okay. We are here, but we can lock up the barrier. Everything will be fine," Austin said in a soothing tone.

"But where is Mr Bert? He runs this place. He is supposed to be here. What if something happened to him?" Ena sobbed out, her tears dripping down to the rug. Austin noticed a butterfly hovering over Ena's head; Austin guessed that it was Ena's familiar. Austin felt like putting out his finger to the fella, but he knew that you weren't supposed to touch someone else's familiar. *What form does my familiar take on?* Austin wondered but quickly focused back on Ena.

"How about we check with Alana? Maybe she knows if he's safe or not. If not, we can go see Peggy and ask her if she's heard anything about it. Maybe he passed through the sickbay?" Ena nodded in reply, but she was still sobbing uncontrollably. Austin continued to explore the room and noticed a picture of a man and his daughters up on the wall. *Wait, I know that girl,* Austin recalled but was at a loss for details. "Beatrice. Mr Bert. And Beatrice's sister." Austin was puzzling the pieces together.

"Her name was Mariah. She was one of the four heroes that day. She died protecting Beatrice. Mr Bert lives on campus; he takes care of all security measures including the lockdown procedures, which never came on. Something must've happened to him. But he is all Beatrice has left; he was a single father to his two girls." Ena's voice now was becoming more clear. The girl resembled her father; they both shared the blonde silver colour hair, but his was short. She also had his stormy blue eyes, which were covered by his glasses.

"Should we check the surveillance or take a copy and lock up before we go to Alana?" Austin asked Ena. She nodded in reply; she seemed much more put together but still fragile. They copied the surveillance for later and shut the barrier as well as locked up. The rest of security would be here soon; they were probably at the sports wing now, reliant on Mr Bert doing his job, but everyone was acting too slow today. Something awful happened, and Austin was going to find out what. They acted hastily when locking up the room, not that it made much of a difference since the assailant had access to the office, but they did what they could.

They rushed off to the front office to use the loudspeaker to try and find Mr Bert.

****

Charlie and Beatrice were at the sports wing, which was now half rubble. A large stadium that could've previously fit 30,000 people was now wrecked. You could see the path the giant intruder took by the massive hole on the far side. It let in sunlight, which shone in on the dead creature, which was limp on the ground. Its body was a massive tree trunk, with two smaller trees that extended from the main body. The head was mostly covered by the bushy and curly leaves. The afro suited the ent; it almost made it look like a peaceful hipster.

68

ALMOST. The creature had massive fangs extending from its mouth. "Kinda scary, huh?" Charlie asked Beatrice, but the girl shook her head in disapproval. The little girl mouthed the words 'Nothing scares me'. Her face was straight and determined. They stood on top of the highest chairs, looking down at the wreckage. The benches slowly descended to the now burning field. Beatrice jumped down stair by stair fiercely towards the action. Charlie followed in her footsteps until they met ground level where they were stopped by the national guards.

"We are the regional bureau of Westbrook Security. You are in a restricted zone; we ask of you to leave," one of two guards demanded; they were both in a uniform: a black suit and red tie-up. The most interesting part of the get-up was a stamp on both of their ties. The stamp had a multicoloured gem surrounded by their official name in gold.

"Actually, as part of the pacifist committee of this school, we would like to ask you a few questions." The girl beamed. The second man couldn't resist the charming little girl's act; he knelt on one knee as if to say 'go for it'. "Well, firstly, how much damage was done? Do you know who was behind this? And was there anything stolen?" The girl dropped the innocent act. The guard rose back to his feet, but the first one answered.

"$500,000. we're working on it, and that is classified," the guard said blatantly out of patience.

"Thanks, officers; we best be on our way." Charlie took the girl's hand, who wanted to ask more questions. They walked away from the field and the dead creature and into the shadows of the rubble back towards the main part of the school.

****

Ena had a list of names, most of which were crossed out. Peggy, Alana, Mrs Rimesdome…

The last name on the list: Beatrice. Charlie and Beatrice were at the language centre when Ena and Austin found them. Ena approached them. "B, I've already notified the school, and the Westbrook police are already looking for him." Ena looked down to the floor.

"Hold up, I need an explanation. What's going on?" the 12-year-old girl asked.

Charlie stood by her side. "What?" he said as he saw both didn't want to answer. Austin spoke up.

"It's still too early to tell, but your dad, he's missing." He looked the girl in her stormy blue eyes. Something snapped, but she didn't show it.

"No, he isn't, new boy!" She stomped on Austin's foot and ran out. Charlie looked at both of them before running after Beatrice. The language room was empty, besides for a room where three men were arguing. Ena sat down at a nearby desk and buried her head into her arms while Austin couldn't help but look. One of the three men in the room had a rough stubble and a raincoat on a perfectly sunny day. He seemed like the one in control, with another larger man with a beard and an oversized beanie on his bald head by his side. The man who wore a beanie seemed like the first man's bodyguard. The other man on the other side of the long glass table was tall, white, pale and wore completely black clothing. The lean man had a dark-coloured phoenix by him, with beady, pure black-coloured eyes. The singular man was accessorised with skull rings on each finger, his hair slicked black. The conversation got heated, and both men got up, but the tall, pale man left. He opened the door to notice Austin as if he knew him. They had a brief moment of just looking at each other before the man walked away. The detective came out of the office looking at Austin with a curios expression.

"I'm Detective Weatherson. You are the student that brought me here, right? Austin?" Without pausing, the man continued. "I've been assigned Mr Bert's case, and I want to assure you that I will do my best to find him and bring him back to safety. He is a top priority case."

"Do you have any leads?" Austin felt hopeless.

"Not yet. We are currently looking into the surveillance; you wouldn't happen to have a copy? Seems like someone has tampered with it, and the original copy is gone," the coated man said. Austin shook his head. "Well, all right then. I'll see you around." The man smiled.

Austin returned back to Ena. "What was that about?" she asked.

"What do you think?" Austin paused. "Met the detective on the case. Who even wears a coat in the middle of a sunny day? He is indoors, isn't he?"

Ena simply shrugged. "What was he doing with Dr Hurt?" Austin could only guess that was the pale man. *What a fitting name. Not suspicious at all,* Austin thought. They got up and started walking towards the dormitories. "We have another meeting after the assembly tomorrow; this time don't be late." The girl in a sombre mood left for the dormitories without a goodbye. He was suddenly left alone again. He questioned everything he was doing. Lying to the officers for a club that he has barely joined and a bunch of people he barely knew. Things at the school seem to be escalating when this is supposed to be a safe space for him. With all these disappearances Austin feels empathetic. It must be why he feels he has to do everything he can to help because the police never helped him.

Chapter 8
Assembly

Everyone formed in the cafeteria for the assembly. A black man stood on top of the stage, ready to present. He had this authoritative aura around him, making him look like the principal. He wore a black button-up shirt with a loose red school tie on; he looked more like an undercover spy than a principal. "Sorry, students, for missing the last assembly. I was on a work trip." The man hesitated on the words 'work trip'. His voice had a strong accent of some type, but Austin couldn't pinpoint it. "Today, we commemorate the anniversary of the four brave students. It's been two years now since Delio, Mariah, Selene and Michael fought against the power of evil to save their fellow classmates. They were our friends, our family, and they were supposed to be safe here. I know I only came to Westbrook this year, but I hope to make us safer than ever." Beatrice stood up.

"Professor Jackson (so that's what his name was), what do you claim as 'safe' because in my definition, it doesn't include an ent rampaging the school, no lockdown procedure in an emergency and teachers going missing." *Teachers? As in plural?* Austin realised there was a lot going on in this school that was much below ground level.

"All of that is being dealt with, Beatrice." The principal forced a smile and gestured for her to sit down. The rest of the assembly was a blur to Austin, just the regular stuff: maintenance jobs (and they weren't making a big deal of an ent rampaging the school. He talked about fixing the sports wing as if it were a normal simple occurrence), timings for certain meetings and other news from the surrounding Westbrook community.

Austin was sitting with Fred and Riona, who surprisingly wasn't even in her sports uniform. Just in the normal girl's uniform. "This uniform is so clingy," Riona said, pulling at her shirt. *I guess there was no sport after the major accident*, Austin thought to himself. Mrs Rimesdome walked up on stage. "Well, I'm sure most of you have been wondering what that big veiled poster is above me." The vice-principal smiled. *Actually, I didn't notice that*, Austin thought to himself. "Well, it is how we will honour and remember the four students, who will be remembered as heroes. Our principal, Professor Jackson, insisted, so without further ado"—she turned towards the ravelled poster—"*LEHAROT!*" The word of the vice principle echoed through the whole cafeteria with such power. As that word was mouthed, the poster unfurled and showed in all its glory the school symbol with a photo of each victim on the corners. "I would like to bring forward the student who designed the poster and could make this possible, Emily!"

The girl walked up on stage and started to explain the poster. "The school symbol and general symbol of Westbrook, the four-headed beast, is the centre of attention representing the four original Westbrook siblings. The gazelle obviously resembles Venus, and the gorilla: Killian, tiger: Terra and bear: Destiny. Everyone knows that were their spirit animals and merged together they made Westbrook. Much like how these heroes each represent a part of Westbrook. Delio." She pointed to the top right corner of the poster. "Mariah." She pointed to the top left. "Selene." She pointed to the bottom right. "Michael." Then she pointed to the bottom left. Emily went to explain the colour choices and font types for ten minutes before finally walking off the stage and back to her seat.

"I don't get it, why do we commemorate four siblings that hated each other and murdered each other?" Riona whispered.

"Allegedly," Jack whispered back; his short brown hair was wet, as if he had just got out of a pool. He had just joined them halfway through the assembly.

"They were the most powerful witches and wizards of all time," Fred intervened. "Good enough reason, even if they had the wrong intentions." The assembly wrapped up, and Austin got up and walked towards the table to meet Ena and Lela, but he could only find Jarred.

"Any leads on who let the ent in?"

"Ohhh, hi." Jarred turned around. "Well…I figured out that whoever let it in had to be working with someone else to guide the ent in, but that's not all, they would also have to have access to the control room." Both students started walking towards the club room. Jarred had short, curly brown hair and for some reason was wearing shades indoors.

"So who has access to the room?" asked Austin.

"Well, there is the whole IT club, school captains Lilly and Tanner, Ena and Lela, Beatrice, Mr Bert, Principal Jackson and Mrs Rimesdome. But that's not the question you should be asking. All those people have a key card access and assuming they're all to be trusted, which I have my doubts, but whatever then, it would lead us to whoever stole a key card. I searched the lost and found on the school website, and a senior named Cheryl-Ann has reported her key card lost, the day before the office was broken into," Jarred explained.

"So what you're saying is that the key card was stolen by the culprit," Austin summarised.

They made it to the meeting on time. Ena and Beatrice were exchanging information, while Lela was talking to other students, two Year 7 girls, who left the room after their quick conversation. Apparently Westbrook had a middle school counterpart not too far away. The schools would work closely together on accelerated programs. It is the reason Beatrice was at the school and other from years seven and eight. "Quiet. This won't be a long meeting, but I would just like to give you guys a few updates on our investigation," Lela said and went over what Jarred had previously said. "So I need two volunteers to interview Cheryl-Ann." She held up a photo of her. She was very pale, with whitish blonde hair and grey-blue eyes and a white choker.

"I'll do it," Austin heard himself say.

"Anyone else?" Lela looked around.

"Well, if no one else wants to do it, I will." Beatrice spoke up.

"Thank you, you two report back to me later. Meeting dismissed," Lela said.

Beatrice walked up to Austin. "Meet you after classes." Everyone left for their classes; Austin's class was potions and brewing classes. He entered the classroom, which was part greenroom and half science room. The greenroom part was filled with magical plants and some ordinary ones too. For some reason, there were potatoes. The plant life was so vibrant and overgrown in a good way. There were plants of every colour and of all sizes, but the main feature plant was an overgrown stalk, much like the fairy tale stalk; it went through a specified hole in the ceiling. The greenroom transitioned into a science room with a dozen posters, a large whiteboard and 15 tables, filled with various equipment. Most of the equipment Austin saw was pretty usual, like Bunsen burners, various vials and scalpels, but some of the equipment was pretty extraordinary. Tubes of various colourful substances hung from the ceiling in an organised manner; an electrical metal conducted cone made up of looped poles stood on a metal platform provided on each table. As well as an ultraviolet circular light with the same outer shelling as the cones beneath them was found above each table. He noticed several students already on their assignments. The teacher seemed very upbeat; she wore a sunflower hat literally made from a giant sunflower, a patchy dress half made out of the mesh that is used with burlap sacks. She wore glasses with lenses that created a rainbow effect on her gleaming eyes.

"Hi, I'm Mrs Legend, but all my students call me Molly. Shhhh, don't tell the other teachers; we aren't exactly supposed to use our first name. Still trying to figure your way around, huh?" She smiled as she put out her hand to shake Austin's. She was overly excited and very energetic.

"Ohh, yeah, hmm," Austin agreed awkwardly.

"You're not in trouble, come here. I will get you to catch up with the work." Molly Legend went on to explain that the coiled cone focused the energy produced by certain plants into a beam only seen in ultraviolet light. Soon enough, Austin saw himself making those beams; all the students around him were testing out from different plants from the greenhouse part of the room. Lela and Ena shared a desk, shooting pulses of energy from a spiky yellow ball plant that Austin had never seen before "A sprangle nut, but don't be fooled, they're quite poisonous and indigenous to Hylenia." Ena caught Austin looking. Austin shook his head and tried some of the potatoes, which for some reason made the largest beams. *Maybe it's all that stored starch?* Austin thought to himself.

"What are we doing here?" Fred walked in late like Austin and decided to join him as his partner. "Wow!" He watched Austin experiment.

"Looking at the energy released from the plants in the ultraviolet light," he said, not even turning away from his project. The pair tested multiple plants before, creating a lab report as their first official practical assessment of the potions class. Austin began to notice that a lot of these classes were very hands on. It was so interesting to Austin who hadn't been surrounded by magic much when he was growing up. Finally, the school bell rang, and the students left for their next classes. The hallway was once again a major labyrinth; he was headed to Troleze class (one of the dialects for the troll nation). Beatrice had other plans; she struck her ambush.

"Hey, new kid, I have a free period, let's go find Chery-Ann. I already got her timetable from Jarred." She tugged Austin's arm in the opposite direction. Her uniform was oversize on her. Compared to Austin, she looked like a primary school student, even if she were a Year 7. Ena had explained that due to her situation where her dad had to live on campus and so did she, she was enrolled as an honorary member till 9th grade.

"But I don't have a free period," Austin explained but was replied to with a face that basically said, 'Do I care?' Austin gave up the argument.

"Let's go," she said impatiently. They headed towards the IT room. The class was filled with different model computers, a giant screen with the coding on it and a dozen robots. Sure enough, Cheryl-Ann was coding a robot with her white choker on. She wore the basic girls uniform, but instead of the regular school socks, she wore white doily stockings. Deep in thought, she did not see Austin or Beatrice approaching. "Earth to ghost lady." Beatrice waved. Cheryl-Ann looked up for a split second before getting back to her robot.

"Uhuh," the girl said uninterested.

"We would just like to ask you a few questions regarding your key card," Austin said.

"Ohh, actually I found it in my locker earlier today. I must have forgotten about it; no worries if that's it." Her eyes were still focused on her coding.

"Okay, thanks for your co-operation."

Austin started to leave as Beatrice stomped her foot and complained, "What co-operation? She did nothing; it's a dead end." Before they left, they were greeted by Frederico, the head of the computer club, aka Fred.

"Watcha doin?" He raised his bushy eyebrows.

"Just following up on a lead, but it seems like nothing," Austin answered.

"Okay, but if there is anything wrong with my club, or it's caught up in any way, I want to know about it, okay?" the Latin boy expressed. Austin and Beatrice shook their heads in agreeance before they walked towards the Pacifist Club to log in the news, but they were interrupted yet again; this time by Detective Weatherson.

"I thought I told you guys to back down from this case; the adults are handling it. It really isn't a place for an abandoned child to be looking for her father."

Austin stared at Weatherson in the eyes. "Actually, you didn't tell us to step down, nor is it in your jurisdiction to tell us to step down, so we will not. This is just as much our case as it is yours because it is our school, not yours." Austin walked past him with Beatrice half pushing him out of the way. The two nearly reached the club room when Beatrice apologised.

"I'm kind of sorry about stepping on your foot yesterday, just wanted to keep your streak with Peggy going." She smirked.

"You know about that?" Austin laughed.

"Yeah, the whole school knows about it, and you know it's an honour. I hardly ever apologise, really thanks for helping." She looked down at her feet, her tone changing sincere halfway through her sentence.

"You're welcome," Austin said, as he turned the doorknob.

"Oh, I'll leave you to log in all the boring stuff, see you." She closed the door behind her before Austin could argue, but he just sighed and logged in all the useless data from their failed mission.

****

Austin found himself staring at the ceiling in his bed; all the wood around him seemed to make him calmer. "Where are you, Dad?" Austin spoke to himself. Things at Westbrook weren't exactly normal; strange things were going on. *What do I do now? The lead was a dead end unless.* Austin jumped out of bed and put on some clothes and left his bed. You weren't supposed to leave the dorms at night, but this was too important. Austin had second thoughts, but he didn't let that stop him; he grabbed his wand. The triangular wooden prism was too large for his pocket, so it stuck out, the engraved symbols showing. In the distance, there was something coming, something big with a low growl. Austin was in the hallway; he had to reach Ena's room; she had the evidence, but he would need to get past the chimera; it was now in vision in the dark hallway. The ivory walls loomed above Austin on each side and doors as far as the eye could see, each unique in their own way. From the orientation video that Austin had watched, he knew that the growl he heard was a species of beast that among others worked for the schools and kept kids in their beds at night, but these things did not look very friendly from the video, and Austin didn't want to see them in person. "There was something in my book about this creature," Austin muttered to himself. He started on a jog to Ena's room away from the growl that came from the distance. Then a second beast let out a roar in the direction Austin was going; he didn't have much of a choice. He continued now running; he wasn't too far from her room, but the beast was right in his way. It was terrifying; it had four legs and looked like a regular lion from the bottom, but it got stranger as from the lion's back sprouted two purple spiked wings, and the creatures drooled from its mouths. Yes, plural. The centre head was a lion with a boar's head to its left side and a serpent to the right. The serpent had green poison-looking drool whilst the boar had red drool looking like blood. They both made sizzling sounds as they touched the red-carpeted ground, but the lion seemed intelligent and old. It didn't drool like the other two heads. Then the thing you would least expect happened.

"Austin," growled the lion.

"Yeah." Austin inched forward; they were now within two-metre distance.

"I wouldn't get any closer if I were you." Just as the lion said that, both, the boar and the serpent, snapped at Austin's head.

"Stop that!" snarled the lion. "Let the boy speak."

Both heads turned towards the middle and asked simultaneously, "Then can we eat him after?" The serpent had a hiss to its voice, and the boar sounded croaky and rough.

"Sometimes I think both of you share half a brain." Both heads hissed in disapproval. *I didn't know boars could hiss,* Austin thought to himself but thought it would be stupid to say aloud.

"Look, I got important information that just can't wait."

"Do you have a hall pass? Detective Weatherson should be with you at your room right about now." The heads continued snapping. Austin just shook his head. *What is he talking about?* A stupid idea popped into Austin's head.

"I don't think that kid has one either." Austin pointed to the roof, and the idea seemed to work. The boar and the serpent looked up; the lion didn't, but luckily, the wings on the lion's back were controlled by the serpent, who started to go up to find the other kid apparently on the ceiling.

"No, you idiots, get AUSTIN." The serpent turned around too fast and hit the boar into the side of the wall. The beast crumpled to the floor, all tangled up. Austin ran and didn't dare look back…He ran up to door number 1282, a transparent rainbow-stained glass door, you could see plants all over the room through the glass. Austin knocked on the door; a minute later, Ena came to the door, dressed in *My Little Pony* pyjamas.

"What are you doing? It's one in the morning; there are chimeras on guard. Are you stupid?" She gave him a sympathetic look. "You have a cut on your arms. Come in, I have a first-aid kit." She led him inside; the interior was amazing, a domed ceiling lined with luscious vines and bright windows that led out to a starry night. The floor was made of moss with minimal furniture. Her bed was a loft made of bamboo, with a rope ladder stringing down. A yoga mat lay rolled up in the corner, next to a small water fountain. She set Austin on a little nook looking out at the night sky. You could see the Little Grobs River streaming down; it was beautiful. She started bandaging Austin up.

"I didn't even realise I got scratched in the fight," Austin said, but he was met with a solid glare.

"What fight?" But he shrugged it off.

"There is something more important. We know that Cheryl-Ann's key card was missing at the time that Mr Bert's office was broken into, right?"

"But I read your log; you said she just misplaced it," Ena stated.

"Well, that's what I thought at first, but what if the thief put the key card back into the locker afterwards?"

"Couldn't this have waited till tomorrow?" The girl yawned as she finished dressing and bandaging the few wounds.

"No, you have the only evidence that can place the culprit at the crime: the tapes." The boy paused for a second. "Detective Weatherson knows you have it."

"How can you be sure?" the girl questioned.

"Call it intuition." Not a moment after, Detective Weatherson's voice called down the corridor.

"Get me those tapes. I will visit every room until I get it!"

He could hear the detective coming towards this room. Ena quickly handed Austin the tapes and hushed him out the window; it was at least four storeys high, and there was only a small ledge across the outside. He decided he would stick it out and hide out here. Austin thought he was done until he heard a familiar creature. The Tachash swooped in to view, its glittery coat reflecting the moonlight. "But how did you get through the city borders?" Austin had an epiphany; he felt so stupid. "Wait a second, Wendy said something about familiars being allowed through the borders; you can't be my familiar, can you?" The unicorn creature neighed in approval. Austin hopped on the creature's back It all made sense seeing them in the wild nearly impossible. The whole flying thing, it felt like a dream. He knew he felt a connection to the creature how could he be so oblivious. Ena appeared at the window. Her eyes wide with shock. That is probably how Austin reacted the first time. A large winged unicorn flapping outside their building. It was something surreal, but Austin just begun to accept all the craziness that had been happening recently. "How? What?" Ena could barely speak as she posed the question not evening taking her eyes off Bob. Austin heard the detective incoming, his voice becoming louder and closer. "Hey, I will explain later okay. Sounds like you are about to have company. I was never here." Austin hopped on the creature's back and quickly said goodbye to Ena before fleeing with the tapes, leaving the school behind. He guided the creature to the edge of Westbrook where a single bunker was left open and a kid was roasting marshmallows on his own by a cosy campfire. Was he talking to someone? But no one stood next to him in the clearing. The boy wore the familiar black outfit with black denim jeans and a leather studded jacket. He faced towards the woods where a tree nymph stood. You could tell he was part of the tree, but he was also in the form of a human. He had chocolate-coloured skin like the tree and looked about 18, but Austin knew he had to be older. He had dreadlocks and a large tattoo of his family tree. That had to be a joke right? He wore a loose open cardigan weaved of leaves, exposing his tattoo. They were deep in conversation until the tree nymph saw him but was shocked when he saw the Tachash. Then Ethan turned to see him land. The Tachash seemed to shrink to fit the landing. Austin knew Ethan ran away to his parents' lodge in Westbrook, but this was the first time he had seen it. Looking at it now it looks more like a cave in the middle of the Westbrook woods.

"I wasn't expecting you, but now that you're here, I think we've got a lot to talk about," Ethan said.

Chapter 9
A Girl Named Unity

"Austin, meet Cato. Cato, this is Austin," Ethan introduced them.

"So this is the boy of the prophecy, huh?" Cato stayed in the shaded woods; he stood on one of his branches, almost blending in.

"So you're a tree nymph," Austin said in response, looking him in the eyes, trying to determine how old he was.

"An ent if you want to be accurate, but some folk stories prefer to use the word 'tree deity'." The boy had a very raspy and deep voice, but yet it sounded very young still.

"Wait a second, I'm confused, so a big tree being and tree deity are both ents?"

Cato looked at him for ten seconds deciding whether that was a question or just common knowledge. Ultimately, he answered, "Ent is a general term for a tree spirit. I'm guessing what you are comparing me to is the big guy that broke into your school? Those are mountain ents, their own species but still closely related. They have never been good news, all that stump zero brain. Last I heard, they were hibernating. I guess not. I am the much more common ent or tree deity." Cato swung down from his tree and landed with a thump. "And who is this?" Austin's familiar had shrunk an incredible size so that it looked like a cat.

"That is Bob," Austin answered, but he was greeted with a low snarl from the unicorn-like creature.

Ethan spoke now; he had been very quiet. "That is a girl, you know that, right?"

"Oh!" Austin was surprised; he felt dumb for just assuming that his familiar was the same gender as he was. "I think a new name is in order then."

"Cleo?" No response.

Ethan suggested a name, "Opal?" Referencing to her coat.

"How about Calypso?" Cato asked; the familiar neighed in approval and cuddled up to him at his feet. Austin still wasn't sure of all the rules behind familiars, but he thought that they weren't allowed to be touched by anyone else, or maybe that was just wizards and didn't extend to tree deities. Cato looked so human he had dark flesh, long dark silky hair and intelligent eyes. Austin had to remind himself that Cato was part tree.

Cato started to speak as he pet Calypso. "It's not a good sign, the mountain ent; they only stir in the times of war." He sat down on the ground, and Calypso curled up in his lap. Austin barely knew Cato. He has barely gotten to know his own familiar, Calypso. Austin hated that he liked the name. He felt jealous of Cato petting her. It was his spirit, Calypso was apart of Austin. The realisation just begun to set in.

Ethan was still roasting marshmallows and handed one to Austin. The campfire was really bright, and it made crackling sounds, which calmed the situation. "Do you remember the last time they were active?" Ethan asked.

"I don't, but I have heard rumours that they were active during Terra's tyrannical phase." Cato spoke up.

Ethan chimed in bouncing off what Cato said, "Weird occurrences have been happening throughout Hylenia: tree spirits going missing, leaving their trees to die; it hasn't reached within the Westbrook barriers yet, but the outside forest is under attack."

"How do you know?" Austin asked Ethan, but Cato answered.

"The nature's council has called it an emergency; these are the biggest nature observers, tree deities, nature spirits from Hylenia, and globally, all of them called a meeting last week to discuss the crisis and found that the number of naturistic attacks have risen rapidly. Whatever is happening, they have targeted us first."

"I think that maybe all of this is all related," Austin said. Cato and Ethan gave him a curious look. "I believe that it doesn't stop there. People have gone missing." Austin paused. Ethan gave him a knowing look. "Teachers at Westbrook, even regular high-ranking citizens. Something big is going on, and there has been talk about it being the OS. I don't quite know who I can trust at Westbrook yet, but it seems that it is the centre of all this. I have been trying to figure everything out, and I may just have the evidence we need." Austin pulled out the tape from his back pocket. Ethan stretched out his hand. "I don't think we can trust the police or any sort of security with this yet."

"What is that?" Cato asked.

"It's like a video projector and memory storage device," Austin answered.

"I know what it is! What is on it?" Cato frowned. Austin just assumed he didn't know what it was because he was a tree spirit. He didn't know what they did; it was his first time talking to one. And this one had a short temper.

"This is the footage from within the control centre at Westbrook. That day, the lead IT/security personnel went missing, and it looked like he left in a hurry, leaving his computer open and his daughter still at school. On top of that, the culprits who were working with the mountain ents would've had to disable the forcefield from within here," Austin explained it all.

Ethan shot a devilish smile. "Let's have a movie night then."

Fireflies buzzed up the night. Ethan passed marshmallows all around, and Austin fumbled the device around before Ethan took it from his hand and pressed a button. A holographic image appeared and started playing the recording. They sat there for hours looking for anything. Austin noticed how calm Calypso was with Cato and she allowed herself to be pet. Austins' annoyance had died down and he settled into detective mode watching the footage. It was mostly just Mr Bert going about his work on double speed until he saw something on his computer and rushed out of the room. From the camera angle, it was unclear what he saw, but he looked very stressed. Austin looked at the time stamp: five minutes before the ent's rampage. Then they saw him. Austin shivered, and Ethan quickly looked towards him. "That isn't THE symbol? Is it?" But Austin just nodded.

"What do you mean?" Cato had been watching from his tree; he was now hanging upside down but was completely serious.

The hologram was paused on someone; they had a mask on and were unrecognisable and, surely enough, using Cheryl-Ann's key card. They wore a hoodie with the same black, red and blue circular symbol as the OS. It was the same symbol that was on the people's backs who kidnapped Irora. It couldn't all be related, could it? Ethan kept the device; he called it a graphicker and promised he would let Austin know if he found anything else. "You know Ethan I'm sorry about how we left it the other day. I know that you are trying to stay out of the radar. I should've thought about that before suggesting you come to the school. I just want what's best for you. You are my best friend after all." Ethan turned his head away just staring at the fire so Austin continued. "Well if it makes you feel any better Westbrook has been crazy. It's hard fitting in and remembering names and not knowing people. Especially when that is all you're used to growing up in a small town." Austin paused for a second. "I wish I had just come to visit but instead I pulled you into all this we should be talking about normal teenage things not gangs and mysteries."

Ethan finally looked up, "Austin, I pulled myself into this before you even showed up. But thank you for everything." He said it awkwardly, usually Ethan doesn't get too sentimental. Austin decided to get going back to school and pretend like nothing happened. That this night didn't happen he didn't need the school figuring out he left unattended. He woke up Calypso, and they both headed back to school and collapsed in his dorm. He only got two hours of sleep before he needed to wake up for school. He showered, joined everyone at breakfast and gobbled down a stack of pancakes. He was heading towards Troleze class the first period of the day before he got interrupted again. *What do these people have against Troleze? Every time I go to this class I am always being interrupted.* Detective Weatherson stared blankly into Austin's eyes.

"We know you have them. They weren't in your room last night. Neither were you." The man squinted as if he were trying to analyse Austin as a piece in an art gallery.

"Well, you see the thing is—" Austin began.

"He was with me. I wanted to go over how the school was treating him." Mrs Rimesdome smiled as she stepped between the pair. "How about we continue our discussion from last night, shall we?" The woman walked away with Austin and shared not a word between the two until they reached the office. "I know you want to be the hero, Austin, but right now, I'm dealing with 20 missing cases reports just from our school. I really need any information you have." The woman's eyes swelled with tears; you could tell she really cared for the school. They both took a seat in leather-lined velvet chairs. Her office crackled with electricity that coursed through the rods that could be seen through the transparent plastic. "You and I both know that you weren't with me last night, and I don't care where you were. I know in the first week kids like to sneak out and talk with friends at night, but I just need any information you have."

"Okay," the boy said. "Pass me a paper and some pens." She complied, clearly interested. He drew out the symbol he saw in the tapes. "A branch of the OS. I presume, they have contacts in this school and are involved with the ent." Austin looked down towards his feet.

"You have seen this symbol before, haven't you?" The woman pointed to the symbol. The walls seemed to be closing in and pressure building up; it felt as if there was no air in the room. The energy seen through the Perspex seemed to be building up like a thunder storm raging all around him and he was in the eye of the storm. Austin calmed himself from hyperventilating and got up from his chair. All he could manage was a nod. "I know the last thing you need is more news, but they're watching you, the counsel," the woman said.

"You're part of that counsel, aren't you?" Austin stuttered.

"I am."

"Who is Caleb?"

"A friend of your parents."

"Then how come I've never met him?" No response. "Why does everyone lie to me, like you all know some big secret! Thanks for your help."

"Your mum was trying to protect you; a war is brewing, and we are just trying to protect you as long as possible."

"Well, everyone is doing a great job of that."

Austin recalled something from his conversation with Mr Trolt. *My dad worked against that organisation. But wasn't he accused of being a spy for the OS? Is this all related?* Austin walked out and headed to Troleze class; maybe he might even get 10 minutes in.

****

"Last period of the week; let's go." Fred pushed through the crowd of students. "Wow, you look dead-tired, bro. Your first week must've been so tiring."

"Tell me about it. I feel like the walking dead. I didn't get any sleep last night," Austin muttered. They were in the sports wing and went into a martial arts den. It was inside the gymnasium which was overcrowded with students with the oval still under reconstruction.

"Tactical class, the most important class you will ever take in your life!" A man in really short shorts and a white t-shirt screamed. He had a red whistle hanging from his neck; he was pretty short, about 4'7" and rocked a small goatee. "Roll on in, kids. Line up." He arranged everyone in height order, but even the shortest kid was taller than him. "From now on, you will call me coach and only coach, is that clear!" A few students muttered something. "I said, is that clear!"

An overwhelming 'YES, COACH!' went up. *Are we on military training or something?*

"What are we working with here a bunch of chum. Good thing they finally introduced a martial arts class here. I've asked for years before I was a mere math teacher," the coach summed up with a snort. A few students chuckled. *Seriously, a math teacher?* "I will pair you up now. I will make it fair; I know this is a mixed-age class." The coach sorted the group into pairs. "Charlie, you will go with Austin." They fist-bumped; everyone was given their own area, while the coach was up the front with some unlucky kid. "We're going to start off with some manoeuvres. I learnt this move in my American Marine training up in Quantico." The coach gleamed, but the boy in front of him looked terrified. The coach grabbed the kid and twisted his leg and smacked him to the floor in one swift move; a small shriek escaped. "You will be fine, kid, walk it off." The kid could barely get up, but he listened. Everyone started practising different manoeuvres from more 'demonstrations', which sent a few kids to the nurse's office. *I'm sure Peggy wouldn't be too impressed*, Austin thought.

"Hey, how do you know Beatrice?" Austin spoke to his partner. Austin's brown eyes connected to Charlie's blue eyes; he knew he had met a touchy subject, but they continued to spar.

"Beatrice's sister, Mariah, was my girlfriend, and Mariah made me promise to look after her little sister when…" Charlie said but tried to distract himself with the sparring.

"I'm sorry." Charlie just nodded in response.

"Hey, you two! Stop talking, that's detention after class!" Coach barked. Austin knew better than to complain. Austin hadn't really spoken to Charlie before he knew that the boy was also in the Pacifist Club and a year above him, a junior. Austin found sparring was a good way to get to know someone, even if they couldn't talk. Charlie was about the same size as him, around 5'8", and although he had seemingly clear skin; he had a bit of acne. Austin also noticed a scar on the other boy's jaw, hard to notice unless you were paying close attention. Austin started to pre-dodge his predictable moves. Although Charlie was a fair bit stronger, he was quite slow and repeated the same moves in a sequence. It was all light-hearted, but by the end of the lesson, Austin was so tired, and now he had a Friday afterschool detention. The class passed quickly, and the coach explained how they needed to reorganise the food closet.

"Sorry." Fred slapped him on the back and left the class, while Charlie and Austin were left to do some chores.

"Here are the keys, Charlie, you know the way," the coach said and walked off. The two boys headed down the hallway.

"Coach was probably given this task and just passed it off to us." Austin smirked.

"Probably." Charlie chuckled.

****

The two boys reached the food storage closet. It was surprisingly big with ladders that moved like you would have in a library to get the hard-to-reach items. It was very cool in the room, with mist curling at the floor, mid-calf in height. Any ingredient you could probably think of was in here. A large shipping container full of new stock was waiting to be unloaded. "Better get to work," Charlie said, but he sensed it too; something was off.

SKSK

Both guys looked behind them, and a can of beans was knocked onto the floor. "HELLO? Anyone there?" Austin called out. Charlie flicked out a flashlight that the coach had given them because the room had no working lights. He searched around the room until he found a girl a few years younger than him, maybe 14. She wore a tattered tie-dye top and denim shorts; she looked petrified and scared. She seemed as if she hadn't seen the sun in a year.

"Are you okay?" The boys walked towards her, but the girl backed up.

"I'm Charlie, and this is Austin; we're not going to hurt you." The boys inched forward.

"Noooo, bad people, very bad people," she hissed. Her skin was a shade of blue; there were no windows in the room. How long had she been stuck here? By the look of the storage area, it looked like it hadn't been restocked in at least a month.

"Here take my jacket." Charlie gave it to her; the young girl snatched it from him and put it on. She tried to stand up but just collapsed; the pair tried to help her up, but she just screamed. A teacher ran in; it was Molly Legend, the potions and the brewing teacher. She wore denim overalls and a green linen top.

"Ohhh my, it is freezing in here. Unity, is that you? I haven't seen you since school started a week ago. Come, let's get you somewhere warm. Boys, pick her up." The boys complied and went with Mrs Legend all the way to the infirmary. Peggy, the young nurse, saw them come in.

"Austin, back so soon, huh?" But her smile dropped as soon as she saw Unity. "Bring her in here." Peggy hurried. Unity had lost the energy to put up a fight. They propped her on a table. "She seems to be hallucinating, with possible frostbite." She placed her hand on her head but quickly pulled away. "Get Mr Tatson!" Molly rushed off to get the head doctor, leaving Peggy to deal with Unity. Charlie and Austin just waited in the corner. Peggy held out her wand and placed it on the girl's forehead; her skin colour seemed to be coming back, but the girl seemed to shift on her table; her skin turned to an olive colour. The young nurse took the patient's temperature, which was extremely low. "If you boys hadn't found her she…" The nurse's voice faltered. "It's just lucky you found her when you did." The girl muttered something lying on the table, when Mr Tatson rushed in; he wore a white coat like Peggy that had his nametag on it, saying, 'Head of the Infirmary'. He had intense blue eyes and short black hair and a stubble. He whispered something under his breath when he saw the girl and quickly ushered all the bystanders to get out.

"She will be okay; she is in good hands." Just as he said that, the girl started to convulse, but the boys and Molly listened and shut the door behind them.

"Austin, we should log this into the data pool. She is the first missing person to be recovered; this could be important," Charlie said.

"You think?" Austin said in a very clear sarcastic tone.

Chapter 10
The Carnival

"Hey, Mum," The boy sat in his bedroom, surrounded by oak, with a few of his possessions filling the room. The gift box that he had received from the school had been raided for all of its treats. His room was completely in order; it really was a reflection of who he was: plain wood, simple, with a flare of all his favourite hobbies, movies and destinations on his poster. There was a waterfall photo of him and his family on one of the good days when they were all together. A Pirates of the Caribbean poster and some of his favourite video games.

"Mum, since I have been here, it's been very strange. I have met people who claim to know you, like Mr Trolt and Caleb. Who are these people, and why am I only finding out that you graduated from this school now?" The wind slipped through the open window from the night sky. The deep, dark sky flooded with stars in the vast distances, lightyears away. His mum dodged the questions and was very vague and ended the call shortly after. "Well, I am safe. I'm at school." Austin spoke into the phone. "Okay, goodbye."

Technically, it was lights out after 10:30 pm, or you had to deal with the chimeras. Austin was not in the mood for that; he took a sip of some water and turned off his phone. He stared at the calendar he put up on his wall; it was given to all the students and just arrived in his room. For each month, there was a picture of some creature that you wouldn't find in the mundane world. The February page had a phoenix, which practically screeched through the calendar. On the calendar was an event circled with a red marker, 'Field trip to golden oak.' It was one of the most famous monuments of Westbrook. The city evolved around that tree literally and figuratively. The tree was the middlemost point in Westbrook, and there was going to be another long walk ahead.

****

"I don't know why we can't just teleport there?" Austin complained. Austin and Fred walked together on foot in a park; the whole grade was there. It was just past sunrise, and the morning breeze carried the sweet smell of the trees. Fred shrugged his head and was about to talk when a girl wedged her way in between the pair.

"They don't allow any teleporting in a three-kilometre radius of the golden oak for 'security reasons', and traffic is bad around here, so it just became a tradition that the excursion became a hike." Wendy had her wand tied up in her bun and wore a short school skirt and a plain white top. "Also, that is why the school was built so far away so we can still teleport within school grounds. So we are well out of the no teleport radius. Also with the current events, school is doubling down on security so now no more teleporting for a while, boys."

"Are you always listening for questions so you can just jump in and answer, or do you just like to stalk us?" Austin asked. Apparently, Wendy didn't register the sarcasm and just waved it off.

"Hey, Fred, I need to ask you about something." The girl twirled her hair. The boys shared a suspicious glance before Wendy took Fred's elbow and walked off ahead. Austin walked for a minute more before the golden oak tree came into view. It was massive, but somehow very camouflaged. It had golden bark, and the leaves were of all colours; it stood roughly 100 metres tall and at least 50 metres higher than any other tree in the area, which was mostly blooming maple trees. *How do they make maple syrup*? Austin thought to himself. A loudspeaker explained the prohibited items not allowed on the premises, which was a major glass pyramid with a wide-open top half that the tree sprouted from. The louvre in France was a copy of this design; the artist Leoh Ming Pei was actually a wizard who stole the idea from Westbrook and brought it to the outside world. It was remarkable; the original design Austin had only read about it. The tree reminded him of Ms Legend's bean stalk. To get into the structure, there were multiple rows of security, like an airport. Austin put his bag through the belt just like all the other kids and walked through the metal detector. Once all the students were through, they walked into the exhibit. Besides the main art piece, the tree, there were all the sites of the battleground and even some relics, like Saigon, the nature amulet that was covered by what Austin could only guess was bulletproof glass, Destiny's wand, and Kilian's ring among others.

"Did you get the news? Unity will be fine, although she is still in the infirmary." Charlie snuck up from behind Austin.

Austin breathed a sigh of relief before he asked, "There's more, isn't there?" The guy may have been stealthy, but he wasn't a good liar.

"She asked to see both of us," he said as he looked down to the floor.

"She is going to be fine, and we will get to the bottom of this," Austin said trying to comfort Charlie. *What am I even referring to, the disappearing people, the upcoming war or just the reappearance of Unity, and who am I consoling, Charlie, or myself?* Their conversation came to an early close when a girl with short black hair and black glasses stepped to the front of the group of students. She wore the Westbrook uniform, and she was here, so she had to be in Austin's grade or the grade above, but he had never seen her before.

"Fashionably late like always " She did a little bow. "You guys know they are trying to distract you with this excursion so you guys don't notice the real problem, right? They say they do this because they don't want mass panic; obviously that's not good for business, well, guess what? I'm sick of it!" the girl ranted. She had black stockings underneath her school skirt and black eyeliner and nail polish on. The chaperone for this school trip, the coach, just seemed to notice the scene.

"ARIA, come here right this instance or more detention."

"Sounds like more excuses and a way to get me out of classes and away from other students. You know I'm right!" the girl screamed as she was dragged away by two security guards.

"That girl has issues," said Fred as he joined the other two boys. "What is she even going on about. Distraction? She is off her head."

"She's not all wrong, you know," Austin said.

"I know," Fred responded quietly. "How about we go shopping for party outfits? You either make the party or blend in, and I'm not one to blend in." The old Fred started to come back quickly changing the topic never staying serious for too long.

"Party, you say? I am yet to go to one of the famous Westbrook parties. What theme did you say it was?" Austin asked.

"CARNIVAL, my friend; you have not experienced life if you haven't been to one of these parties. They are everything they say they are and more. Tonight will be uber fun. I'm so excited!" Fred smiled. The boring tour was just about to start, and with the coach focused on Aria, the three boys slipped out and headed to the main shopping street conveniently nearby.

****

After going shopping all day, the three boys walked in in their new outfits. Fred had a steampunk retro look, with a red frill top under a black suit while wearing silky oversized black pants with a monocle on. Charlie wore dark makeup around the eyes under a hood attached to an avant-garde coat and an armour chest plate and black studded pants with a metallic look. Austin wore a chain link bronze and gold chest plate over a thin see-through coat with a gothic buckled chained cargo pants. The scene was like out of a movie; everyone dressed up to the theme with feathers or ringmasters; it was truly amazing. Westbrook really new how to deal in a time of crisis. It was a great initiation, Austin was still getting use to the school and a party was a great way to get to know everyone. Food and game stalls were sprawled out everywhere on the yellow grassy plains. Red velvet curtains gave the feeling that it was inside, but the open air suggested otherwise. Lightbulbs were everywhere, buzzing up the night sky, and the smell was like a cross between a Brazilian market and a circus. A few rides were spread out across the grounds, including a love boat ride, a g-force coaster and a Ferris wheel. "Hey, I'm going to quickly check out the food stands; you guys want anything?" called out Fred.

"I'm good," the two boys said in sync, but Fred had already walked off to the stalls. A minute later, Beatrice came running towards the pair.

"Hey, Charlie, can you take me on the G-FORCE? They said I needed an adult to come with me because I'm too short." The girl watched herself kick the grass at her feet. Charlie just shrugged and took her to the ride, leaving Austin. Austin started to walk around the carnival until he spotted a familiar face, Lela. She was dressed in an elegant, feathered dress with a matching headpiece. The sleeveless teal dress extended until her knees; her makeup was also a shaded blue and green with lots of glitter. She looked completely different from her serious pacifist group look. She stood alone, sipping on a red gooey drink in her high heels that made her just as tall as Austin.

"Hey, I didn't expect to see you here." Austin smiled.

"I do have a life, you know?" The girl laughed it off.

"Yeah." Austin gave an awkward shrug. "Hey, you want to go on any rides? I hear the boat ride is pretty cool."

"NOT WATER!" The girl shrieked. "I mean I don't want to go on any water rides." The girl pushed a weak smile. "It'll ruin my makeup." The girl made up an answer to avoid the real question.

"Okay, that's fine. I get it. I hate heights; anything in the air is super scary to me," the boy confessed. A moment of silence and understanding stood between them. "Fell out of one too many trees as a kid. So good luck getting me on that slingshot ride over there." The boy pointed at the ride on the far corner of the carnival; it was lit up with bright colours; two girls who seemed familiar to Austin were screaming at the top of their lungs while swinging around in the air.

"I guess it's my turn, right?" The girl studied the ground.

"Not if you don't feel comfortable," Austin replied.

"No, I do want to." Lela took a shaky breath and pushed some of her feathers from her dress away from her face. "When I first came to Westbrook, at one of these carnivals as a Year 9, I thought it would be a great idea to stay after the party died down and try to operate the rides with a friend of mine. In the dead hours of the night, we snuck onto the escape box ride, which was an enclosed room filled with water. You had to escape before the time ran out, and the box filled, but I couldn't figure out the puzzle, and the machine got put to work. The box filled with water, and my friend out of panic assumed I was dead and fled. In that desperate moment of this room being filled with water I couldn't figure out the clues, it was a dumb ride. But there was a pocket of air which I breathed in for close to an hour. With no one to open the emergency exit from the outside I was trapped. My pulse was down, I was hungry and could've even died from hyperthermia. No one at the controls; I was truly alone. It's safe to say I hate water. This is the first time I'm at this carnival since that night." The girl's sombre tone died down until both students stood in silence. After a few minutes, Fred approached with food as promised; he handed Austin and Lela a wiener with no bun. Lela didn't find this unusual at all and started on her bun-less hotdog.

"How about we all go on a ride, the spooky coaster?" Fred suggested either oblivious to the mood or in spite of the awkward tension. The line was 30 minutes long, but they eventually got on the ride, Lela and Austin in the front two seats and Federico in one of the back seats of the four-seater carriage. The three squirmed in their seat for the first half of the ride until the first jump scare, where Fred practically jumped out of his seat and let out a massive scream. The ghost prop just hung loosely in the air now.

"Are you serious?" Lela smirked. "I just thought of a good nickname, banshee boy." The two in the front started laughing, while Fred crossed his arms.

"If I'm banshee boy, then you're the feathered feline." The girl shrugged in response.

"You haven't even seen me attack before, only then will I really be feathered feline."

"Then what am I?" Austin asked.

"Hmmm," Federico said, "maybe the goth—ARGGGGGGGH!" The boy was interrupted by another jump scare. Fred took a second to regain his composure before talking again. "The gothic knight."

"Fair enough, but you can't be talking; you look like a weird inventor who believes their machines will come to life and kill half the town," Austin argued.

"That, funny enough, was the look I was going for." Fred grinned for the first time on this ride. The ride came to an end, and Federico jumped out of the seat as soon as he could. "That may have been one of my least logical decisions tonight," the banshee boy stated.

Lela turned to Austin and said, "That was the most fun I've had in a while." The boy's stomach filled with butterflies, and he forgot how to talk, but he didn't need to because Lela leaned in for a kiss on the cheek.

"Wow. Well, you're quick, Austin," a girl's voice interrupted. Wendy appeared; she was dressed in a black corset and a very short skirt, with high, black, studded heels going up to her mid-thigh. Her hair was dyed a deep red, which matched her coloured contacts. "You look stupid in your outfit," she directed at Fred.

"I don't remember asking for your opinion!" Fred barked back. "Wanna catch a ride?"

"Yeah," the girl said, before the pair said bye in sync. She interlaced her arm into his, and the two walked off together, not even another glance back.

"That I did not see coming," Austin said, stunned. Lela seemed not to care about the odd couple but looked to Austin. She suggested they visited some more of the various stalls. The night had only just begun, so much to do, see, smell and eat. It was the first time that Austin really let his guard down and just have for the rest of the night.

****

Mr Rhike's classroom was a bleak, four grey brick walls. He wore his rock 'n' roll t-shirt, this time, *Kiss*. 'Buzzzz', the school bell rang, the first period on a Monday. After a minute, students flooded into the class. Wendy sat with Fred at the back. Austin sat at the front, with a seat empty next to him; all the seats filled up behind him.

"Okay, today, I will be doing a presentation. Let me just—" The teacher pulled down the screen for the presentation, but it was graffitied with 'THIEF' in red. The class started to blow up with laughter, and after a minute, it died down. A girl with red lipstick and very heavy eyeshadow leaned on the doorway with a small smirk.

"What did I miss?" Aria asked. The professor gave her a look that could kill.

"You're late, take a seat next to Mr Bolden." The girl just shrugged and sat next to the 17-year-old; she held her hand out for a fist bump. Austin complied.

"Your makeup up is pretty edgy." The guy gave her a head nod.

"I know." Her short black hair was at shoulder-length; she had a fierce look in her eyes and made it a point of redoing her red lipstick.

"You two stop the talking." The professor pointed towards the pair; he was setting up a mechanism that projected his presentation onto the board, which had magically had the graffiti removed without Austin even noticing. The projector hovered mid-air, near Aria's head, and the light shimmered much like Mr Davon's wand projector and the graphicker that had the footage. "Everything in our universe is made up of atoms…or so the mortal world teaches. While it may be true that nano-particles are responsible for having substance to matter, there are elements that do not follow these boundaries of science. Magic, it is a substance without matter; it isn't anything, but it gives power to those who know how to manipulate it. Only those who have wizarding blood can control it, with the rare exception of a few mortals. The magic gravitates towards the wizard's blood because it has a percentage of true magic from the flowing River Grobs. Now we know the government has extracted all the magic from the river and it has no natural powers, but it still has remnants of the original power. Nothing with that much power can ever truly be distinguished…" the professor explained. The dim-lit setting seemed to close in. "The thing is, wizards aren't the only thing with magic in their blood; monsters have them too, which makes them just as dangerous." The professor went on to explain the different sorts of magic and who has it…until the school bell rang, and the professor dismissed the class.

"Hey, new kid, where are you going?" Aria stopped Austin from leaving the classroom. Before Austin could even respond, she slid something into his school jacket pocket and left the classroom.

"What was that all about?" Fred walked up to Austin with Wendy holding his arm. She wore a vest with a stitch of the school emblem, the beast with a bear head, a tiger head, a Gazelle head and a gorilla head. Next to the emblem was a second stitch-on, a singular vertical line and a horizontal infinity symbol passing through it. Austin didn't know what it was, but he guessed it supported some sort of movement. That seemed like Wendy's style.

"I don't know? What does that symbol mean?" Austin pointed at the girl's stitch-on.

"It represents the endless cycle of the government's oppression against the native people of Hylenia and the restrictions put in place. The symbol is called the Deltic line, and the symbol for the followers of the Delta; we hold protests and stuff."

"Hey, a few of us are throwing a little bonfire later; would you like to come?" the boy said changing the subject, as the girl leaned onto his shoulder. He had clearly had this conversation with her.

Austin replied with a simple 'Yes', and the trio walked towards their next classes.

****

The fire crackled in the night, little embers floating through the air with the sweet aroma of maple trees coming in from the vast distance. Several mats were sprawled out near the fire, next to a fold-up table with snacks and fizzy drinks. Soft music calmed the mood. Riona and Jack the twins were fighting about something the way siblings do, knocking each other out, with many elbows everywhere and many insults flying like the embers. Carter sat next to Charlie; they both looked very similar; they had the same sort of build and haircut, and both had blue eyes. Both of them were in the grade above. Austin had barely spoken with Carter, he briefly met him on orientation day, Charlie though was part of the pacifist club so he was starting to become his friend. Charlie had acne and brown hair and was a bit taller than Austin and somehow he always had a goofy smile on his face. Him and carter who Austin barely knew seemed to be in mid-conversation about some school sports game. Austin brought Lela, who also invited her best friends Ena and Jarred; they were doing each other's hairs. Ena had hairs in a crown braid with a laurel wreath around it, and Jarred's was currently being put into these short braids. Lela sat in Austin's lap, and she laughed at a joke he had just made. Wendy looked like she had actually let loose, and she was playing a game with the 'banshee'; apparently, the nickname was catching on.

"Hey, anyone want some marshmallows!" exclaimed Fred as he held a few packets high up in the air. A unanimous cheer went up, and the bunch shared out the goods and toasted on some sticks. There was something about marshmallows that made the people of Westbrook crazy.

"Okay, let's play a game." Jack stood up. "Let's all go around and say something about ourselves that no one else knows," the boy said. "Let's start with you, my sister." The fair girl stood up, her hair looking more red with the firelight shining onto her face. She looked like a tough girl who dominated in all the sports and wanted to prove something of herself, but today, she seemed relaxed, just wearing a simple floral dress.

"Well, I just got elected as the soccer captain." Another cheer went up, it was clear Jack started this game to celebrate his sisters new achievement. "I know it's a bit different from my usual sports roles, but I wanted to try something new." The girl shrugged. She sat down, and everyone took their turns one by one, all standing up until it came to the final person, Lela.

"Well, I may have a little crush on someone in this group" The girl grinned as she looked down at Austin. A few laughs and compliments made it obvious that it wasn't a secret and everyone knew, but it did get the group all giddy.

****

Everyone had left the campfire, and it was just Lela and Austin lying down, looking into the sky, with the after smell of the burnt gooey marshmallows wafting through the air. The couple had spent hours talking and waiting for the sunrise over the orchard of maple trees, pulling an all-nighter, but they were sharing, and they had more in common than he originally thought. After the hours of warm conversation the mood had shifted to a deeper side. "I don't know where my dad is, and now more than ever, I need to know. It just seems important and connected to everything that's going on. I know he was always on missions for long periods of time, like now, but it feels different. My mum is really worried, even though she doesn't say it. Their marriage wasn't perfect, but they were happy together before all the army stuff." The boy's mood turned sombre, with his intelligent brown eyes working at what his gut was trying to tell him. The girl leaned over on her side and stared Austin in the eyes.

"As you probably already know, my brother, Delio, died last year. He was called a hero. He is now on every freaking banner at this school; every hallway I turn to, I can never forget the guilt I feel. He was my older brother, and I'm what he chose to protect, his useless, unworthy, unpopular sister. I owe him everything, yet I can't thank him. I can't hug him. I still have this empty feeling inside of me, and no one will ever truly understand it. He was my best friend. I can't really ever tell anyone how I feel because then I won't be strong and that is what you need in a leader. I can't live up to everyone's expectations." The girl had tears in her eyes; her face was puffy; she had grass in her hair, and the cold wind now blew in and made the night shiver. The couple shared a feeling of empathy, and they held hands; the boy's hands held both of hers in between his, keeping her warm as he squeezed them. There was nothing that could be said to make it feel better but that feeling of understanding. They shared eye contact until Austin broke the silence.

"You are so much more than what you make yourself out to be. You are the strongest person I have ever known; you come into the Pacifist Club room with a fierce and determined look; you are amazing…If he hadn't saved you, you wouldn't be here at this moment, and that was his final gift he gave to you, so don't waste it." The boy was met with a kiss, and the night went on.

Chapter 11
Guilt

Rain trickled down the classroom window. Austin stared outside on the cloudy day; the Little Grobs River, which acted as the school barrier, was rushing with water. The clocked went around ever so slowly. Austin thought a lot about yesterday; it was deep, but perfect. The nostalgia would linger on for a while. While Austin was staring out the window, he put his hands into his school jacket and felt something in the inside pocket. He completely forgot Aria had slipped something in the day before. It was a plain piece of paper with the words 'GET OUT WHILE YOU CAN.' The room felt still; the teacher, Molly, who was wearing another weird, bizarre plant hat, dismissed the class. He walked the halls in a daze; he couldn't tell if this was some sick idea of a joke or real. The ivory halls filled with students like always.

"Austin! I can't find Wendy," Frederico gasped. He started mumbling something in Spanish and appeared to be hyperventilating until Austin placed a hand on his shoulder and looked him in the eyes, which seemed to calm him down. Austin's books were in his other hand, and now he was completely out of his mood and in person, focused.

"She didn't turn up to class or respond to my texts. I went to her room, and she wasn't there; no one has seen her. This isn't like her, Austin." The boy paused for a second. "I think she is missing." There was a brief moment of silence, but the world shifted back to normal with the same usual pushing and shoving, especially with the teleporting being completely banned as a new restriction on keeping the students safe. People were dispersing and began to enter their classrooms, and the boys stood there in the hall until Austin spoke.

"Come with me." He led the frantic boy to the Pacifist Club room; he had received a key, so he let both of them in. The child's plastic table was still there; a few new additional bean bags were put in, but Austin went straight to the computer and booted it up. Fred went to the evidence board and started looking for the pattern. The highest chances of finding Wendy were within the next few hours. "When was the last time you saw her?" asked Austin; he didn't look away from the computer screen.

"Yesterday night, at the bonfire." The boy was starting to hyperventilate again.

"You called the police, right, or at least campus security?" Austin started to panic as well.

"Of course I did! What do we do? Right now, they are overrun with missing persons' cases, at least 10 more victims each day. It's never going to get investigated; they're understaffed." The Mexican kid looked down at his feet.

"Look, if anyone can handle themselves, it's Wendy, don't worry. I will get the whole Pacifist Club on it; we will work through it." As his sentence finished, the lights went out. *A blackout?* Not half a minute after, the lights came back on. *The backup power generators?* Austin guessed. Both boys were shocked and didn't talk for half a minute. The only sound was their heavy breathing and the computers whirring back to life. Then again the lights went out; the backup power generators had failed. This was not just a power outage; this was done on purpose. The darkroom was soon met with a faded glow from each of the boy's cell phones. Click. The door locked; that was the fail-safe in a situation like this. They were locked in for whoever knew how long. The soft blue light led the pair to the door; that was the only exit. The key didn't work; it was a digital lock, and only two ID cards can override it, and that is Mrs Rimesdome's and Professor Dark's cards. The Mexican kid twitched.

"I can't be stuck in this room. How about I try something?" The sentence was more like a statement than a question of permission. He double-tapped his shoulder before trying to ram the door out. The door wouldn't budge.

"You know that won't work; those doors are designed to be reinforced against an atomic bomb, so you won't even make a dent. Not even with magic." *I guess that tour with Wendy came in useful for something, after all. Oh, Wendy.* The pair focused their time hypothesising into possible locations of the kidnapping and tried to create a timeline, although it was pretty empty. A new space on the board had already been made for this. Not much got down, but after two hours, a search group opened the door, and the vice principal greeted them.

"Well, we have been looking for you everywhere; we didn't know where you were because you certainly were not where you were supposed to be: in your allocated classes." The day came to a quick end with students still evacuating. The boys walked out of the building with Mrs Rimesdome, who stayed at the front entrance. "What happened out there?" asked Frederico.

"All questions will be answered in tomorrow's mandatory emergency assembly," the woman stated. The rest of the day was just many people reuniting and Austin calling his mum, who had already called him several times, probably out of motherly love and worry.

The signal was blocked out when they were locked in the room cliche.

As Austin was making his way back to his dormitory, he bumped into Unity, who was already looking a lot better. She wore the girls uniform, and it was a bit loose, even though it was magically supposed to fit the size of the wearer. Her cheeks were sunken, and her hair looked frail; her eyes always looked around, looking for people. "I'm so sorry, I haven't gotten to visit you sooner. I have completely spaced out with everything going on. Are you okay?"

"I am, thanks to you and Charlie. I already spoke to him, but I really wanted to tell you how appreciative I am that you saved my life."

Austin gave her a sympathetic look, but he felt guilty that he wasn't really the hero she made him out to be. "I'm glad I could help."

"I want to be like you; I want to join the Pacifist Club. You guys really are making a difference."

"I'm not sure we are supposed to be taking new members or even be allowed to function now, but you should as soon as you can." Austin was going to start going towards his dorms before Unity stopped him again.

"That's not all, I have some information." Austin was intrigued. "When I was kidnapped, there were two people that put me in that pantry. A boy and a girl. I couldn't tell who they were because they wore a face mask, but they were young, no older than us, maybe even a student here. They left me to die in that cupboard. I was alone for over a week, no light in the cold. I think they wanted to keep me silent; maybe I was getting close with my research. I was doing an article for the school newsletter. Although I can't remember now, and all of it is gone, not that that matters anymore. I hope that helps." Austin listened to everything she had to say patiently and answered her.

"That is maybe some of the most interesting intel we have had yet, but what most matters is that you are okay." Austin left for his dorm once again needing a restful night now.

****

101

The assembly was first thing in the morning. Everyone was still in shock, and chatting was kept to a minimum about the disappearance of Wendy; no one was truly safe. Once everyone was seated in the cafeteria tables, a man entered the cafeteria. He looked vaguely familiar to Austin, but he couldn't quite pinpoint it. He had a visitor's tag on himself, but Austin couldn't make out the small print. The principal said his speech in regards to the loss of another student and that went on to explain the details of the outage. "The system did not simply malfunction but was set off, and we believe this was a distraction so that while others were evacuating the building amidst the havoc was a plan to steal a priceless artifact. The spell book of Terra; we had this artifact shipped here when it was excavated from the Sigon battleground. We will be implementing several new security measures, including more guards and monitors. Everyone is to stay alert and contact either me or Mrs Rimesdome immediately if you notice something suspicious. In other news, we have an important visitor, none other than Mr Spirit, the head council member of the Council of Justice." *That's where I know him from; he was the man speaking in my dreams.* The principal stood down from the large wooden podium as Mr Spirit took the microphone. The man tapped the microphone, and it sent a loud screech throughout the room. It surely got everyone's attention; the man himself didn't flinch, his face solid.

"That is Wendy's father," Fred whispered over; everyone else at the table was still covering their ears, Austin's ears were ringing. The whole crowd shuddered when the man first spoke.

"My daughter Wendy was a pristine student, perfect grades as supposed to be, but it has come to my attention that she has gone missing. No stunt she hasn't pulled before to get my attention, but with other evidence of missing people's cases, it appears that this may not be of her doing. So if anyone of you knows any information about the whereabouts of my daughter, do not hesitate to contact my assistant; she will be here after the assembly." He gestured towards a petite Asian lady in a suit with many contact cards in her purse. "Now I better be off. I have an important meeting." Mr Spirit was a large man, very unlike Wendy, although they had a few similar features. He had a professional businessman cut look with nothing but the best clothing. He acted very coldly, like he didn't really care; it seemed as if the councilmen only made an appearance at this assembly as a gesture for the press. The man walked off the podium and across the cafeteria, casually checking his watch every few steps until the far exit; his shoes echoed across the hall. No one dared move or speak whilst this happened but only after the door slammed shut behind him. The vice-principal walked up to the stage and concluded the assembly; she seemed very disturbed while closing the assembly, her eyes puffy, red and sad. She was the first to leave out the side entrance, followed by Mrs Legend, who left her funny hats back at home, attempting to consolidate the vice principal. The cafeteria began to clear out with only a few people coming towards Mr Spirit's assistant, including Austin, Riona, Jack, Carter, Frederico, a few members of the Pacifist Club taking notes and about half a dozen kids Austin had never talked to walked up to the lady.

"Please, one at a time…My name is Kelly. Everyone, please take a contact card and please send all the details to the email provided, and if we find interest in your information, we will contact you and initiate a call if we find anything relevant." Everyone followed her instructions and took a card, but even with all the kids taking a contact card each, there were still a few hundred left. Another middle-aged blonde lady in black started to weep; she was previously sat next to Kelly during the assembly. She joined the small group teary eyed. Austin guessed this was Wendy's mum. She had the same facial structure and features as Wendy as well.

"Please tell me anything that will help," the woman pleaded. "Ohh, Frederico, please!" The woman recognised him through her tears. It made Austin think that their relationship had been going on a while way before Austin even arrived at the school. It also must've been kind of serious so much so that he made it to dinner with the parents. Her eyes pleaded to him but he gave her a hopeless look in return. "PLEASE! For a mother to be reunited with her daughter." The woman begged everyone, but Kelly took the lady out the back, letting the kids be dismissed. Austin felt something vibrate in his pocket; instinctively, he took out his phone while walking out one of the exits and saw that it was a text from Ethan. He had never sent Austin texts lately, so it must've been important. The text read:

Meet outside now!
I need to tell you something…come outside the side gate.

Austin snuck out the side gate as requested in the text and was met with both Cato the tree spirit and Ethan. It was unusual for a tree spirit to be so far away from their source, but then again, it wasn't unheard of. You could see the strain on his face concentrating on staying and not being pulled back to his life essence by an invisible gravity-like force. Cato skipped greetings. *Apparently, pleasantries aren't a thing for trees?* Austin thought. "The forest is stirring. Trees are going into hibernation. Just last night, the Western Wolf Pack roamed the forest; things are getting more dangerous. Many of the tree spirits are not willing to fight back, and whole areas of forests are burning. I have many sources, but everything is being covered up to stop mass panic."

"Wait, hold up; what is the Western Wolf Pack?" asked Austin.

"A practical myth for centuries until yesterday, that is. The strongest alpha pack of the hybrid beast, chimeras, much like the ones on duty at your school, but larger, more trained and ancient," answered Ethan. The word 'ancient' rolled off his tongue and seemed to leave poison in the air with a metallic taste.

"Things are stirring up here as well…A visit from the head member of the Council of Justice, Mr Spirit, his daughter just went missing; it will make big press with the next 24 hours, also the spell memoir of Terra was stolen. Probably one of the most protected artifacts that just shows you how nothing and no one is safe. It hits home." The pair took a second to register what had just been said. The tree spirit spoke up.

"We need to rally up strong allies; we seem overrun. If we don't, we won't stand a chance. The Other Side is rallying all of the most dangerous and untamed enemies to the Westbrook community and Hylenia, especially with hatred towards the council. Anything and anyone that has been exiled is teaming up." The way the tree spirit said 'anything' rattled Austin to the core. Everything that he had ever read about was now opposing him; this was the reasoning behind why he would always sleep with a nightlight on and cower under his covers at night when he was just a kid. Those myths, that to him were just stories without a second thought could be real and be a part of this 'war' that everyone seems to be talking about. A cold wind blew through the air. Ethan was wearing a black leather jacket and black pants as usual, but with the addition of a dark wooden wand, which Austin guessed was for additional protection. Cato wore simple baggy pants made out of what looked like a recyclable beige mesh. He wore a woollen green shirt, which seemed a size too small. His body looked human enough but with the skin complexity of a tree trunk. Neither of them were cold, whereas Austin, who was in a basic white school shirt, shivered. The three considered many options for the next half an hour and discussed all the events in detail about any attacks of the sort that seemed suspicious or that would give them any clue to find their friends and stop the enemy. Every so often, they paused to give Cato a break; he was under a lot of strain being far away from his source.

****

Austin walked back through the empty hallways after meeting with Ethan and Cato, his mind racing and unfocused. A middle-aged man dressed in a simple blue linen top bumped into him. *Wait, wasn't that…*He remembered this man, from his visions; the one with his mum and the other in the council. *Caleb* that was the man's name. He was very tall and buff; he made Austin look like a plush toy. His voice came out deep. "Watch it." But he continued to walk; Austin didn't breathe until he turned the corner. This overwhelming feeling came over Austin, and it continued through the night. *He is here to keep tabs on me, isn't he? For my mum.* Austin was still running that same question through his mind, throughout the day, until Detective Weatherson approached his room and snapped him out of it. "I will be needing to speak with you, just a routine check-up questions in regards to the stolen artifact," the tall man said dryly; he wore a grey coat today, with his usual stubble slowly getting more scruffy. The case clearly showed wear on his face, bags forming under his intense dark eyes, crows' feet forming on his face. The man did not make it sound like a suggestion and led Austin to an empty room, where he began to question him.

"Where were you during the power outage?" the questions started off simple enough.

"Trapped in the Pacifist Club room with Frederico," the teenager answered, shifting in his chair that he sat in, one of those wheely office chairs that creaked every time it moved.

"Why were you there and not in class?" The detective leaned forward.

"Because I was skipping class," the boy lied trying to avoid the truth. *The detective can't figure out the Pacifist Club was still functional.*

"You have been a major topic on the council; apparently, you are a powerful wizard," the man continued his interview.

"That's not even a question what—" The boy wanted to speak.

"I already questioned your friend, the Mexican kid."

"Frederico."

"He said he wasn't with you during the power outage. So you are lying, so where were you? The question that I can't figure out is why you would want the spell memoir, then it clicked, you are stealing it for the traitor father of yours, aren't you?" The interview got intense.

"That isn't true!" The boy stood up, soon followed by the man.

"This interview is over, but I will be talking with you soon." The man left before Austin could talk back. The school day was over Austins' mind was still racing trying to process everything the detective had said. He was clearly lying about Frederico, trying to make Austin break. He wanted Austin to know he was looking into him start making him nervous, scare tactics. Austin stayed in his room till the sun had set it was a beautiful view but Austin was zoning out. He just stared into the night sky was dark, the stars mostly hidden behind clouds. He had a million things running on his mind his body feeling restless. Austin pictured this school to be some sort of safe haven and it looked like it. In all its grandeur, the drum towers, the amount of stories, the over exaggerated arches, the walls which look like they were made for giants. Though Austin walked in on one of the schools' largest scandals. With missing artefacts, teachers and students. All these new experiences with magic was very overwhelming as well and talk of him being a part of some prophecy. Austin doubted it but that didn't stop the council. The boy stared out the window barely getting any more tired.

****

The boy fell asleep but not without dreams. He found himself back at home, his mother still up in the kitchen on a call with someone; it seemed important. The old setting made Austin feel nostalgic, for when he and his friends would come back for some peanut butter and jam sandwiches after a long time playing all day. The red wooden cabinets, the island with a deep sink, the simple grey stone granite floor and simple surround lighting made the place feel like home. Newspaper or little figurines used to always fill up all the tabletop area, but now it was empty and clean. He felt like he was supposed to be there with his mum; something felt missing in that house. "Irora, she was with him that night, that poor girl. It was one of the first kidnappings; you think it could have anything to do with what's happening now?" Natalie spoke into the phone, concern on her face; she must've heard the news. A moment of silence before she continued. "Just keep an eye on him for me; you haven't seen him yet, have you?…No?" The woman seemed disappointed. Austin didn't know how he did it, but he willed himself away from the scene, which shifted to the morning news being passed from door to door with none other than Mr Spirit on the front cover.

'COUNCILMAN SPIRIT IN GRIEF WHILE VISITING BELOVED DAUGHTER'S SCHOOL.' read the title. The newspaper went on to explain the bravery of the man and the efforts he put in with not even a mention of Wendy's name or any of the real news of what was going on within Hylenia. The dream slowly faded.

****

The morning classes were slow; he sat with Lela, who had joined Mr Davon's class: elemental magic. Ever since the incident, they hadn't tried anything, like harnessing magic but rather focused on theory and how to control their powers. The morning was cold but sunny, their shoes on the solid dirt, sun seeping in from the open roof. The Gaia Mother Earth statue was in its place near the door, facing towards the vibrant fish tank at the back. Mr Davon would always let the group feed the tropical fish after class. It was so nice, the coral and the vibrant, diverse fish. The hearth was at the centre of the room still on fire, spreading a slow warmth towards the surrounding kids. The teacher sipped his coffee as he read through the textbook. The short, stubby man did not comb his black mid-short hair today, but he didn't seem to care. He wore a grey Disney shirt and had his wand like usual. His wand seemed special, like a metallic obelisk, with open glass to reveal a piece of dirt, some water, some empty capsule and a never-ending fire, all in their separate areas. Lela leant on Austin's shoulder. "What's wrong?" She could tell something was off; she had only known him for a week, but she already understood his moods.

"My mum is keeping tabs on me with this shady guy, Caleb, who seems to have just shown up as everything started going bad. Detective Weatherson is also really suspicious of me and is on my back. On top of that, school work and all these disappearances; there is a war coming, and everyone is just acting normal!" The pressure somewhat got lifted off his shoulder now that he had finally told someone everything running through his mind. Just her being there on his shoulder seemed to ease him; she grasped his hand.

"Do you have something to share, Mr Bolden?" asked Mr Davon, not lifting his head from the text.

"No, sir." The rest of class went by, not once did Lela's hand leave Austin's, squeezing it at random intervals.

After class, she gave him a kiss on the cheek, which made butterflies fly in his stomach, and she whispered into his ear, "We will talk after school and after the pacificist club meeting. Do you mind starting it for me? I will be a bit late. Jarred will fill you in on everything you need to know." With that, she left for her next class after Austin replied with a nod. Soon she was lost in the crowded hallways, everyone small compared to the high ivory ceilings. So much detail was engraved into every part of the castle, Austin wondered how long it would've taken to build everything from start to finish. Not ten seconds after Lela left, Austin was also lost traveling between classes.

****

After school, Jarred was already waiting outside the Pacifist Club room. "You are one minute late." The boy shifted his weight onto his right foot, his hand on his green jeans. The boy wore a pink top and simple runners; he had short and very curly hair. The blonde-haired kid opened the door with his key card; A shiver ran through Austin, the last time he was here he was trapped for hours.

"How come I don't have a key yet?" the curly-headed kid asked.

"Maybe dating the club leader has some benefits." Austin winked and walked in and sat on one of the colourful beanbags. "Well, I can't exactly do that, now can I?" The boy also sat on a bean bag chair. The room was starting to feel more homely and familiar, the small arts and crafts table, the two monitors on the far end of the room, the four white walls covered with drawings and quotes. The fridge, which now had snacks for the meeting, which the pair broke into and took some before the other kids arrived and of course the evidence board with the new addition of a photo of Wendy. So many disappearances and strange occurrences, hard to keep track, but this was the new normal. Jarred continued to speak.

"So update, that's why I am here. We have a lead that Wendy may have gone to get her books after the bonfire to study. So we need two people to interview whoever she got the books from. I think her name was Riona. So in summary, we know that she never went back to her room but instead went back to get her books from this girl's room, as reviewed on the new cameras put up in the dorm hallways."

"And this was at what time?"

"10:45."

"And she was at the bonfire until 10:30, that leaves 15 minutes until she picked up the books. What about any time after that?" His brown eyes fixed on the evidence board, a timeline slowly beginning to build up.

"Well, we have no other confirmed sightings of her, so from 10:50, when she left Riona's dorms and 8:00 am, when Fred checked her whereabouts, we have no knowledge of where she was. Not in any of the footage but what I did find out that is that Lilly was making out with Tanner, Billy's ex." The gossip left his mouth with such a passion. "They were in the hallway in the middle of the night, quite brave, cause if one of the chimeras came around—"

"Okay, so nothing important, or sightings of her," Austin blurted out.

"Well, her books are still missing, meaning that if they are found, we will know a position of where she was, so I already sent some scouts to the main places, libraries and classes," Jarred continued while the group started flowing into the room. Austin began explaining the missing case of Wendy and that they should be on the lookout, ask around, put up photos and finally asked two individuals to interview Riona. The meeting went on for 20 minutes; everyone exchanging information. Austin finally summed up the meeting with Beatrice and Charlie being the obvious choices for the interviewing job. Everyone dispersed and got to work, while Lela walked up to him from the back of the group and kissed him.

"You did great; how about we hang out and dig into this Caleb guy, or we could go study for your schoolwork? We have a few tests coming up." She paused for a second. "You shouldn't be worried about anything; the club will get to the bottom of this. Detective Weatherson wishes he had our detective skills." The girl giggled, and suddenly, Austin didn't feel like he had to put up any brave facade. They locked up the room and escaped to his room. They studied for a few hours, testing each other and getting distracted a bit, but both of them listened to some music and mostly stayed on track before they decided to go for a sunset walk. During the golden hour of the evening, they walked around, embracing the warmth of the sun, the freshly cut grass and its smell wafting through the air; the environment felt still as if time just stopped. Kids were walking in pairs, laughing, probably coming back from activities and fun get-togethers usually finishing around this time. The ivory school stood tall, decorated with vines and greenery. Leaves were falling from trees, a true setting until it was broken.

"Lela, I need to interview you with regards to the disappearance of Wendy Spirit," the detective said, standing very stiffly. The couple shared a nervous glance before she let her hand out of his and left, and Austin could only continue back to his dorm. Lela and the detective walked the other way; Austin didn't trust that man at all, but there was nothing he could do. He walked all the way back to the side entrance of his dorms and met a crying girl in black fishnet stockings and running mascara on her face. Her short, black, messy hair turned as soon as she noticed Austin; she tried to hide it.

"No, no, no one ever uses this entrance," the girl made out. She wasn't wrong; there wasn't another person in sight, but Austin decided on going the scenic route, which was apparently her hideout.

"What's wrong, Aria?"

The girl broke down again, covering her face and resting her head on her lap. "I can't say." She wasn't breathing properly, and her legs were shaking; she seemed to be checking her surroundings every so often.

"Tell me, Aria, you can't stay silent. What's going on?" The boy noticed something very wrong; she was scared for her life and kept flinching as he came closer until she calmed as he finally sat down next to her.

"I did something bad, very bad." Aria looked away. "I hurt someone." She continued to weep.

"Aria, who is it? Are they okay?" The boy leaned closer.

"Yes, despite me abandoning her."

"WHO, ARIA?"

"You're dating her, for god's sake. I was the one, okay, don't try to consolidate me. I'm an outcast. I nearly killed your girlfriend. We used to be best friends; we went to that carnival together, and I fled like a coward. Everyone knows the story." The boy was shocked; it was her. *She use to be friends with Lela? She left her for dead?* Austin wanted to feel angry, but he couldn't. What was wrong with him?

"Is that why you left the note?"

She ignored his question completely. "Now they are coming for me." The girl's hands were shaking.

"The Westbrook Security? Detective Weatherson? Campus police?" Austin kept on asking, but she never answered and fled the scene. Running into the night, the sun had set, and the boy was left alone once again. *What happened at this school? Why had no one told me? I just assumed that that person had left the school. All along it was Aria? Who was after her?*

****

The golden hours were bright but still had a cold breeze. Charlie and Beatrice found themselves at the soccer stadium, where the girls' soccer team was practising, all the girls with baby blue jerseys and white shorts. The renovations were already finished due to the school's productive attitude and use of magic. They really had made it their top priority. Riona had the ball and was dribbling down the field; she was doing well. She was getting close to the goal until a much larger girl shoved her in the abdomen with her elbow and stole the ball away with ease. Riona seemed to notice she had spectators, and she went for her water bottle and walked up to the interviewers. "You two are here about Wendy, aren't you?" she said as she took a sip from her water bottle.

"Yes," Charlie said, his short, wavy blonde hair looking golden.

"WOW, that was cool; you have to show me how to do that," the small girl asked. "I mean, if you have time." Riona met her with a smile.

"Of course, kiddo." She messed with the small girl's dark hair.

"I mean she seemed normal enough. I left the bonfire a bit early, and she came to pick up the books from my place like she said she would; it was at my place because we were studying the night before, so yeah," the girl started off her story looking at Charlie.

"Did she seem in a hurry at all? Did she tell you where she was going?" Charlie tried to figure out the whole story.

"Well, she did mention something about meeting up with an old friend of her mum's. I think his name was Caleb, but I don't think she ever got there. Is that all the questions, because I have to get back to practice."

"Sure, get back to practice; we got what we need, and kick her butt!" Beatrice spoke up pointing at the larger girl who previously shoved Riona.

"Of course, that's why I am here." The girls smirked and shared a fist bump. The pair left, and Beatrice started for the school entrance, half running, half skipping, forcing Charlie to keep up. It was cold anyway; the night was already

111

set. After five minutes, the pair found themselves nearly at the entrance of the school, the golden doors open. Something fell off the roof or was it…The crowd was gathering around something. It was Aria! Her dead, lifeless body lay spread on the floor.

Charlie quickly shielded Beatrice's eyes and screamed, "Someone call the Campus police!" Just as he said it, Mrs Rimesdome came down the first few stairs and let out a shriek and with shaky hands held back the kids from getting close.

"Everyone, back to the dorms immediately, except you, Charlie, the police will want a witness." Everyone hastily followed the woman's instruction and went through the door, including Beatrice, who headed towards Ena's dorm; it was where she was staying while her father was missing. With a wave of the women's wand, the golden doors shut; they were dim in the cold night sky. It was so fast, kids crying and emotional, blood everywhere, messy and terrifying. The body was completely disfigured. But it raised the question of who did it, or did she do it. Mrs Rimesdome put her jacket over the body, only half covering it and spoke into a walkie talkie, initiating a lockdown.

****

Lots of chatter and gossip filled the cafeteria; the morning assembly was sombre and mournful teachers red-eyed, students sharing their memories with the girl. Before her death, no one seemed to notice her, but now something had changed. Lela sat next to Ena, red-eyed; the girl used to be close with the victim until the incident, and now she is dead. The principal walked onto the wooden podium; he was going up there too often. The black man stood tall and made her death formal. He brought up the autopsy report, which basically stated that her death was caused by a major fall (blunt force trauma). Something bothered Austin though: within the autopsy, it stated that there were previous abrasions not from the fall; they ruled it out as a suicide, even though knowing her mental state history and given that there was a suicide note on her bed. But there was no way she could've put that suicide note after her talk with Austin, so either she put it there before or someone else did it for her. Also when Austin saw her, she had no abrasions right before the fall, which meant someone did this to her, but the case was already closed. "We now know the culprit of the ent incident; it was Aria; it was revealed as a confession within her note, as well as her being an

112

agent for the Other Side," the principal stated. Maybe she was the one they were after; she seemed nervous before she died, like someone was going to do it to her. All of this was too neat. "There will be grief counselling opening up tomorrow to whoever needs it. That will be all." The assembly was dismissed, and everyone went to their morning classes. None of this made sense; she couldn't have been working alone; she had to have a partner that led the ent in while she dismissed the cameras.

Chapter 12
The Aftermath of Aria

That was it, the chapter of Aria; it was as if the principal could now cross that off his to-do list. Mrs Rimesdome must've took notice of how Austin was still on edge about the whole scenario, so she interrupted his last class of the day and sentenced him to a mandatory visit with the therapist. She checked in with everyone, briefly talking in front of everyone on a more personal level before leaving and going to check another classroom, which left the class with Mr Hurt. He was the man that was originally interviewed by Detective Weatherson when his fellow staff member Mr Bert went missing. The man was lean and tall and was quite intimidating; he had this dark glare. He had very pale skin, which only contrasted his dark circles under his eyes some more. He seemed very tired and drained; his persona was very sombre. "Welcome, I'm sorry this is our first class this semester, but I had many issues in my personal life. Unluckily, I have come to the capacity amount of vacation days for this term." The man laughed dryly. "Well, enough about me. You all signed up to learn about the mystics magic, usually not the most-liked topic. A bit of the black sheep…Can I get a show of hands of who has done any work on this subject previously, just so I know where everyone is at?" A few kids raised their hands in response, lifting their hands up as if they were reaching for the ceiling, which was twice as high as a normal ceiling. Austin sat next to Lela at a double desk, their timetables really matched up, as well as Charlie also sitting on the other side of Austin. Other than Lela and Charlie, Austin recognised a few people who he had briefly talked to during his first week, but most of the class Austin hadn't spoken to. It's not what you'd expect a mystical magic classroom to look like; it had high open windows bringing in sunlight, shining in on metallic flooring and plastic tables filled with students. The teacher himself wore all black and accessorised with different rings, mostly just gems Austin couldn't name. "We will start with the basics for today. Nothing to worry about; our magic works a little bit different to all other classes here because we don't use the same magic source. Other classes use the substance of magic and link them with emotions and use certain fields to control different aspects of matter and mind. Our class, however, calls upon power from another source, a more ancient source than magic, a more unreliable and deadly source, from the supernatural. We are all taught here about supernatural history, but what if we can control these powers that men once controlled to such an extent that they made mutations within themselves, werewolves, vampires and chimeras. I will be your guide in your own journey in unlocking your inner ability to connect with this source of magic so that when all else fails, this will be a powerful defence." The teacher walked up to the blackboard at the front of the class and drew a symbol, a five-edged pentagram, with an infinity symbol going horizontally and vertically, intersecting the pentagram. Mr Hurt mumbled some words and the rune lit up in a sudden fire and after it vanished as soon as it started. "In this case, I created this runic symbol and gave power to it through words, but this power came from the internal. My inner being and everyone's inner being has some connection to this source of power so everyone can create some magic; all you need to know is how to access this ability. For a larger incantation, we would call upon an external force that holds more power than you. This is more dangerous as these 'sources' are not always friendly, so control is key, which is why you guys will build up to it; this is pretty high-level stuff. The third and last source of this magic will be certain ingredients and objects; some ingredients enhance powers, and some objects have a spirit, unlike the usual magic, much darker, so this will be a combination of internal and external forces to harness this specific category of power…" The professor paused for a bit, taking a breath. "Now that wasn't too hard, was it, all three categories of the magic that we source our power from in this class. Everything mentioned will be in a slideshow emailed to you for studying purposes if you want to research and refresh your mind. Moving on, we will be practising our first practical assignment, and we will circle back for more theory later. Today, we will learn a hard lesson, a very hard lesson, so this internal magic that everyone has is released when someone dies their magic becomes an external force. We will harness that and properly let it go, but to do so, we will go to her place of passing, the school entrance." The teacher got everyone up and brought the class to the site, the school's front entrance. The day seemed regular enough, the sun beaming and the trees standing tall. Many kids seemed nervous and uncomfortable with their familiars in sight and close to them; one girl had a small dragon curled around her neck, and another boy had a cockatoo perched on his shoulder. The lean man held a simple, matte, black wand in his hand, holding it with his gemstone-covered fingers. He enchanted a spell, and immediately the area darkened with just a few words. It felt as if like the sun had been switched off, the area dampened. Austin felt queasy; a nauseous feeling overwhelmed Austin when the area felt quiet and silent. The usual sounds of birds and wind depleted; it felt very secluded. This was all a new concept to Austin; he hadn't even chosen the subject; he was just assigned it limited to the school schedule and other classes being at capacity. The blue mist started curling up from the floor, strain showing on Mr Hurt's face from the incantation. The mist suddenly vanished, and everything returned back to normal, as if nothing had ever happened; all the other kids seemed just as confused as the teacher. "This…This…" The professor couldn't talk; he stumbled a bit but regained focus. "This wasn't the place she died. This spell is supposed to show us the spirit realm, and if she had died here, then a part of her would still be here, a concentration of magic, but the spell failed. Every place her body was transported, you will be able to track her essence but only in small amounts. She had to have died somewhere else; this was all staged. This wasn't suicide." He rubbed one of his rings and rubbed his eyes; he sounded startled. "I knew it." The man kept on talking to himself, rather than the class of 20+ students in front of him. Austin stood next to Lela, who gave him a knowing look after this new-found information. Mr Hurt dismissed the class and headed towards the vice principal's office, heavy with his footsteps.

****

Nothing else didn't mattered anymore. Mr Hurt was on a mission. He powered through crowded hallways until he arrived at her office door. A crying student came out, leaving the door open for him. The man shut the door behind him as he walked in; it was just the two of them now inside the electric room. "I already told you, Hammond, you cannot have any more days off; you have already reached the extended amount for a regular sabbatical leave. We sympathise with you, but we can't let these students get any more behind in their work; it's unfair to them. What happens when they go out of these school walls? They can't protect themselves. The committee is contemplating firing you, and

116

after they have made their decision, I can't change it. I am doing everything I can here." The woman was strong with her words but was still saying it with care, like a protective mother. Mr Hurt hadn't even started, but it was clear they had similar conversation to this.

"It's about something else, Madeline. Inside this school, they aren't safe, let alone outside. If you haven't noticed, Aria Hurt, my daughter, this wasn't of her own doing; she was dead far before the fall. You and I know that these detectives don't care about actually solving this case; they just wanted to put that 'solved' red stamp plastered into the folder. I cast an incantation that indicated that the fall wasn't the reason she isn't here." The man held back tears, blinking his red eyes.

"She was murdered and pushed off that building; there were previous abrasions not caused by the fall. Please just bring it up with the council and tell them to open up the case. If not for me, then for the safety of the rest of your students." The man took a seat in the leather-lined chair, but the woman was uneased.

"I need evidence to open up the case again, and I am sorry, but dark magic is unreliable and can be interpreted differently. It is unclear, so in court, it will be nullified meaningless. We will still need stronger evidence." The man shifted in his seat.

"But we have multiple witnesses who stated there were no previous abrasion, and with the autopsy report, there must've been a fight. I know what I saw, Madeline."

The woman responded, "I believe you, Hammond, I really do, but it is not enough, even more so that you are the witness as a grieving father trying to open up the case again with your testimony. The court will classify it as an unstable emotional witness; there is nothing I can do. I am sorry."

"I know she wasn't perfect, but she didn't deserve this. Even the graphologists state that the handwriting doesn't match her suicide note," the man exclaimed.

The two exchanged words for another half hour before Mr Hammond had to leave for class; he couldn't get fired as well; he had to continue to work or else he would be not only out of a family but jobless.

****

The therapist's door was open; from the room, a warm light was emitted. The room was filled with colourful posters and simplistic ceramics on bamboo shelving. The room had carpeted flooring so patients would tend to take their shoes off at the door. On the desk was a plaque suggesting the woman's name who sat on top of the desk in the centre of the room, cross-legged. Kiara Clark. She had dark skin and appeared to be meditating, her brown curly hair reaching her shoulder; she wore a purple t-shirt that seemed quite child-themed, but she made it work. The woman looked young, probably in her early 30s. She sensed someone entering through the door and opened her eyes in response; she saw a kid she had never seen before; he was about 5'8" or 5'9" and had messy dark blonde hair and brown eyes. He looked athletic like one of the footballers, but she knew that wasn't the case; she often accompanied the team on their interschool matches as a supervisor. He seemed a bit nervous and awkward waiting at the door. "Austin, Mrs Rimesdome said you were coming. Please take a seat." Austin complied with her instructions.

"Nice office, feels very homely," Austin complimented; he wanted to shift her attention from him to her room. She had a powerful glare, but it wasn't necessarily threatening; it was as if she was staring into his soul. She finally looked away after 10 seconds of silent eye contact.

"Yes, it's all the ceramics made by students as presents; they know how much I love them." Her voice was soothing, slow and quite quiet; her voice echoed through the room. She focused back towards him. "I want to discuss a few things, but first tell me about yourself, why did you come to this school?"

"Both my parent's met here when they were students, and my mother said I would be able to reach my full potential at this school. We have links to this school, and in ways, I guess, I was destined to walk these halls as my parents did those many years ago," he explained, looking anywhere but her glaring eyes.

"Are you making friends?" she asked, no change in tone. She was still calm and cross-legged on her desk.

"A few."

"How are your studies going?" It sounded as if she was going through the general questions' list in her head.

"Fine, not what I'm used to, but I'm adjusting."

"Have you joined any extracurricular activities?" The questions started to get more personalised as if she knew the answers but wanted to see how Austin would respond.

"Um, technically no, but yes. I joined the Pacifist Club, which Detective Weatherson is trying to disband," he answered sceptical of the therapist's intentions. She simply nodded in response, which was the first sign that she had actually acknowledged anything Austin had said.

"I'm sure you must be concerned about all the disappearances, including your father's, even though he left you at quite a young age." She adjusted herself and sat back in her chair, which was a leather-lined reclining chair. She was waiting to see how Austin would respond.

"Why am I really here?" Austin leaned forward, completely ignoring the jab at his father's disappearance, "I know this isn't grief counselling."

The woman didn't try to act shocked; she held herself together very strong. She had a mysterious persona about her, like she was always holding something back, but she told him, "It's about the prophecy." She paused for a second then began to explain the source of the prophecy. Something immediately clicked in Austin's brain. Although he was never magically inclined and never kept up to date with the news, hes still knew about the Great Prophecy. It was a big deal in Hylenia; everyone had their own opinion; people argued about the legitimacy of the prophecy. Conspiracy sites were dedicated to everything about it, no detail left unnoticed. "The future is the most difficult type of magic, and even when perfected, which few wizards have, it's still obscured and never defined. There was one prophecy from before the times of Hylenia…An immortal wizard crossed paths with a Nepalese monk who wrote scriptures about the magic of this man. Although many of his findings and work were destroyed in a fire, one of the remaining scriptures was a prophecy that seems to relate to this time. Most wizards have memorised the famous prophecy to pass down the information orally."

'Two angel-blooded being separated in thunder
The new world will yield to the one who holds the power
The big war arising full of plunder
The chosen one goes forth to scower
Ancient ones arising from the dawn of the first era
The shadowed ones will come and bring terror
It begins with the creation of the first chimera
When it comes into contact with the element bearer.'

The therapist sat forward in her leather chair, her dark skin glistening in the light. "Obviously that is the translated version. You know, no one quite knows what happened to that unnamed wizard. As far as I know, immortality is a myth, so how much of this prophecy do we really believe? Not many people think like me and idolise this information with their lives dedicated to studying it. People have taken notice of you, Austin, a wizard with such power, an element bearer, rare. You can control all the elements, which makes you special."

She came clean, and now Austin was starting to comprehend the enormity of the situation.

"I wouldn't exactly say I'm able to control them but—"

The woman cut him off ignoring his sarcasm. "You met him, didn't you?"

"Met who?" Austin was convinced this woman was actually insane.

"The first chimera, Rhicon, you met him in the hallway; he works as a guard for the school. The oldest of his kind. Big lion head and two unintelligent other heads; boar and a serpent's." What she said was starting to make sense. "The council is concerned that you will turn against Hylenia, but you have some pretty powerful people fighting on your behalf. I was administered to you. To get what you know and your intentions." The boy couldn't look at the counsellor in the eyes; his leg was shaking.

"I am the only person since Terra that could control all the elements; I guess that makes me the element bearer, and if that line links with the second line in the prophecy, it means Hylenia will be at my judgment." The boy only began to grasp what diplomatic matters were occurring all around him.

"You might not necessarily be the one who holds power, these prophecies are hard to get a proper reading. I mean, the original four siblings thought the prophecy was about them that is when the first chimera came into creation. This is just all one big precaution. What more concerns me is that these other lines are starting to make sense especially: 'Ancient ones arising from the dawn of the first era' and 'The shadowed ones will come and bring terror'. Something big is coming, whether it is the prophecy or not, but I just hope you are on our side." Austin took that as a cue to leave; he was at the door.

"I am on your side, but I'm not who you are looking for," he said as he closed the door behind him.

****

"Hey, babe." Austin hugged Lela from the back; it was in between the many flocks of high school students in the tall hallways.

"Did you see the data put back onto the pacifist data cloud system?" Lela asked. "From the interview, another lead on Wendy. She met up with Caleb, the same person that randomly showed up to our school when everything started going wrong," Lela said with a concerned voice, elaborating on her first statement.

"He is lying to my mum as well. Apparently, he was a family friend to her."

Lela nodded in reply. "This isn't good news; we shouldn't tell Fred. He will worry too much. Now Caleb is officially a person of interest. We have to bring this to Westbrook Security, but anonymously." She remained calm and logical, with a straightforward attitude; she sounded so sure of herself, a true leader.

"Or we could contact Wendy's mother directly so as to not involve the media; they are backtracked on cases, anyway; it would never get investigated."

They locked eyes and said in sync, "Class can wait." The pair rushed to the library to call Kelly, the short Asian assistant; Lela had the woman's contact details saved in her phone and dialled the number once the pair got to a quiet place. The phone was finally answered.

"Mr Spirit's office, this is Kelly speaking."

"Hey, it's Lela; we need to talk."

Lela spoke to the Asian assistant for two minutes before hanging up.

****

Lela and Austin sat on a bench under a pavilion near the school surrounded by the sweet-smelling maple trees. Kelly was dressed in a professional black and white feminine suit; she stood opposite them.

"Here is the deal, the Westbrook Security is very tight about working with external forces. So there will be private investigators on Caleb, but as of now, there is not enough evidence to get a warrant. What I need you two to do is something the authorities can't legally do." The woman sighed, showing signs of guilt in her voice.

"You have to break into his house and search for any evidence that could blow the case right up. If you two get caught, it would completely decriminalise Caleb if any federal investigators found out. And you mustn't leave any trace of the evidence, or it will have been believed to be tampered with. If you do find something, contact me and I will force the Westbrook Security into a joint investigation." She gave Austin details to Caleb's apartment and left for a meeting.

Lela began to speak. "Well, she is intense!" The pair laughed. "I have a test next period, so I am going to the library to study till then." She moved her hair from her face.

Austin kissed her neck. "Good luck, I will try and follow Kelly's instruction."

"Are you sure you don't need any help? Also, how are your studies going, you aren't falling behind or anything?" She was taking notice of his lousy attendance.

"Maybe a study session or two couldn't hurt." The boy leaned forward.

"I would love to, but we are never productive with those." She laughed it off and messed with the boy's hair as she stood up. "Maybe we should get you a tutor?" He nodded, and the girl walked away.

Austin took the rest of the day off and snuck off campus outside of the boundaries; the weather was very chilly, almost a snow blizzard, much different to the weather-controlled campus area. The 16-year-old was not ready for the cold weather; he was still in the short-sleeved Westbrook uniform. Kelly gave the all-clear to break in; apparently, Caleb wasn't home, so it should be easy. The address wasn't too far from the campus. He reached the complex building, which was built out of concrete; it was a massive plot of industrial-designed apartments. Austin found the door number and opened the door, stepping inside and instantly feeling warmer. It wasn't locked or anything, like he didn't have anything to hide. The area was very cosy compared to the harsh outside cold weather; the apartment was filled with wooden oak bookcases with every sort of book you could think of. The floor was filled out with a plush olive-coloured carpet; in the corner, a reclining chair and a floor lamp stood empty. There was a small kitchen and island to the far side of the room and one door leading to Caleb's bedroom. Austin was filled with anxiety, even though he knew no one was home. He reached for the door handle, his palms sweaty as he twisted the metal knob. The room had lights on showing from under the doorway, but there was no sound. Austin quickly swung open the door, like a band-aid; he couldn't handle the suspense. The room was tidy, unlike the rest of the small apartment, but still empty. There was a single door leading to an ensuite bathroom and a box TV. *Weren't those a bit outdated?* Austin thought to himself. The apartment was designed by an old soul, completely different from the exterior of the complex. There was no kidnapped Wendy in sight; just as Austin nearly gave up, he noticed something on the wooden oak nightstand. A school book, the same book Wendy took from Riona that night she met up with him; this was definitely incriminating. Austin checked the first page, and sure enough, it had Wendy's name, which placed Wendy and Caleb together the night she went missing. Austin was careful to leave everything where it was so it didn't look like there were any intrusions and took a photo of the evidence before leaving and shutting everything back up again.

*¤**********

The morning was cold and mundane; they had already removed all of Aria's belongings out of her room, leaving it open for another resident. Four boxes were packed, and the room was empty. As soon as the removalist squad left, Austin wandered into the room, and everything was so boring and bland, black walls, empty draws, a singular bare mattress. Only one of her possessions was left behind, maybe by mistake, a dreamcatcher on the black glass and steel table. Austin slipped it into his pocket; at the time, he just felt like it was the right thing to do. He didn't know why he even came in here, but he felt drawn to her room. There had to be something here, a clue to what happened to her; something that tied Caleb to her, anything. After what seemed like an hour of searching, Austin finally lied down on the bare mattress and stared at the ceiling. Nothing. The outside scenery was blank, just plain fields, and beyond that, just the stream, the Little Grobs. The boy checked his pocket for his phone; he decided he should show up for Troleze class. He walked towards the school hallways and was soon pushing and shoving his way through to get to class. *They really should get the teleporters back up again; it would clear the hallway traffic so much,* Austin thought to himself. He saw a familiar face also heading towards Troleze class, Charlie. The pair walked through the hallways talking till they reached the class; the teacher still hadn't gotten there. Austin started practising; he was behind in the class, struggling. He missed too many lessons; it wasn't that he wasn't putting in the effort, it was simply too hard. Too stressful, how did everyone balance keeping up to date with all subjects without sacrificing one? Troleze, potions and brewing, scientific matter and magic, elemental magic, supernatural magic, and even the tactical class with coach. Just as Austin was overthinking and stressing about school, a familiar friend walked in through the door. Mr Trolt entered the class; the short blue troll wore a suit and tie. He had shoes hitting the tiled flooring.

"For those of you who don't know me, I am Mr Trolt. I will be your substitute teacher as your old Troleze teacher isn't here and is on a leave of absence for an undisclosed amount of time. So I will be here for the rest of the semester." The troll propped himself onto the teacher's desk. "I want to get to know everyone and for you to get to know each other and just start a bit of an introduction. I know everyone has already started learning Troleze, but I teach a little bit differently, so we will start over. But before anything else, I want to say a few things about myself. I am the mayor of Troll Village, and not to worry, I have many advisors and council members taking care of the village while I teach here at Westbrook. I am very excited about this position and being able to teach the youth about a passion of mine. How about all of you? What brought you to choose this subject?" Mr Trolt questioned. A few hands went up, and he chose Riona to answer.

"Well, this subject is the original language used to practise magic, so it makes it easier with my other classes and fits in with my time schedule, plus it gives so many points to my end of year mark." Mr Trolt did not seem impressed with the second part of the answer but still nodded with satisfaction.

"How about you, Mr Bolden?" the substitute teacher asked.

It took Austin a second to respond to that name, but he answered surely, "It is necessary to know the language to communicate; it is widely used across the whole of Hylenia. I wanted to learn to be able to communicate. That is the point of learning any language, isn't it?" The professor let out a smile and moved on to the next student. The class went on for a while; it was a double, but Austin definitely learned more in this lesson than any other lesson; the teaching style just suited him better. Mr Trolt held Austin back after class to talk with him.

"Hey, how you holding up? I heard everything that is going on with the council," the troll said. The teenage boy held his right arm in his left and stood stiffly.

"There isn't much I can do right now; the prophecy worries them so it is best not to do too much to spark attention, especially when everyone is keeping close tabs on me, so, for now, all I really can do is act like a normal teenager in Westbrook and just do school work," the blonde boy answered. The troll stood up.

"Well, if you need anything, I can help you. I will be more than willing to help to try and return the favour of your dad." There was a mutual agreement, and Austin walked out. He headed to the library after school ended; he had planned to meet up with Lela. By the time Austin got there, she already was sitting waiting for him, deep into reading a book about the usage of wands and control. She wore her hair up and had a coffee next to her, but she made no attempt to drink it. It was probably just there for motivation; she only noticed Austin after he sat one foot away from her. She put her book down onto the desk; the book was suffering from the equivalent of a computer overheating. Lela laid her head on Austin's shoulder.

"Don't you think that it is sort of suspicious that the guy that kidnapped you now happened to randomly show up as your teacher?" The girl furrowed her eyebrows.

"Well, I was intruding in his territory, so they sort of just held me captive and questioned me; it made sense, plus he was a close friend of my dad's, even though I have never heard anything about him," Austin exclaimed with much sarcasm. "But I respect him purely for supporting my dad when no one else had. Plus, trolls are very loyal, at least that is what was written in my book," the boy defended his new substitute teacher.

"I saw what you loaded into the cloud yesterday. I already contacted Kelly, and it's a joint investigation, which means the club can finally get some freedom." The girl's eyes sparkled. "And I think I found you a tutor, and you're starting now. You know Leslie, right?"

The boy felt betrayed. *You ambushed me with a study session?* Lela left the table leaving Austin with the approaching Leslie. She wore a green turtleneck, the same uniform when Austin had first met her. She wasn't accompanied by her other friend Jill; they almost seemed inseparable.

"So what's the deal, sporty kid." Austin was definitely not used to being called a sporty kid; he wasn't really that athletic; he was just naturally built bigger.

"Well, I believe I have been set up. Ummm, I am falling behind in a few subjects; I guess not being here at the beginning of freshman year really set the pace for this year so far, and I really want to be prepared for the exams for this term," Austin replied. He shifted awkwardly in his cushioned seat.

"What sort of subjects are we talking about? I can help you with just about everything except tactical class, then you're on your own." The girl brought about 10 textbooks and placed them on the table for a nerd; she could definitely carry a lot of textbooks; those things were like weights. She had her honey-coloured eyes set on a few of the textbooks, her glasses magnifying her darting eyes. She seemed very enthusiastic about tutoring, which was refreshing.

"Scientific matter and magic class is proving to be very difficult and also elemental magic; I am falling behind with the theory side of things, let alone the practical side, and don't even get me started on the supernatural magic; so much history, how does anyone know all this stuff? Westbrook Academy really wasn't kidding when they said this school is exclusive and advanced."

"Okay, let's start with elemental magic. I heard about what happened, even though I am not one to know about drama." She snorted. "We will study every Sunday, Tuesday and Wednesday. Is that okay with you?" Before letting Austin respond, she had already opened up a textbook. Her social ques were a bit off, but she seemed sweet.

****

Austin had an epiphany. He was with a few kids in a common room after his study session had finished. He was sitting on a red couch; behind him was a soda machine, and low-hanging lighting surrounded the room. There was puzzle-shaped carpets where Beatrice sat next to a low table, even though there was still couch space. Charlie helped her with her homework, even though she was incredibly smart for her age and skipping a year. Riona braided Beatrice's hair while she was still zoned into her work. On the other side of the room perched in front of a flat-screen TV were Jack and Carter. Austin had never really noticed how short Jack was compared to his best friend. Jack had a very mature face, with strong bone structure and had so much confidence that no one underestimated him. He was still in uniform like most students with a jumper, but Carter had found time to change into a sports jersey, which Austin guessed was for the team that was playing. They were both arguing which team was going to win the game; so far, it was all tied up in the last quarter.

"Are you kidding? The Jets are definitely going to win; they are such a strong, united team!" Jarred intervened.

"See, Jarred knows what he is talking about," Jack continued the argument, and both tried to pull people to their side. Carter tried recruiting Ena, but she wasn't having it.

"Why bother following American sports, anyway? It's dumb." Her statement set off more arguing; the environment was very playful yet competitive. Fred and Austin were throwing a ball between each other while Lela tried to catch it, a classic game of piggy in the middle. It was surprising the ball didn't hit any of the low-hanging lights. A few minutes later, a teacher was walking past the room and stopped the game, so Austin sat down next to a few kids talking about their dreams, and something clicked in Austin's brain. His eyes lit up.

"We can figure out where Aria died." Everyone looked up except Beatrice, who was still focused on her work. "Her dreamcatcher, I read somewhere that trolls have been practising dreams and psyche through dreamcatchers for millenniums. If we find someone that could figure this out, we can enter her spirit and find her place of death."

Lela looked at him concerningly. "That is really dangerous, Austin, even if we can find someone to help us do it. I don't think it's a common practice anymore, anyway."

"We need to, all of this is connected, and she knew something. We have to do it for her sake and Wendy's and anyone else that has gone missing." All the students nodded in agreement.

"I know where we can start," Frederico exclaimed. With that, Austin and Lela got up and headed for the exit. Ena put down what she was doing and joined Lela, Austin and Fred, who were all heading for the staff office. *So much for a normal afternoon.* Austin thought but he knew his compulsion to get to the bottom of this mystery was the only thing on his mind. He knew the others in the club felt the same. He had this drive built into him that made him feel as though he had to do something among all this chaos. He had to, it felt like no one else was doing anything. Honestly Austin was surprised that the school hadn't been shut down as a precaution. Already some of the international students were leaving. He looked at his little group of friends, classmates, group members. He felt more confident, everyone supported his new idea.

"Wow, the Pacifist Club really isn't a joke; they are serious," Riona said, which resulted in a small punch from Beatrice who finally looked up from her work.

****

They found Mr Trolt eating lunch in the staffroom; it was troll cuisine; it smelt good, but Austin had no idea what it was. The kids explained what they were trying to do and explained that they needed his help. "Do you have any experience with this sort of magic?" Austin asked.

"I'm sorry to disappoint, Austin, but this tradition has not been practised for a while; no one has done anything like this in hundreds of years. With all these technological advances in magic, we left this form to sort of die out. It is something you read in books about Trolls but it isn't accurate." The troll looked saddened by his words.

"There has to be someone who could do it or at least someone who has seen someone doing it." Fred was now desperate.

"Well, I have seen a book about someone doing it in my youth, but these were some of the most prestigious and knowledgeable trolls of their time, and now no such trolls exist. It is incredibly dangerous."

"We have no choice," Ena said.

Mr Trolt understood the circumstances and described how they would need someone close to the victim and suggested Mr Hurt, her father. Austin was very surprised at first when he found this out, but it made sense.

"Okay, Lela and Ena, there is a list of things you will need for this ritual. I will send it to you, and I want you to retrieve them, no matter how obscure. Fred and Austin, you find Mr Hammond and see if he agrees to do the ritual. If he agrees, we will all meet up in the boy's locker room on the second floor in the sports wing after dark. I will go into the troll archives and see if I have one of these spell books still." He gave each of them a hall pass and described how no one must know what they were about to do or the school would shut them down. The girls and boys split up and did as they were told for once.

Fred and Austin headed for Mr Hurt's apartment in the school, and finally got there; the staffrooms were separate from the student dormitories, which just meant more walking. They finally arrived at Door 2341, a steel bolted door. They reached for the cast iron door knocker in the shape of a harpy, a winged hag, but the teacher opened the door even before they rang it. He had puffy red eyes and wore a sleek, black, loose shirt and pants. "If you are here for the test, I haven't marked them yet, and even if I did, I only give them out on school time." The man was about to shut the door, but Austin held it open.

"Wait, we have something you might want to hear."

The man listened intently to Austin's plan and the risks surrounding it; he kept adjusting the purple gemstone ring on his left thumb. "I will do anything for my Aria. She was really sweet and fierce; not many people knew that side to her, but I did. I know that something is off about her death, and I will do anything to put her at peace. She deserved more."

*＝**********

The day turned to night quickly. Austin was in his room; just at lights out, he finished off a call with his mum then headed out. He went to go meet up with Lela at her room so they could walk together. He knocked on her dried bamboo shoot door; it took a minute, but she answered, her deep brown hair in a messy bun. She wore a simple pale pink tee and long tracksuit pants. She handed him some of the objects she had retrieved and carried a few in her own hands. Austin noticed some spices, a bunch of candles, a lighter and purple feathers. Austin had no idea what these were all for, but he had trust in the process. She locked up her room and put the key into her pocket and finally laced her left hand into Austin's hand. "How did you pass the test to get into this school?" Austin chose a light-hearted topic to distract both of them from the very risky ritual they were about to perform. He could see the tension release from her face as she started to explain.

"Well, at my primary school, they taught a little magic, so when the day came, I was prepared. I was lucky enough to have some magnets in my pocket when I was in the test. I really liked the design of my door, so when I figured there was no end to the hallway, I traced my way back to my door and slipped a magnet into the locking mechanism. I used an *avidanen chatum* spell to—"

"Control the magnetic field to get your door to unlock. Brilliant, and you didn't even blow your door into smithereens!" Austin finished the sentence.

"Exactly, I see the tutoring with Leslie paid off so far." Lela smiled.

"Actually, I learned it from the nurse, Peggy, long story." He laughed.

He went on to explain the story of how he got a magnet stuck in his throat as a kid, and they both talked about random childhood experiences. They were both sharing stories until they heard a low growl in the distance; it still sent shivers down Austin's spine. "It's fine; we have hall passes, and even if we didn't, I'm sure that you could manoeuvre your way out of it again," Lela tried consoling him. He squeezed her hand in reply, and they continued walking to the very dangerous hybrid, the first chimera. Eventually, the guard met them in the hall.

"Austin, definitely not a first, and Lela Moon, do you have hall passes?"

"Actually, yes, Rhicon; here they are." Both students presented their passes.

Both of the unintelligible beasts hissed in response. "CAN WE STILL KILL THEM?"

"Definitely not."

Austin still wondered why they would let Rhicon be allowed in the school; they could really harm some student. "So Austin, why are you out here tonight? I have noticed a few students out today, why is that?"

"Just extra-curricular and studying," Lela intervened.

"Well then, I guess you two are free to go." Their wings flapped in disagreement, but sure enough, the pair were on their way. Austin could still hear the hissing of the drool meeting the ground. It had a very high-pitched sizzle both from the serpent and boar.

Once they were out of earshot, Austin broke the silence. "Rhicon called you Lela Moon, not Lela Bishop, why?" Austin asked a detail; he may have already been overlooking in the class rollcalls.

"My dad's last name is moon, and it's my official last name, but I also go by my mum's maiden name since they split up, Bishop," Lela said as they continued their walk. Austin felt so dumb that he never knew this; every time he thinks he knows everything about Lela, she always surprises him.

"Cool," Austin said in a low voice. Austin felt a bit of tension and distance between the two. *Cool, is that really all you had to say, Austin?* He thought to himself, hyper-fixating on every detail now. He felt dumb not knowing what to say, but he was grateful that Lela changed subjects. Lela finally got serious, one of her characteristics as a leader.

"So you think this will work?"

"It has to." Austin looked down towards his feet as they walked for the next two minutes until they arrived. Everyone else had arrived and were finishing setting up. Fred was helping Mr Hurt to move the freestanding bathtub that was already filled out with water. They placed it on a large drawn-out dreamcatcher, drawn out from purple chalk. There was a massive dreamcatcher painted across tens of hundreds of bricks in the centre of Troll Village Austin recalled. It looked very similar to the one Mr Trolt drew out. The book Mr Trolt promised he would bring was opened to a specific page on a nearby counter. Austin placed the candles he and Lela brought on specific points on the drawn-out symbol directed by Trolt. Lela took the ingredients she had brought, the purple feathers, star anise, thyme and a dusty powder, into a makeshift cauldron someone else had brought and lit a flame underneath, continuously stirring it.

"A dreamcatcher focuses on mind and emotion; it is said that a troll has a strong link to dreamcatchers due to this. A dreamcatcher can interpret hidden messages and is a form of psyche," Lela said, to which Ena continued reading from the open book. "We brought the dreamcatcher connected to Aria's spirit here." She gestured to Austin. "Mr Hurt is put into a dream-like state in the bathtub, which acts as a conductor for the spirits to intersect. Hopefully, if done right we can figure out the last place she was alive or some other clue to how she died." Ena shivered, either because she was really cold as she was dressed in a matching black crop top and short bottoms, or that she was really creeped out. The boy pulled the dreamcatcher out of his bag. It was woven with purple string in a symmetrical form, with beads and feathers hanging from either side.

The troll now took the spotlight. "It took a lot of convincing, but I was able to get this ancient runic book from the counsel; it has the steps of the ritual and everything we need to complete it. Though I can't promise it will work." He now referred to Mr Hurt directly, "I will warn you though, the emotions and feeling you will experience as you go through the ritual is overwhelming, so you need to find an anchor or your consciences will be lost in the dreamcatcher. Austin, would you hand me the dreamcatcher?" Austin complied, and as soon as he did, it glowed in the troll's hand, making a small buzzing sound. "These are Barminian feathers, a very powerful bird, rarer than the phoenix, and with more power. That is why we have it in our spice mixture." He gestured to Lela, who was still stirring. "Are you sure you want to do this?" The troll seemed empathetic.

"I am sure I have to do this." There was a mutual agreement between the teachers.

"I was hoping you would say that because I didn't set up these vessels with water and get everything in order for nothing." The troll started to laugh, but the others were too nervous to join in. They started the ritual. Mr Hurt wore the same thing as before except he lost the shoes before he entered the water.

"Why is the water so cold?" the man shrieked.

"It's a better conductor of magic. It has something got to do with molecular structure at different temperatures." The man was now submerged with just his head above the water level. Mr Trolt spoon-fed him some of the mixture then he started the chant reading from the book. He was focusing carefully on each word of the passage, standing in front of the egg-shaped tub at the head of the purple chalk symbol. Mr Trolt finished his chant, and nothing happened for a few seconds until Mr Hurt's head was dragged underwater by an invisible force. As that happened, the cold water started to bubble. Ena rushed forward, but Fred held her back.

****

Hammond woke up in the bathtub, but not in the locker room, rather back at Aria's room, her possessions filling up the room. The tub seeming so out of place, he exploded out of the water and jumped out of the tub soaking, dripping, shivering. Aria didn't seem to notice the new decorative bathtub in her room or her father. Hammond felt like he was in a dream but still felt fully conscious. The dreamcatcher experience was strange and uncontrollable; you just had to follow the storyline; it was all he could do. There were three skull posters hung up on the dark walls that belonged to her favourite band. The girl herself sat on her bed, leaning up against the wall with someone standing opposite of her. She talked fast-paced and in a hushed tone. "You were there that one night; you took her. She was never going to tell you anything. Now we are responsible for kidnapping her. All for our employer who has got too much over us. The cycle will never end; we don't even know their name. I want out; this is not what I signed up for." The girl got up and started to pace the room; she walked right through Hammond like he didn't even exist. He couldn't move; he could only observe the memory, which felt like it was taking over; it had strong emotions. Hammond could feel the fear and anxiousness radiating through him. The girl continued to speak. "Look, Tanner, you think you can just ignore this until it goes away? We have to take action now, otherwise we will continue to be puppets for the OS." The man was in shock. Did his daughter really do such things, and for them? The vision began to blur, and he was losing focus and was fading; he heard the screams of those that were in the locker room, but that felt like a decade ago. One voice rushed him back into concentration.

"Find the place of her death; let her be your anchor!"

He tried speaking to Aria, but it was like his mouth was glued shut. He just wanted to speak to her; the vision was blurring, and it felt violent. Hammond closed his eyes and focused hard on the Aria he knew, not this double life of hers. He was now back in Aria's room; she was still on the phone, but she placed it on speaker and kept it on her bed as she paced the room. "The Other Side isn't just something you sign up for! You don't have a choice; you need to play along for your own safety because I can't protect you anymore. You are out of favours; we have been lumped into this together. There is no end; this is our life now." The boy sounded so irritated, but the girl was frantic, pacing. This was the same outfit as the day she died. "Listen to me, Aria, it's your last warning!" The girl hung up the phone and left her room. He followed her out the side entrance and saw her interaction with Austin, taking in the old news of Aria's betrayal. He then followed her to the forest where she ran; she was paranoid, looking around, screaming at the trees like they were going to hurt her. The sun was soon to set. She continued running and tripped over a rock, landing on her face, her clothes getting scratched. Hammond wanted to turn away; he didn't want to watch, but it was as if he had no choice. She stumbled into a clearing, then limped over to a particular tree and leaned against it. On a heart etched into the bark was A.H. & L.M.B. BFF 4 EVER. Two men dressed in the Other Side uniform, pure black from head to toe except for the circular symbol consisting of the three colours: red, blue and black. They were on either side of her, flanking her. Her eyes showed she knew that her fight was up. One man stepped forward and snapped her neck. The man snapped back into reality and yet again shot upward from the tub. Ena and Fred rushed to him to help him to his feet.

The man tried to start explaining, "She, she was working with this other student, and there were these two men..." The man started to notice his surroundings; everyone looked like they saw a ghost. "And you on the tree and..." The man started to speak in tongues; he pointed at Lela. Mr Trolt intervened and tried to help Mr Hurt get to his room with Fred to let him rest.

"The rest of you clean this up, not a trace to be left," Mr Trolt stated. They started to leave, but the teacher wanted to stay and explain.

"She was—"

Lela began to speak. "We know; we saw everything." That seemed to put the man at ease, and all three boys left. They could over hear Mr Hurt as he was escorted away, "why didn't she come to me. I would've helped her." Ena started to break down.

"He was underwater for over an hour!"

Austin tried to comfort her. "We know, but he should be fine by tomorrow. He just needs some rest; he is going through some major grief." Ena nodded in reply, and the three students finished cleaning up in silence, not leaving a trace as Mr Trolt had said.

Chapter 13
Truth

"Look, I didn't do anything, I don't know what you are even talking about. I barely even knew her!" the six-foot jock stated.

"That's not what our source tells us," Ena questioned the boy; she was short compared to him. She stood confidently, not showing an ounce of doubt. She was doing most of the interrogation while her best friend stood back and observed Tanner. His body movement, his eyes and his facial expression gave it away. They stood in the long corridor during the second period; the best friends tracked his schedule. It was eerily empty in class time, the marble floors not crowded with shoes. Ena's rainbow pendant necklace hung loosely around her neck. "I'm going to ask you one more time." The girl took a deep breath. "How were you involved with Aria, and what do you know about her death?" The boy was one of the jocks, a footballer, tanned, always friendly and had those outdated puka necklaces. His green eyes stared ferociously at Ena, accusingly denying anything. If they hadn't had the information with Trolt's help, it would've almost been believable.

Lela stepped forward now. "Listen, we know exactly what you did. Does the name Irora Winter mean anything to you?" The boy's face went white like a ghost. "Well, how about 12/12/2020? The date she went missing." The girl shifted her black hair out of her fierce face.

"Look, I only met Aria like twice; we were on very different ends of the social spectrum, but we were forced to do a job together. They said it would be the last time; they were going to kill us. We disabled the forcefield and let the school boundaries fail; after that, we thought it was done, but we were wrong. They wanted us to steal some scripture in the archives room, but we didn't do it, and as a result, she died. I haven't heard from them since. I know it wasn't a suicide, but I didn't kill her."

Ena took over again. "Who made you do this?"

"You know exactly who is behind this." He towered over her threateningly.

"Do you want to elaborate, big boy?" the short girl said in a sarcastic tone.

"The Other Side, they offered me a place in this school if I did that one job in Mertamic, but it just kept on going. I never meant for it to get this bad." The boy's tone turned to anger. "You can't prove anything! So if I were you, I would leave this school because I don't like loose ends. I only tolerated Aria because I had to. I don't have to tolerate you." Lela tried to step between the two, but Ena still insisted.

Lela slipped her hand into her pocket and tapped on her phone; it was recording everything. The boy lunged for the phone, but she dodged. "I wouldn't do that. One tap and it will be sent to every student and staff member in this school." The girl didn't seem intimidated at all. "Principal's office, now! And would you mind walking one metre ahead of us, with both hands in the air?"

"Come on, gals, I wouldn't hurt a fly. I'm not going to try anything. I will live up to my actions." The jock did as he was told.

"You know what, Lela?" Ena stood by her side.

"What?"

"The thing is that Tanner sort of did hurt someone, and it could've been a lot worse than just the sports wing; who knows what the ent could've done?"

"I think you're right," the pacifist leader replied.

"Okay, I get it. Can we just go and get this over and done with?"

"Well, what are you waiting for?" Lela raised an eyebrow.

****

The principal's room was large; it was the highest point in school and had 360 degrees views. The rest of the school was on break and filling up the green fields, all cheerful, completely oblivious to the matter at hand. It was much like the rest of the school, ivory tiling, but what differed was the massive chandelier which was twice the size of a yoga ball. Austin had already explained everything when the girls came in with their hostage. He sat on one of the three seats in front of the principal, who had called in Mrs Rimesdome, who stood nearby in the corner, observing the situation. The principal looked like he was vacationing in Hawaii; he had a tropical shirt on and khaki shorts with a red tie to make it look more professional. The black man stood up when they all came in. Ena took a seat, and Tanner sat in the middle seat, with Lela standing behind him, her gaze like a hawk.

"What you guys are accusing Paisley of is very serious!"

Ena couldn't contain her laughter. "Wait, your name is Paisley? No wonder you go by your last name."

"That's enough, Ena." The principal gave her a stern look, but Tanner didn't seem fazed at all by what she said. Lela placed her phone unlocked on the table and opened up on the recordings app with only one tape there. There was a very tense moment of silence before the principal hit play. They let the recording play through until the end. Mrs Rimesdome spoke first; Austin almost forgot she was there. She had mostly observed the events from a corner in the room, looking out the window while listening to the tape. She wore a regular, white, button-down, silk blouse with loose black pants, very professional attire.

"Well, Tanner, I really thought you had a bright future here; you should've come to us for help, but now we have no choice but to follow protocol. It infringes safety codes of the rest of the students if you stay here."

"You will go pack your bags now, and Mrs Rimesdome will escort you to the council, where a hearing will be heard to understand all your knowledge on the Other Side. You will not be allowed back at campus, unless your name is cleared. They will question you about the whereabouts of Irora Winter, who would've been one of your classmates." The principal pulled her admission file out of his draw, the approved stamp still bright and green. "I expected more from you; you went against every moral of our school values, risking the lives of your peers. You may go now. The rest of you three, stay here." The principal adjusted his plain red tie.

Mrs Rimesdome chaperoned the traitor outside, the echo of their footsteps sounding the silence. After the vice-principal and the boy were out of earshot, the principal began to speak. "I don't know who you think you guys are; playing this is a dangerous game. I don't know what your sources were, nor do I want to know, but you have to stop. The Pacifist Club was shut down and for a reason by the Westbrook Security; you are lucky I am not going to inform Detective Weatherson. He believed that you were behind the security incident. In his words he said, 'It's very convenient that he was in a place without cameras and not where he was supposed to be.' You have to stop putting yourselves in these situations, or you will end up like Tanner. And girls, you need to be more like an upstanding model for your peers. Leave the detective work up to the adults." He didn't sound like he was putting any room in for argument, but Ena was one for speaking her mind.

"I just find it funny how everyone is saying let the adults handle it, but so far the only ones that have actually done anything so far are us, the students. I mean I would've settled for a thank you. The sad part is that you are threatening to put all the blame onto the only person that is actually helping this school." Ena looked like she was only getting started, but Lela, who was still standing, put a hand on her shoulder and signalled her to stop before they got into real trouble.

"There is a lot more than you know happening behind the scenes. We have access to the access codes and log of the security room. We tracked it back to Aria through Cheryl-Ann's key card. The girl was sloppy and volatile, but we needed to see how things panned out under supervised watch. There are many things at play here and many powerful people; I am doing my best to keep a lid on things."

"So you want to just cover everything up? Aria may not have been innocent, but she still deserved your protection!" Lela had now started.

"I think we are done here," said the principal. The students got up and started heading for the exit.

"You should really take your job more seriously and adjust your priorities," Austin said before he shut the door, leaving the principal to contemplate on what Austin had just said.

****

The rest of the classes that day went pretty quick until the last class, supernatural magic, most people were still very anxious about the class, but Mr Hurt took it easy with some textbooks and history in this class. Mr Hurt arranged the classroom desks in a horseshoe shape, all facing towards him as he explained some creatures in history. The light was shining in from outside. Austin was keeping up with this class after going through a few of these stories with Leslie already. Lela sat to the left of Austin and tapped beneath his plastic desk; he reached under, and sure enough, there was a sticky note that she had put there sleekly. It read: 'Meet after class in the music room. Jarred is performing a song he wrote.'

He wrote on the back and pulled the same manoeuvre she had done.

'Can't, have tutoring'

She shrugged it off, but something else caught her gaze. Austin followed her direction of sight; there he was, in his usual grey coat and his familiar stubble. He entered the classroom, forcefully slamming the door open, and it sent a shudder through the class. The light shining from outside, not seeming so bright anymore. The footsteps thudded against the metallic floor, asserting dominance. Two men followed Detective Weatherson, both wearing security badges. The detective made quick eye contact with Austin, which spiked Austin with anxiousness, but when the detective spoke, it wasn't directed at him.

"Mr Hammond Hurt, you are under arrest for the murder of Aria Hurt. Anything you say, can and will be used against you in the Council of Law. You are going to regret reopening this case. After further testimony from Tanner and a further observation of the autopsy report, we have concluded that the fall does not match the cause of her death."

"Not right here in front of the students; I didn't do this. How could you think a father could do this to his little angel?" The other two officers turned the teacher around and placed the handcuffs on him, ignoring the students, all with shocked expressions whilst they filmed it.

"Students, you are all dismissed for the day; your teacher will be taking a short leave." The detective smirked, and like that, they left. Lela turned to Austin, still in shock.

"This is a complete abuse of power and misinformed information." She stood up from her chair. "We have to do something!" But she could tell something was holding Austin back. "What?"

"I'm not sure there is much we can do right now; we will testify, but right now, we have to remain calm and not bring attention to ourselves." Austin hated those words coming out of his mouth, but he felt like he was out of options and second lives.

"I can't believe you right now. This is not just incompetence; there are active members in the council trying to cover this up. We can't let this happen. I don't know how you can just sit on the sidelines as an innocent person we know was just dragged out of his classroom. Maybe you aren't the person I thought you were!" She pushed her way to the door, storming out and not giving Austin a chance to respond. Austin heard the bell ring and finished packing up his things and left for the exit, moments after, trying to catch up to Lela, but she was already lost to the crowd of students fleeing their classrooms.

"She will come around, just give her time." Charlie placed a hand on Austin's shoulder, obviously noticing the fight and not even trying to hide that he had just eavesdropped.

"I know, but I hate this feeling, because I know she is right."

Charlie gestured to the hallway, and the boys walked out together. Austin continued his rant.

****

Austin was now feeling like a school regular finding his way around without following or asking anyone. He sat in the library on some plush red cushion chairs in the corner. Leslie had brought a tower of books and placed them on the table. They had already been working for half an hour. Every so often, she would get distracted by the books around her, but she was a good tutor, dedicated and passionate. Her honey-coloured eyes were full of knowledge and curiosity; she had her hair in a ponytail, deep in thought. Austin noticed she had a new necklace with a crystal pendant attached.

"I like your necklace," the boy complimented.

"Thanks, it's a new thing I'm trying; it's a rose quartz crystal used for attracting love among other uses." The girl held it in her hand. "Can I ask you something, not tutor-related?"

"Umm of course," Austin hesitated but answered surely.

"Do you think I have a chance with Charlie? He became my potions and brewing partner; it made me get to know him more, and I really like him. Although Jill and I had a fight, she was upset that I would change partners, saying it would bring down both of our grades, but I followed my heart. I know you are friends with him, so do you know anything that could help me?"

This was news to Austin, but he replied, "I know that he is single, and he is a really sweet guy, and I think you might be his type. I think you should go for it, what's the worst that can happen? I know where he is now, and I think I may have just made a huge mistake; we should go together."

"Like right now?" The girl started to panic. "I look like a mess. I can't meet him like this. I haven't prepared what I'm going to say and—"

Austin looked her in her eyes and said, "Just let the words spill out of your chest; it's the most authentic and raw way to express yourself."

"Okay, fine, but we are going past my room first quickly; there is something I want to give him."

The pair gathered the books and hauled them to Leslie's room; she said initially it would only take a minute, but Austin waited outside her room for 10 until she finally came out. She slipped a little box in her pocket, but she wouldn't tell Austin what it was. She dressed in fancy casual clothes, a whitewashed pair of ripped jeans and a green floral strapped top. Austin had never seen her out of uniform; it was either the purple and green turtleneck or the basic uniform.

"Did you have a shower?" Austin noticed her wet hair. "You said you would be quick."

She shrugged it off. "Well, we better hurry before the performance is over. I read somewhere that music makes a place 50% more romantic, and I am counting on it."

Austin was so confused by how she knew that fact but didn't get a chance to ask her because she was already running for the hall. They reached the hall halfway through the last song, and it was quite the opposite of romantic, which made Leslie frown. Jarred was singing some Swedish heavy metal punk rock, certainly not what Austin expected, and since when did Jarred know Swedish? The room itself was dark lit, with large blue tiles on the walls for acoustics, Austin guessed; the flooring was tiered and slowly lowered as you got closer to the stage. About 30 people were watching. Beatrice was standing close to the stage while Charlie sat at the end of the front row next to Fred. Carter and Jack, the goofy best friends, were right behind them, playing air guitars and jamming out. Jack was standing on one of the fold-down chairs; both of them were practically exerting testosterone. Lela and Ena were sat in the first row as well, with Riona; the girls didn't seem to be enjoying it, besides Ena. A bunch more kids filled the seats. Austin recognised Lilly the cheerleading captain; this wasn't usually her scene; it bothered Austin for a few seconds, but he gave her the benefit of the doubt that she just liked Swedish heavy metal. Leslie thanked Austin before going to find Charlie, which wasn't hard since he was so tall and stood out in the small crowd. Austin himself went to go sit behind Lela; he tapped her on her shoulder, which made her reflexes jump into action quite literally; she jumped out of her chair as she turned around.

"You made it!" she said practically screaming just to be heard.

"I'm sorry!" Austin screamed, but Lela shrugged pointing to her ear, suggesting she couldn't hear him. Sign language. Austin had learned it in his primary school as one of his core subjects, so he knew the basics. Not knowing if Lela would understand, he signed the words 'I'm sorry.' To his surprise, she understood him and signed something back quite fast, but all Austin could make out was: 'I knew you would be on board…Together, we can…make a burrito?' While Austin was trying to process what she said, Lela laughed seeing his face; he must've looked so puzzled. Austin decided to wait for the song to end before continuing. "I feel like a coward. I now know we have to do something; you were right." She went in for a kiss, and he obliged; maybe Leslie was right, music does make a place more romantic. The world ceased to exist for Austin for a brief moment before a girl made her presence very known.

"PDA much." The blonde cheerleader looked the couple up and down; the girl was born with proportions like a barbie. She had her hair in a high ponytail, trying so desperately to fit in the popular girl stereotype. "That's funny; you two are in a relationship when you decided to ruin mine."

"Lilly, what are you on about?" Lela shot back.

"Tanner; you got him expelled; you never even thought to consider how good of a person he is; he boosts our football team ranking; he was on his way to becoming junior school captain, but most of all, I was his girlfriend, but I'm sure you loved breaking us up, didn't you two?"

"For one, we didn't break you and him up; we just brought the truth to light, and two, these are the consequences of his actions," Lela said to the girl head-on. Ena and Riona noticing the action stood behind the pacifist leader.

"You two act so high and mighty with your whole club, but it was shut down temporarily, wasn't it, and I have proof of all of you performing illegal activity on campus." Lilly was practically screaming now.

"Go ahead, but we have immunity as of today; the club has full power again since the 'force-field case' has been solved," Lela said with a firm stance. "You can't blackmail us because you're heartbroken." Lela made a point of having a condescending tone.

"I will come for each and every one of you!" She left the room very dramatically. The crowd started to disperse as Jarred and his crew started packing up their equipment. Austin leaned into Lela's ear.

"Should we finish that conversation now?"

"Of course," Lela said, whispering back.

"I think we need to begin at the start; there is still so much we don't know about the prophecy, Caleb, Aria, Tanner and Irora." Lela tensed at Irora's name.

"Emergency club meeting, a quarter till lights out," Lela said, already starting to text all the members on the group chat she created, 'Peace Warriorz'.

"Also, how do you know sign language?" Austin asked.

The girl hesitated for a second glancing at her shoes, one untied; she bent down to tie it up before answering, but Austin joined her on the floor, helping her tie it up. "My brother had Meniere's disease so only one ear worked; the doctors were scared that it could progress to the second ear and he might lose his hearing completely, so I learned it from him. He was always so calm and collected about it, so confident, and he never seemed down about it. He really was always so positive all the time; it makes me feel so unsure now. I feel like a traitor in his footsteps. Who am I even kidding? I can't be the Pacifist Club leader; I barely even know what I am doing half the time." The girl seemed frayed and on the verge of a breakdown. "I'm sorry I overshared a bit." She let out a weak laugh. The boy responded with a hug, giving physical reassurance.

"Don't be sorry. You are the most confident headstrong person I know; your brother would've been so proud. No one is perfect, but you have so many people at the club. You aren't alone; you can rely on others more than you know. And I feel like an idiot for not realising how much pressure the job was putting on you. But know now that it will never be like this again." The two sat there embracing each other for 10 minutes before finally going back to Lela's room to watch the sunset and run through a few things before the meeting.

****

The familiar Pacifist Club now felt like a general's tent, a strategical battleground. Names and dates were written down on the main flip whiteboard. There was sound of computers whirring in the background and two students doing some research into Terra's spell book. Something new was that the children's table was exchanged with a convertible pool table/regular table. It was Ena who called the meeting this time. Lela stood against the back wall, overwatching everything, not making any attempt to draw attention to herself. Austin took a seat at one of the 10 spots on the table. The whole group was at 22 kids now, some already dressed in pyjamas.

"We have multiple issues, and we are sorry to have called this meeting this late, but we need to go over a few things now that we are actually recognised as one of the clubs of the school again." That got a few cheers. Ena went on to explain what happened with Tanner but left out the whole ritual thing with Mr Hurt.

"So they have an innocent man in custody! We will not stand for it, especially since it is one of our long-term staff members who has been a part of our community as long as some of us have been born. I need two members to go to every court proceeding as guests and provide summaries for everything, as well as gather as much information as we can." Two volunteer freshman raised their hands. "Thanks, Stefan and Grace. Now if there are any ideas, I'm open, but I say we have a school fundraiser." She left the spotlight for anyone to speak up.

"How about a protest? There is clearly insufficient evidence against Mr Hurt to keep him in custody. We just need to get more media attention." Charlie spoke up; he was one of the oldest members of the club now. Austin noticed that he had a new leather necklace on; it had a tooth belonging to some kind of animal, possibly a tiger, as a pendant.

"That is good. Do you think you can organise that, and Jarred, can you organise the fundraiser, may be a food stall?" Jarred nodded in agreement.

"Now onto the next topic, Terra's spell book was stolen as we all know that was the whole point of the power outage fiasco. We are trying to figure out why the Other Side would want it and what they plan on doing with it. We are also attempting to track it down; it has something called a magical footprint, all ancient and powerful magic objects have them. So we are already doing research into it." She gestured to the open computers at the back of the room. "We have reason to believe that the book is still within school grounds because the magical footprint never left this vicinity, but there seems to be some interference blocking the exact whereabouts of it." Little groups of kids talked amongst each other seemingly nervous.

Ena coughed to gain the attention of everyone again. "Furthermore, we have a new member: Unity Light." All heads turned. She was sitting towards the back of the room, a simple woven cardigan covering her frame; she looked a lot better now fully recovered from her kidnapping. She stood up, Ena trying to give her a bit of courage from the sidelines. She had frail blonde hair and a very unique eye colour with her pupils being a shade of crimson and her irises being a light blue. She had her hands crossed around her waist, holding her cardigan tight.

"I guess you all know what happened to me, news travels fast." She let out a weak laugh, then went on to explain, "I was locked in the closet, assumed kidnapped, lived a nightmare, and now I want to take back my power. I want to bring the fight to those who oppose us and bring council and justice." She got a round of applause and went to sit back down. While everyone in the room was applauding Unity, Jarred caught Austin's eye; he was by the printer now.

"Everyone listen up," he said. Something was printing out of the printer; something was faxed through old fashioned. "It's an article about Mr Rhike as a baby, a twin; it showed a second child, Caleb Rhike. They are brothers! Austin, isn't that the guy that has been lurking around school?" Jarred passed the attention onto Austin, his turn now.

"It is." Austin was hesitant, still processing the news. "He has some connection to my mum. I can try and get more information about him. I also know he has some connection to Wendy; the Westbrook Security is looking into him with all sorts of background checks. He also has a connection in the council, but that is all I really know; he is sort of a mystery. Also, on a separate note, we have reason to believe that the ancient prophecy could be happening right now." More whispering and low conversations sparked, but Ena controlled everyone to focus back on Austin. Austin recited it again:

'Two angel-blooded being separated in thunder
The new world will yield to the one who holds the power
The big war arising full of plunder
The chosen one goes forth to scower
Ancient ones arising from the dawn of the first era
The shadowed ones will come and bring terror
It begins with the creation of the first chimera
When it comes into contact with the element bearer'

"My ex, Irora Winter, and I were a target for kidnapping, with her being taken during a thunderous night. We are both angel-blooded, a witch and wizard." Austin hated referring to himself as a wizard; it didn't feel right; he barely knew any magic, let alone knew how to control it. In his mind, wizards are grey-haired old men with a beard and a cape. "The new world refers to Hylenia the land of magical creatures and all things not mundane. The land we live on will be at the mercy of a single individual, and we don't know who it is yet. Furthermore, the council of Westbrook is trying to keep it hidden, but there have been monsters from the first era, the so-called untameable vicious creatures that haven't been seen in aeons. The ancient ents, one seen at our school, the

Western Wolf Pack, aka the shadowed ones, are believed to be behind the kidnappings within the forests of Westbrook. Even fire giants, the Vorhiëns, born from the first flame in the River Cynex. Some of you are lucky enough to not know who the first chimera is, Rhicon, but he came into contact with me, the element bearer. Did I miss anything?" A deep silence stood in the club for 10 seconds before the usual chatter erupted.

"Hey, everyone, I have something I want to say." A girl named Grace tried to grab the attention of the very busy room. Her voice was timid; she was just a freshman, had shoulder-length lavender purple-dyed hair and glasses. Austin noticed she was on the computers researching into the Terra book before the meeting had started. "Hello!" She finally gained the attention she was trying to get. Austin saw her fear of having every head towards you; it's scary; she seemed very frightened. "There is one very classified spell in Terra's book which I believe could be the reason whoever stole the book did so. It is a reanimation spell needing 50 sacrifices, hence the disappearances. All sacrifices are to be burned at once on an altar made of holy wood. The spell is one of the most powerful in the book, and I believe it could be used to recover all the ancient scriptures that were mostly lost to the world. It would give whoever the holder is the knowledge of ancient power and magic. Those scrolls would become the most dangerous weapon of our time, especially if it were to get into the wrong hands. That is just one possibility though; it could really conjure anything bad; it's some bad voodoo."

The crowd was low. If this was true, it matched with the current circumstances. This was so much bigger than just them; it was the fate of the world. No one made a sound, just the humming of the printer and a few computers in the room. Ena took the spotlight again in a desperate attempt to be optimistic. "Well, if they need a minimum of 50 sacrifices being the missing people, then that means all the captees are still alive as they all need to be sacrificed at the same time, so they are all being held somewhere. Right?"

The question was rhetorical, but Grace didn't seem to think so. "That is assuming this is related to the kidnappings, and it is the spell I am talking about."

Pessimism wasn't in Ena's vocabulary. "This is all we have to go on, so I have to think this. We need a small team to see if there is a pattern in all the captives. We need to try and make some sense of it." All heads turned towards Unity's direction, being kidnapped and rescued, still a hot topic. Now Lela put her hand up and looked to Austin to do the same. She was keeping awfully quiet this meeting, but she looked frustrated, like a thought was bothering her, and once she had something in mind, she needed to speak it. "All these disappearances have been from Westbrook besides…Irora Winter. So is it possible that all the missing people could still be in some facility within the boundaries, because it's not so easy to get in and out the security; it's pretty high tech."

This time, Jarred answered, "Even if that is true, Westbrook is huge; there are a million places they could be. Also, there are gaps in the city borders. But to smuggle tens of people, maybe not. So it is something to go on."

Ena started to summarise the meeting. "Okay, so we have our volunteers, maybe the next meeting will be next week. Until then, focus on the fundraisers and the protest we will hold in Mr Hurt's name. Meeting dismissed." The children all left the room in small crowds, and after two minutes, it was just Austin, Ena and Lela who remained.

"That was nowhere near as easy as you make it out to be; all the eyes on you to have a strategy, a plan for the impossible, where even the authorities are failing. All the while keeping a smile and moving onto one of the many topics of discussion." Ena sighed; she let her hair up into a messy bun after presenting herself as a leader for the past 15 minutes.

"I know, but we will talk about it in the morning; it's almost curfew. We don't want any more meetings with Rhicon," Lela said in an urgent voice but then laughed a small laugh under her breath.

Chapter 14
The Protest

The first lesson of the day was Troleze. They did some class reading about ancient troll history. Austin was starting to get used to the language. It was similar to English; it was a mix of foreign and regular English words. The original language adapted to the modern world, so Austin was picking it up pretty easily, especially the tutor lessons he had been having with Leslie really helped as well. Mr Trolt was explaining the conjugations of different verbs, which was way too confusing for Austin for it to be the first lesson of the day. He watched the sunlight outside, teasing him, making him jealous that he was inside still learning. The lesson was a double, and by the end of it, Austin was ready for a break. The bell rang a bit prematurely, but Mr Trolt let the kids go. Austin walked up to the teacher to go over a few of the study techniques he had explained.

"Hey, how is Julian doing?" Austin asked, reminded of the nightmare he had had, immediately feeling guilty that he hadn't checked up sooner.

"Last I heard, he was still back at home. Fine, I suppose." The troll didn't seem quite sure of himself, but Austin let it go. "Also, be sure that your mother sends digital verification for that trip later in the week."

"Will do. See you." Austin smiled and left for the gazebo to meet up with Lela for the break. He had taken a liking to the gazebo ever since he and Lela had talked with Kelly, strategizing against Caleb. It hadn't worked, but Austin was still determined. Austin pushed his way through the crowd of students and slipped out of the corridor through a side entrance not many people knew about and walked through the stone pathway that twisted through the many maple trees all the way till he saw the white pergola providing shade against the unusually warm day and beating sun, which was strange since the whole school area was weather-controlled. Nonetheless, Austin joined Lela, who was lying down on one of the benches, her white top covered in multi-coloured glitter. Austin guessed she was doing some sort of arts and crafts instead of joining in the lesson for Troleze. As if reading his mind, she answered, "Preparations for the strike or demonstration, whatever you want to call it. I made a sign, which Ena insisted needed galaxy-coloured glitter, which got everywhere." The girl emphasised the word everywhere.

"Well, hello to you too." The boy sat at the far end of the bench, just near Lela's head, one foot on each side of the bench and started to play with her jet-black hair.

"Tell me you are at least coming to the excursion; it will be so boring without you. You can't skip that, no excuses."

"I promise I won't skip. I already made the glittery signs." She put her hands up in defence. They spent their 15 minutes with harmless banter and soft music until they were reminded by that dreadful bell to go to class. The pair split up, walking in different directions for different classes. Austin headed for the elemental magic class, always nervous for this class as he never felt normal in this class. He entered, the familiar exposed floor meeting his shoes, the fish tank ever so colourful and full and the heat radiating from the furnace easing his nerves. Austin was a bit early, so he picked a seat first. People filtering through one by one, made it very clear that they didn't want to be seated anywhere near Austin by choosing the opposite end of the class; people gave him side looks. Even though they only had theory classes since the incident, people were still wary of Austin, as they should be. Even Austin was scared about his own abilities and his lack of power to control them. After a few minutes, the classroom was full, with the chairs furthest from Austin filling up first, and eventually, the seats near Austin were reluctantly taken up. Even Riona had stayed clear of him and was by the windows. Austin still felt guilty, even though Riona had forgiven him and told him it was only an accident. The teacher walked in himself, minorly late with Peggy accompanying him. Peggy wore the usual nurse outfit: the white coat, a size too big and dangly gold hoop earrings to accompany her outfit. She stood by the side of the class, trying not to draw attention to herself, but it wasn't working; the classroom started to stir. The teacher himself wore a plain grey tee and jeans; he had a short stubble growing and seemed like he was half functioning on caffeine. He placed a coffee thermos down on his desk and began to speak.

"Good day, class. Today, we will be putting into practice all of what we have learned in our theory classes. It's coming up to midterm progress reports and I will need to mark you all on something besides just the theory exams. So we will be working as partners; everyone will be working with the opposite element. If you are a fire student, you will work with an air student, and earth and water elements will work together. Hopefully, this will counteract each other and create a balance so we don't have any, erm…issues, and we have student nurse Peggy here if anything goes sideways."

There were many side conversations going on and looks particularly towards Austin's direction. Peggy made a wave to the class and then took a seat by the side; she put her hair up in a ponytail and started making notes in a notebook she had on her lap.

"Everyone will get to choose their own partners, so go ahead." The students erupted from their seats and got into pairs around the class. Austin stood up; none of the water kids dared to look in his direction. They all stood by the water tank. After about 30 seconds of awkward nudging, Riona volunteered and went to Austin; they stood together, and Austin mouthed thank you to her.

The rest of the students sorted themselves, but all eyes were still on Austin and Riona. One of the other water students, Calvin, called out across the classroom, "RIP, Riri, for a second time." Mr Davon sent him out, but it made Austin feel so exposed and judged. No matter how many times people stared at him, it never got less frightening.

Mr Davon spoke up. "So, we are going to keep it simple this time. In your own way, show your ability to master your element, whether the fluidity or the solidity matter of it. Take everything we have learnt into account to show both elements complementing each other. May I also remind you this spell may only be used under supervision in this classroom. We have had reports of a few of you using it unrulily. Okay, you may begin one at a time, starting with…"

Don't say my name. Please don't say my name, Austin prayed in his mind. It didn't work.

"Austin and Riona. Earth and water signs, you may begin." The teacher had his wand at the ready. Kids backed up while Riona began with the water, saying the spell, focusing her face on the water, and sure enough, the water erupted, but she managed to steer it into a small rotating sphere; her face was scrunched due to the effort she put in, her eyes closed, her body shaking slightly, her nerves showing through her body language. She stabilised the orb, calmed herself and straightened her back, still focusing on the water but letting out a sigh. All eyes turned to Austin now. He watched the ground, the soil shifting uncomfortably under his feet; he had a clear vision in mind, a memory of nature and dirt under his feet, a camp he went to when he was younger. He was trudging through a forest on a hike; he was maybe 12, but it felt so real, the details ever so specific like it happened yesterday. Oak trees rooted in the ground and standing tall, the air crisp; in that second, he felt alone in the room, and he muttered the words to himself, "*Entacio Chatum*." The boy put his hands on Riona, bracing her as he lifted the ground up from beneath them; they levitated on the ground. Austin gestured to the girl. He nodded towards the ore and then to the soil they stood on. They stood deep-footed on the floor steady, ready for Riona's next movement. She adjusted the water towards the ground, but instead of soaking up the water, it moved like the air above it, like waves. The ground shifted beneath them as Austin made a mini cliff that went up to knee height, and the water rushed off it like a waterfall; they had created a mini-ecosystem, a river, a waterfall and a little reservoir. Finally exhausted from the effort, the weight straining on Austin, he let them down, not so gently, and Riona also gave way, and the water soaked into the thirsty earth. The whole class was stunned, even Peggy looked up from her notebook. Then a brief moment later, everyone snapped out of the trancelike state. Mr Davon started clapping, and everyone joined him. Austin was relieved and could now just sit and watch everyone else. Mr Davon wrote down a few notes on their performance, Austin presumed, for his grade before the next two classmates presented. Fred, his element fire, and someone Austin couldn't remember his name, but Mr Davon announced he was an air element. Fred started off holding two fires, one in each hand with ease. The flame danced around above his hand, but he didn't get burned for some reason, and he merged both the flames into one orb erupting, not wanting to stay in a singular geometric form. The other classmate started creating a mini tornado from the ground up to chest height, and Fred put his fire into the tornado, spreading and multiplying like a wildfire. The cyclone was nearly a full red colour, spinning like crazy on the spot. The duo finished off their performance by entering the blaze and leaving unharmed, much to Austin's astonishment. The rest of the class went through their performances; some were impressive, some not so much. With the anxiety off his chest, the class was quite entertaining and enjoyable. Peggy only needed to tend to a few burns and one nasty cough caused by one of the water kids but nothing like the first practical assessment. When the bell went, Austin thanked Riona one last time before leaving with Fred down the hallway.

"How did you not get burned? Bro, that was insane!" Austin asked Fred, walking with his textbooks under his right arm.

"Well, the thing is, me and Gray actually practised before knowing the assignment was coming up, so we did this trick where I controlled the fire so close to my skin, giving the appearance of it touching, and the heat of the fire is actually kept at bay because Gray has a layer of air between my skin and the fire, which doesn't mix with the fire unless he wills it to. So like any mundane magician, it's just an optical illusion." He handed Austin his books so he could do some jazz hands. Austin saw that Frederico had the same energy as he did when Austin first met him, smart and energetic, but now something was missing; it didn't seem the same, but rather a shadow of him. Austin knew that the boy had a long history with Wendy; apparently, it went all the way back to pre-K. Her disappearance had taken a toll on the boy. They had a love-hate relationship, which Austin didn't know too much about; besides that, it was passionate. Frederico now didn't have the same glow to his warm natural skin; his complexion was darkened by bags under his eyes. His eyes were bouncy, always looking for clues. Austin felt sorry for him, but the Latino boy didn't like showing his emotional side. He kept on this friendly persona that only a few people could see through. Austin then saw something he didn't believe he would ever see in the hallways. The students that were walking through the hallways all parted to one of the sides, leaving a clear path for a strange sight. It only meant one thing: Mrs Rimesdome was heading towards them.

"Austin." The hallway filled with electricity; it had a taste to the tongue like burnt water. *Of course, why can't I get a break?* Fred grabbed his books back and putting his hands up, left Austin standing by himself. He followed the lady with greater powers than any other witch or wizard: the power of parting the hallways of Westbrook Academy. "I hate walking these hallways during peak hours," the woman said to Austin. Austin knew what that meant. It meant that this couldn't wait, and that was hardly ever good for Austin. The walk to the vice principal's office wasn't long, but it felt like he was walking on a tightrope above a chasm. When he entered the office, Lela was already there, not good, but that meant it was about the Pacifist Club. The vice principal cut Austin's guessing games short and got straight to the point. "I know about the demonstration that you are planning, and it's amazing to see your passion for our Westbrook community and respect for the staff here, but this is not going to happen. This is up to the court, and the last thing we need is publicity." The woman was in an uncomfortable position, her body shifting in her seat. Austin could tell that the woman was in a position in her job where she couldn't show her real intentions and thoughts about her old friend, Mr Hurt, for the school's sake. She couldn't let the controversy get the media's attention; it would affect the school, even though this was right.

Lela spoke up. "That is where I respectfully disagree with you. You know what it sounds like to me?" She posed the rhetorical question and paused for a dramatic effect. She made a show of checking her nails. "Sounds like you are just scared of bad press. You know the news reports will show everyone what is really going on here. How you are failing your job to keep your students safe, the lack of security, and most of all, all the secrets being kept here. So what are you doing? Sacrificing justice so you can keep your job. You know Mr Hurt, so why are you letting them pin this on him?" She let the steam roll off her words. Lela leaned forward onto the desk; Austin couldn't help but smile. She was so confident in her words, the way she composed herself. The two women held intense eye contact; Austin counted ten breaths before the principal spoke again.

"This demonstration will not happen; it violates the student code of conduct. Maybe if you two ever read a few chapters of it, it would save you visits to this office. This protest is potentially harmful and puts you in potential harm's way. I don't need to be dealing with a riot on top of this."

"Sounds to me like you aren't dealing with anything but just covering everything up." The student glared at the woman. Austin put his hand on Lela's shoulder, trying to convince her not to push too many boundaries before it was too late.

"Disrespect like this will not be tolerated! If you do this protest, anyone who participates will be expelled. There is your ultimatum; now leave the room."

The pair stood up in eerie silence, even the electricity running through the walls seemed to have dimmed down. They shut the door behind them, standing in the still-busy hallway; they still had their next class to get to. She grabbed his hand in an awkward position, leading the way, charging through the halls, heading for Ms Legend's class. Potions class wasn't really for Austin, but it was always fun and exciting. She led them through an alternate route, then the regular hallways, an offshoot path lit by the sun shining through the transparent glass arch surrounding them. Vines grew on the outside of the hallway on either side, crawling up the glass. It was a lot quieter here. Austin thought back on the conversation they had just had with Mrs Rimesdome, weighing up the consequences of their actions. "We aren't really going to cancel the demonstration, are we?"

"You read my mind. I think it is best to move it forward to the date of the excursion. We could get more publicity this way. As a bonus, Mrs Rimesdome's rules will not have a hold over us outside of the boundaries. Think about it; we won't only get the attention of the school but of greater Westbrook and even might reach all the citizens of Hylenia." She looked back to him, her hand still in his; she let out a sly grin. They made the rest of the way to class plotting the new schedule.

****

It was lunch break, and Austin found himself at the fundraiser Jarred had set up. Lela went in line to get some freshly baked pastries. Austin had no idea how Jarred made all this possible in less than a day, but it was a success. About a hundred kids congregated at the front of the school, 20 feet away from the giant golden front doors. The stall was a fold-away table covered in a colourful woven tablecloth. There was a huge handwritten sign presenting all the pastries available. The variety was impressive; it had everything, from doughnuts to croissants. He saw a few of the other Pacifist Club members lining up. Grace was in line, her eyes analysing the options through her studded glasses. Unity standing next to her was also waiting impatiently, tapping her foot, waiting in the queue. Lela came back with two apple-filled filo pastries. "Jarred's stall is a success. Finally, something turned out." She took a bite out of the pastry, the filling oozing out of the log-shape treat.

"This is definitely a success," Austin said, the warm dessert giving warmth to his hands; the day was a bit colder than usual.

"Jarred said he needs us to help pack up, do you mind?" Lela asked.

"Not if it includes us getting the leftover pastries," Austin joked around. They spent the rest of their lunch eating and laughing, waiting for all the kids to clear out. They noticed Tanner's old friends coming back from practice, their gear still on. With their lacrosse sticks in their hands, they headed towards the stall. *Was it already lacrosse season? When did the football season end?* Austin thought, his obvious lack of knowledge coming through. Austin had met most of the players on his first day; he tried to recall their names, possibly Bobby and Scotty.

154

"If they are anything like Lilly, this is not going to turn out good." Austin was observing the scene closely. Lela nodded in agreement and left with Austin for the encounter. They arrived a tad too late; the jocks were already making a big scene. "So you are the same people who landed Tanner in prison officially today but also the ones trying to cover up the real evil man behind this. You can't actually be trying to have a fundraiser to cover the costs of a lawyer for that creep teacher. It's a joke, and you are all hypocrites."

Austin stood between Bobby and Jarred. The jocks all wore this buff blue and red jersey, each with their names and numbers in bold letters at the back. "Hey, you need to back up. I know you all have a collective of two brain cells, but if you actually used them, you would know that your buddy Tanner endangered everyone. He even confessed it. Mr Hurt is a grieving father, not a cold-blooded killer, so yes, we are standing up to this injustice."

"You guys are just as evil as your favourite creep of a teacher." The boy pointed at Austin and his friends with his stick. Just then, he slipped the stick behind one of the glass displays with croissants in them and knocked it to the floor, sending the croissants spiralling and the glass to break. Many kids were already gathering around to see what was going on.

"Whoops," Bobby said sarcastically. The only one laughing was Scotty, cackling behind him. Scotty had a buzz cut and was built like a wrestler, his gear only adding to his mass. Bobby was a bit smaller and clearly more in command. Austin rushed to pick up the stuff that was sprawled onto the floor; his first mistake: turning his back on his opponent. Austin felt a quick attack land on his back; it was a cold but sharp hit. The lacrosse stick drew blood from Austin's back. Austin acted in reflex, quickly stumbling to his feet, adrenaline rushing through him, ignoring the pain.

"*Entacio chatum,*" Austin murmured, and the ground beneath Bobby shook. Austin noticed a dark figure hurtling towards him from his peripheral vision. Scotty's fist landed on the right side of Austin's face, instantly breaking Austin's concentration and thus the spell. Austin was knocked to the ground, the air escaping his lungs. He held his eyes closed, waiting for a third blow that never arrived. Austin opened his eyes and attempted to get up, but he fell back down.

"Stay down; you might have a concussion," a familiar voice said. "We have already notified the nurses; they will be here soon. Just lie down." Austin couldn't see this person who stood behind him, but with his head facing forward, he saw both jocks suspended in mid-air. Lela held them there, her face trickling with sweat, her wand extended. Time seemed to be passing slower; every movement of Austin's was an effort, the pain taking a hold of him. The air he breathed into his lungs seemed to be in short supply. Austin heard the voice behind him, comforting him and telling him to keep his eyes open, but all Austin wanted to do was the opposite. He could make out that the voice was feminine but didn't recognise it. He lay on her lap, looking towards the blue sky. After what seemed like forever, the nurses arrived and held a torch into each one of Austin's eyes, temporarily blinding him. He felt himself get put on a stretcher and taken indoors, but after that, everything was a blur as he drifted into dreams.

****

Austin felt this strange outer body experience he had already had a few times, but still he was not prepared; he felt like a ghost. Stuck in a dream where he was conscious but still pretty much bound by the laws of physics. He looked around; he was in a vast cavern, jagged with rocks and stalagmites hanging from the ceiling, dripping with a cold fluorescent liquid. The air was very thin; it was strange because Austin didn't feel the need to breathe, but he chose to anyway to make him feel more real. The floor was covered in moss and the occasional mushrooms; it was beyond Austin how anything could live in this climate. It was almost pitch-black, but that didn't seem to bother Austin. It was as if he could see through the darkness. Austin felt something beyond his five senses, a radiation of power almost calling to him. He was attracted to it like a magnet; he stumbled a few times, and even though he was in a dream, he still got hurt just as much as in real life. His shoulder was scraped, drawing blood. Somehow, all of Austin's previous injuries from the fight ceased to exist in this reality. After what seemed like a long time, Austin stumbled into a more manmade cavern. There were supports and symbols carved into the walls. A small light coming from a podium illuminated the room. It glowed a red hue and bubbled like a liquid. *Is that lava? No, Magma; we are underground.* The podium wasn't built for a human though. Austin walked all the way up to it, and it was very much off scale, twice the size of Austin in height. Then he heard a thunderous movement. Then again, not a second later, coming from a second entrance on the opposite side from where Austin had entered. Soon enough, two enormous figures rose from the shadows. *The Vorhiëns*, Austin knew immediately; he had studied them during primary school, one of his obsessions as a kid. They were remarkably

156

similar to the illustrations that portrayed them in his book. Their bodies seemed to be made out of gravel; they had more or less human features, a huge jaw, deep eye sockets without eyeballs, two arms extended from each side of their body and two giant legs that were slightly too large in comparison to the proportions of the rest of the body. Their bodies glowed with lava-like veins, visible under thin layers of gravel. Then, the most surprising part of all, they talked in English, although slurred. "How could you let something like this happen? It's bad enough that the progress rate is slower than predicted, but a captive escaping under your watch. This looks bad on all of us. The boss is going to be mad." The first monster was slightly larger than the second one, the guard.

"She will never find her way out of the cavern; anyway, it's a maze down here, and she certainly doesn't have the ability to navigate it. Right?"

Austin was in a crouched position, leaning against the podium and trying to avoid being seen, even though it was all just a dream. He listened in on the conversation, the low, rumbling voices still approaching closer and closer. One more loud thud and a foot came down, barely missing Austin and causing him to stumble and hit his head against a groove on the podium. The monsters looked in response with their non-existent eyes; it seemed like their vision wasn't too good, but they could smell him and hear him. They were tracking him down, bringing their noses close to the ground and following his footsteps. Austin was crawling backward, his hand behind him giving him stability; he stared into the pits that were the eyes of the Vorhiëns. It finally sent one sweeping motion with his hand, passing right through Austin.

"Never mind," the monster grunted.

The scene shifted; he was in more or less a familiar setting of the Westbrook woods, the maple trees branching over his head. He spotted a petite woman; she was a businesswoman wearing a sophisticated grey blazer and had broken glasses. She looked like she had taken a bad fall, but she still held a folder in her hands. She seemed very disorientated; she was trying to get away from something that should've probably scared Austin, but he felt invisible. She stalled for a second, standing five feet from Austin's face and looking at him confused, but then continued running right through him, and it was at that point that Austin saw what she was running from. The infamous Western Wolf Pack. Austin knew all the conspiracies about the pack; he had read up on them as well, but that was when he thought they went extinct aeons ago. They originated in ancient China during the Shang Dynasty, a curse put onto theirs, but the villagers of their village began to fear them. One night, the villagers took their own fears to the sub-humans. That night, those werewolves got their first taste of human blood, but it didn't stop that night. Night after night, they lost all parts of their humanity until they were full-on ravagers, the source of all werewolf myths. With each kill, they grew stronger and took on the life span of their prey, but then again, that was only one of the myths speculated about them till now. They made their way through many continents throughout many centuries but ultimately settled in North America pre-colonisation till presumed present. But that was also just speculation; not many people knew much about the history of the monsters, but one idea was clear throughout all the theories: these beast were no longer humans and could not be tamed. Their features were terrifying; they moved on all fours, moving with incredible agility and very stealthily, not doing as much as breaking a branch as they leaped over six metres at once. Their white fur stained with blood, they took a final leap at the woman; about seven of them in total, the woman stood zero chance. She threw her binder at one of them, which caused a snarl, but they didn't attack. They picked her up from her blazer, then dropped her, knocking her out, then once again picked her up and retreated with their new-found captive at an incredible pace. The whole interaction lasted less than 20 seconds, but Austin was in shock, taking in all the details, studying them and cross-checking their features against what he remembered from his book. The monsters although very fast couldn't run backwards, only forward or towards the sides, but they weren't designed for running backwards. But that was the first and last of their weaknesses. Austin didn't like his chances against one beast, but seven as a team, he was a chew toy.

The scene shifted once more; he was back in the underground maze, but this time, he was in a bigger room than before, branching off in a dozen directions. The same familiar stalagmites hung from the ceiling, but this floor was tiled in grey stone-like ancient tiles. Through the cracks in the floor, sprouted weeds about knee height. In the middle of the room was a large grate. Austin decided to further inspect it, and there, lo and behold, were all the hostages. Austin counted 48 altogether. He recognised Mr Bert from the picture up in his office; he certainly had seen better days. Wendy was nowhere to be seen, nor was Irora. *Could one of them have escaped?* He noticed the petite woman also in the cell, still knocked unconscious. The people showed zero compassion; they were already used to it, the hope drained out of their eyes. Nearly 50 sacrifices. Austin didn't have much time. Everything connected, and all of Austin's and the Pacifist

Club's suspicions had been correct: the Western Wolf Pack were working with the Vorhiëns and the boss, which Austin guessed was whoever was trying to cast this spell. This would be the most significant downfall in Hylenia's history if it succeeded. All of Austin's biggest fears and the security were not coping with their jobs. Fighting these ancient creatures was not in their job description. How the boss could control and get all the creatures to fight alongside each other was beyond him, but right now, Austin needed to communicate to get any information he could on the hostages' whereabouts. He had done it before in his dream at the council building. People had seen him, though he had never held a conversation, but he had to try for their sake and the world's.

"Hello?" No response.

He tried a new approach. If he was this apparition, he needed to communicate like one, and since he saw no Ouija boards on hand, he decided on the lights. This room actually got electricity, which meant that it must be connected to the Westbrook grid, which meant that someone on the outside was working with them. Austin got up to a low-hanging, soft white lightbulb. He didn't know Morse code all too well, but he did know the combination for SOS. He unwinded and wound the lightbulb three short times, then a bit slower three long strobes and then again, three quick flashes. That seemed to get the attention of some of the prisoners. They began to sharpen their senses and tell the others. Some thought the rest were going crazy, so Austin did it once more. In the moment, hope re-entered everyone; they didn't know what happened, but they knew that their SOS had been reached. Austin tried to focus really hard. He didn't really know what he was doing; every other time people seemed to sense him, it was always different. In frustration, seeing it wasn't working, he screamed, "Mr Bert!"

The teacher was bewildered; his mouth stood open. He pointed, but no one saw what he pointed to. "Can you hear me?" Austin asked.

The man shook his head in response. "Are you real?"

"Yes, and I know your daughter, Beatrice. We have been trying to find you all. Can you tell me exactly where we are?"

"What are you?"

"I'm just a regular wizard. I think I am in a dream, but I am communicating with you," Austin said in an unsure tone.

The professor, just recognising that Austin had said his daughter's name, got onto his knees and put his head into his lap. "Beatrice, my little Beatrice." The rest of the people went back to sitting down, helplessly looking with strange looks at Mr Bert, but no one dared say a thing.

"Yes, but if you want to get back to her, I need any details I can get so I can get you back to her, okay?"

"Tomorrow, sunset," the man said, looking up; he was still on his knees.

"What is happening tomorrow?"

"The beginning of the end." The man's blue eyes pierced straight through Austin's soul. He had a grey, tattered shirt and a terrible bruise beneath his left eye. It was a living hell here; Austin noticed that they were given food, water and a bucket but no other luxuries; a blanket wasn't even a thought. Before Austin could ask any more questions, he was transported back to the world of the living.

****

Austin woke with a gasp; he saw the familiar setting. He was fed up with waking up in the nurse's office, but he had a feeling it wouldn't be the last. When Austin woke, a silent alarm was sounded, which sent Penny rushing into the room. "What day is it?"

"Sunday. You were asleep for two days," Penny said, trying to push him back into his bed to check his vitals and do some tests, but Austin had other ideas.

He looked up at the clock on the wall; it read 8:57 am. He still had time; he needed to get going now. He tried getting out of the bed, tubes still in his arm. "Nah, uh, superman, you can't just wake up from a two-day coma with a concussion and start walking. I know you may be bummed, but I prescribe you to take a day off for anything but resting. Including the excursion today." She read his emotions, and he certainly wasn't laughing; he had cold sweat forming all over his body. "It's okay; the boys who did this to you have been suspended, and everyone else is fine."

"No, that's not it; everyone is going to be sacrificed tonight. I saw it in my dreams; they are all going to die." The boy was struggling now, trying to push the nurse off him.

"It is perfectly normal to have nightmares. It's okay; you are back in the real world," Peggy said in an assuring voice.

"No, you don't understand. I have been having these dreams where I know I am in a dream, but it's like the real world. I saw where all the missing persons have gone."

"Austin, if you aren't going to calm down, I will have to give you something."

"Okay, okay, I will, but you have to believe me," Austin pleaded. She placed a hot towel over his forehead.

"Okay, I believe you, but you need to start by telling me when these dreams started."

Austin calmed down, sat up and told her all his stories, about his mum, about the courtroom and his most recent encounters at the cavern. Peggy took five moments before she responded; it looked like she was running through different scenarios in her head. She was in deep concentration, deciding if Austin needed to go to a mental hospital or to contact the authorities.

"I will tell the head of Westbrook Security, but even if all this is true, we don't know the whereabouts of the hostages. Maybe we can take your descriptions and lay them against any of the underground maps of the city, but there could still be a dozen possibilities, and like you said, the deadline is tonight. I do trust you, and if you believe it…" She trailed off with her words. "Doesn't mean the authorities will." She paused. "The most important thing for you right now is to stay in bed until I can finish all your tests. Promise me you won't do anything stupid; you are in no condition for a fight."

"I promise."

He complied with all the tests. She took a quick blood sample, which came back with all negatives. She took his blood pressure and a few other tests; she had already taken a CT scan while Austin was out, which didn't show any fracturing in the skull or internal bleeding.

Most of the small injuries she had already healed, but the major injury on his back had stitches. He could walk fine. He had a few bruises, but he felt okay to go on the excursion; he couldn't miss it. Peggy made him take minor pain medication before she left for the security station. He made his way out to the foyer to meet up with everyone before they held their strike; he couldn't miss it with all the planning that happened. He met up with Lela, Carter and Riona; all were in a group together, finalising all their plans, when Lela pulled Austin aside for a second.

"You are awake! What are you doing here?" Lela embraced him in a hug.

"I'm fine. I'm coming."

"Are you sure you can go?" Lela said concerned; she had a backpack, most probably filled with signs and possibly a megaphone.

"Yeah, I feel fine," Austin lied. The injury on his back ached every time he moved, but he wasn't going to pass up this opportunity.

The whole grade was assembled, a couple hundred in total. Each one was sorted into one of three groups. Charlie was going to meet them at the rendezvous point with Beatrice. Lela had explained their plan.

A teacher Austin didn't recognise got up on a little stall so she could be seen by everyone. "We have a few changes; will all students listen? If you have your name called, you will be moved to group three. Ena Marigold, Frederico Diamond, Austin Bolden, Jarred Skies, Carter Sea, Jack Stolt and Unity Light. The supervising teachers for this group have also been changed. Coach will be with group two, while guest Detective Weatherson and our vice principal, Mrs Rimesdome, will be in charge of group three. Now group one with me; we better hurry, we are already off schedule."

Fred and the rest of the group joined Austin and Lela. "I don't know how you did it, but you did it," Austin said, bringing him in for a bro handshake. Frederico's part of the plan was to move everyone into one group. A success, but Mrs Rimesdome was also in charge now with Weatherson, which is not good.

"Well, being the head of the IT club has some pros to it. All I needed to do was switch a few names in their system; it really wasn't that difficult at all with the right kind of access, which I have." The student's eyes beamed with glee. "Now are we going to do this, or what?" The boy posed the rhetorical question. The first kids left for the buses, shortly followed by the second group, then finally Austin's group. He had adrenaline rushing through his system, knowing what they were about to do.

"Does it change anything, you know, Mrs Rimesdome?" Austin whispered to Lela.

"All the kids were warned as to the consequences; we can't turn back now; we will just have to find a way to get around her," Lela whispered back. They were passing out the security borders for Westbrook Academy, and finally, all the students filed into the bus, and they were on their way. This was the first time he would actually see the city centre; he had only been to a historical sight and a few shops around the area, but now he was actually seeing all the tall skyscrapers and the magical city with his own eyes. Austin had always seen pictures of the city skyline on posters and on the internet, but it was different to see it in person. There were so many buildings Austin couldn't count them all, all unique and different. Austin didn't see one regular-style building. They were all shaped weirdly or made out of crystals or some other defining feature. The bus passed through several busy intersections with no less than six lanes each way. There were plenty of pedestrians flooding the streets; the sidewalks were crowded with stalls for food, which smelt amazing. Austin stuck his head out of the bus window like a dog, just to breathe in the city air. The bus driver dropped them all off at some important landmark, which just looked like two lumps of metal next to each other, but nonetheless, tourists took photos of it, even some of his classmates. Austin hadn't gotten the memo. Mrs Rimesdome did a headcount before they entered some museum, where, sure enough, they met up with Mr Trolt. He explained that this building was a troll heritage centre and the first embassy to the wizards from the trolls. There were many famous artworks created by trolls displayed on the walls and objects of all sorts of significance. Austin noticed a few dreamcatchers. He never wanted to see one of those again. Then something caught Austin's eye on the display plaque for the dreamcatcher. In small writing, under all the description and information, it displayed the museum name followed by the endorsement company: 'Trolt Industries'.

"Hey, Mr Trolt, what's with your name on all these plaques?" Austin enquired. All the other students rushed to the displays, and everyone started noticing them as well.

"Well, yes, Austin, you have quite the eye. Apart from being the mayor of Troll Village, I am also a businessman. I am the founder and co-owner of Trolt Industries." This seemed to even surprise Mrs Rimesdome; she herself looked at a plaque belonging to some painting. The detective, however, was nowhere to be seen. *What a chaperone.*

Mrs Rimesdome spoke up. "I think it best that everyone can go explore the city, but don't go too far; meet back at this point in 30 minutes, not a minute late." Kids rushed out in groups of two or three, while Mrs Rimesdome walked away with Mr Trolt in a heated argument. The only ones left in the room were Austin, Lela, Ena, Unity, Jack, Riona, Carter, Jarred and Fred. "Guess this is our chance; let's go meet up at the rendezvous point."

Chapter 15
The Cavern

Austin debriefed the group and their deadline on the walk to meet up with Charlie and Beatrice. Some doubts spread through the group, but Lela promised Austin they would figure it out after the protest. The group met up with Charlie and Beatrice at a corner of two major streets where they had set up near a news van. They unpacked all the signs; each one having its own short message. 'Hammond Hurt Is Innocent', 'The Westbrook Council and Security Is Covering up the Major Prophecy', 'Release Hammond Hurt', 'The Other Side Is Behind the Disappearances', and Austin's favourite, 'We Are All Going to Die', a bit pessimistic but it gets to the point. Austin held up a sign with the names of all the disappeared captees he recognised some from his vision. "Are we really about to do this?" Fred asked very concerned. Austin's heart was pounding; he didn't answer, instead he acted by putting the sign above his head with both his hands and standing in the middle of the intersection and was shortly followed by all his peers. That got the attention of the news reporter. One stranger got out of the car and joined them by picking up a sign saying 'Where Are They?'. Lela took to the megaphone.

"This isn't normal; the Westbrook Security is doing nothing. They were our friends, our family, our sons, our daughters, our teachers, our colleagues." They started on their march through the streets; the cameras were now turned on. Lela continued on the speaker, "Hammond Hurt is an innocent victim to the crimes of the Other Side yet he is being prosecuted. It had been kept a secret by the council, well, no longer." They walked past an electric billboard with a breaking news story showing their faces; they had reached nationwide news. *That was fast.* Their small group on the news. Lela passed the megaphone to the stranger who had joined them in exchange for her sign. The woman was on the verge of tears; she was an elderly woman but still in full health.

"My daughter Tanya Tierlo was abducted a week ago. All the Westbrook Security had to say was their condolences as if she is already dead. I don't believe that; I feel in my bones that she is still here somewhere." Lela held the woman around the shoulder with one hand. They were certainly gaining attention now, but because of some not so happy drivers, they made the decision to head to the very large park ahead of them. A few more pedestrians added to the group, and by the time they reached the park, there were about one hundred people in the protest. Lela kept at the megaphone while Jack, Carter and Riona made their way to Austin.

"We have to make it back to the group," Jack said with a look of guilt on his usually mischievous face. Unity, Riona and Carter were behind him, looking at the time, not wanting to be late.

"Don't wait up," Austin stated dryly. The few left, and the protest continued but was pre-emptively stopped when the Westbrook Security arrived. Lela, who was standing on the podium, immediately got down stopped with the megaphone and took Ena's hand the crowd started stirring. Everyone stood still for three seconds before they realised what was about to happen. The press was going to love this story, the demonstration wasn't violent at all but the authorities still took to it with pepper spray and tear gas they were armed with shields and fully dressed in riot uniform. Austin noticed that in the city magic wasn't used he didn't see many people with wands it was much like the outside world if you ignored the magical architecture. It wasn't really what Austin imagined; it was almost mundane. Westbrook Academy was really one of the last wizarding schools that still taught magic. Two guards stood opposite Austin. They held their shields high and rushed at Austin; they had smirks on their face. Austin had his wand at the ready, trying to focus on some of the spells that he learnt, but his mind was blanking. Then he noticed a bush beside his foot treaded with thorns; he recalled the type of plant from one of Molly Legend's lesson. One of its properties is that it grew fast and faster if you knew the spell. "*Crescere rubus.*" And like that, the bush erupted, blocking the guards on the other side. People ran in all different directions; the crowd was already hazy from all the smoke. Austin needed to find his friends and ditch; he ran towards the crowd. He ran and found Frederico, who was in awe, stunned by the bush that Austin created. Austin grabbed the Mexican kid's arm and ran towards Charlie. Never hard to find him in a crowd, he stood above everyone; he was with Beatrice, protecting her from the hysteric crowd. The four of them all together searched for the rest of the group. From the corner of Austin's eyes, he noticed Caleb. After all the investigations, he was still out on bail, but why was he here? He was gone in a second; people were rushing everywhere, blocking Austin's view. A moment after, Austin saw the emergency flare that Ena had packed, smart. The four of them all headed to where the flare was set from, and they joined Ena, Lela and Jarred. Lela screamed to be heard; her megaphone was nowhere to be found.

"Where is Jack, Unity, Carter and Riona?"

'Gone,' Austin signed; he knew the word in sign language because he used it nearly every day in primary school class. She nodded with her head in a gesture saying 'let's go'. No one argued; they ran away from the authorities, leaving behind the protest, which most definitely got media coverage; their job was complete. They all looked like a bunch of misfits. Ena had her shirt tied up to look like a crop top, her face painted with war paint, always enthusiastic. Jarred also had war paint, his mid-length hair in locks. Lela had a camo jumper on top of her school outfit. An unstoppable trio, the real power and minds behind the Pacifist Club. Charlie, the bulk to the group, his sleeves rolled up showing his muscle, but secretly, he was also the heart. Beatrice was certainly the voice, the youngest of the bunch; she had this tough attitude, her grey eyes building up a storm. Frederico, the most determined, his uniform was tattered from the mob when they were escaping. Austin, the most powerful, his face still bruised and cuts and gashes still apparent from his fight. The group had left the crowd and made a beeline for an alley which was an offshoot from the park. The Westbrook Security were at all the main exits arresting people. The back alley wasn't really an exit; the group had to jump the park fence to get out. The small street was wedged in between the backs of two buildings and ended in a dead end.

"Well, now what?" Frederico exclaimed.

"Check all the doors!" Lela ordered. The group complied to no avail; they were sitting ducks. Everywhere was locked, no way out except back to the park.

"With any luck, no one noticed us enter here, and we can hide out till everything has calmed down," Ena said, her hands reaching for her pendant necklace. As if jinxing it, two policemen scouted their hideout and jumped the fence. They had thorns in their suits, but it didn't seem to penetrate their gear. They no longer had their shields or smirks; they were here for business.

"We are arresting you for disturbance of the peace and instigating a violent riot," one of the officers said closing in on the teens.

"You and I both know that the demonstration was in no way violent. We are trying to get some accountability for people like you," Lela practically spat out. Everyone was moving towards the back wall.

"Now that is no way to speak to an officer," the second man said. "How about you all get on your knees and put these handcuffs on." The man dangled seven pairs of handcuffs in between his thumb and index finger. "Or my friend over here gets to have some fun with his new toy. It would be a shame though; my boss wants you all in one piece, but a few burns can't hurt; actually, it can." He gestured to the other officer who was now holding up a silver canister; Austin did not want to know what was inside. "There is nowhere to go." The man laughed. "Choice A, or choice B?" All the kid's back were against the walls. Charlie sheltered Beatrice with his body. They all looked to one another. Lela was right beside Austin. She gave him a concerned look and then took her knees to the ground; the officer threw a pair of handcuffs on the ground in front of her. Jarred soon followed and put on his own handcuffs.

"Good choice, kid," the man grunted, still holding the can at the ready, his arms extended keeping the canister far from his body. Ena joined the people on the ground and so did Beatrice; they held hands before both applying their handcuffs. Than Charlie, than Frederico.

The second officer continued, "Don't even try anything again, kid."

Austin was about to join his peers, hope dismembered. Then he felt something hit his back, a hand, which pulled him backward; he fell on his back but did not hit the wall. Both officers gawked their eyes at what they were seeing, and in that moment of weakness, all the kids fell backwards, not hitting a brick wall but rather into open grass, the confrontation disappearing in front of them. A portal, swirling purple magic dissipated into thin air as soon as Ethan stopped concentrating. The handcuffed group lay on their backs in a familiar clearing to Austin. The campfire still set up but all ash now; Ethan's cave home was now more homely with glass doors, a wooden bed and a small kitchenette. Cato hung on two legs from his tree, a crystal necklace hanging upside with his simple woven tunic. Ethan had his usual black leather jacket open, a grey button-down underneath, with some band name Austin didn't recognise etched into the design. "Thought you guys might need a hand, saw you on the news, plus I needed to talk to my buddy here Austin." The boy stood over Austin, who was now on his back.

"You could have called."

"Would you have been able to answer once your hands were in cuffs?" Ethan said with clear sarcasm.

"Do you even get service out here?" Austin snarked back.

"Platinum screen TV, fully connected to my own green power grid of solar panels." The screen was mounted in Ethan's room, still playing the media's coverage of the riot. "It's amazing how much trouble you can stir up."

"Actually, it was really all Charlie and Lela. You all haven't met Ethan; this is Beatrice, Jarred, Fred, Charlie, Ena and Lela, my girlfriend. Guys, this is Ethan, my old friend from Mertamic I was talking about, and this is Cato." Cato waved with a genuine smile, still on his tree, hanging upside down.

"That was so cool," Fred said, now on his feet with his hand out for a handshake through the cuffs. "How did you do that?"

"Cato took me to the elders, and I have been learning ancient druid magic; it's the same spell that runs the portals at your school except I am the generator instead of all that technology," Ethan said. "Well, let's get you all free. I have some lockpickers, and we will get everyone set up."

"Hold on, so you have a spell for portals but not to get us free from locks?" Jarred said; he was now in a sitting up position.

"Even if I did know one, which isn't general practice here in the forest, those are enchanted; no spell will work on them," he said as he was searching through one of his drawers. "Ahh, here it is." Austin wasn't even surprised that his old friend had a lockpicker. The teen began working at Beatrice's hands. "This may take a while so catch me up to speed with everything." And they all took turns explaining everything from Wendy's disappearance to Caleb's suspicious activity and his secret twin brother at the school to Mr Hurt's trial, even Austin's dream and deadline. By the time everyone was done, Ethan managed to get through most of the handcuffs, except Charlie's. It was a slow and aggravating process, and they were losing precious time, but it was all they could do. "It's as I thought. That is what the elders said as well about this deadline of sunset tonight the night the blood moon rises. This spell that you are talking about scares them; They have also speculated it. This dream that you talk of, the setting sounds familiar. Cato, do you know anything about underground caverns with leaking magical stalagmites?"

Cato joined everyone. "If it's where I am thinking of, you do not want to go there. Ancient sacrificial grounds before wizards inhabited the island, and the land was known as Hylenia, back when it was the troll kingdom ruling over all the tree spirits and nature. There are very dark tales about it; it was a story told to me when I was little to scare me into going to sleep."

"Your parents told you nightmares to go to sleep?" Frederico asked.

"Yes, like most parents, it's tradition to keep the memory of the past. Although I believed that place was abandoned centuries ago, it will be difficult finding an entrance."

Austin spoke now. "I think I might know someone who knows the land really well. Mr Trolt."

"Yeah, he would definitely know; we need to get to him before it's too late," Lela agreed.

Ena interrupted, "We can't trust the police though, or anyone; those men back there, they worked for the same people kidnapping all those people. They could be related back to the Other Side organisation." Ena was completely serious, no optimism now. Her face was now a black mess; the war paint had smudged all over her.

"That is true; everyone is compromised till proven not," Ethan said.

"Weatherson and Mrs Rimesdome are going to be looking for us," Fred said.

"That will be the last thing you will be worried about; you guys are talking about going into the lair of a known O.S. operative who has evaded the Council of Justice and has rounded some of the most infamous monsters in history." Ethan talked to the whole group with a sense of obvious doubt. "Look, I will transport you to wherever you want to go, but that will be as far as I go. You will leave in an hour, sunset is 8:21, which leaves you an hour. I will need to rest, till then everyone wash up and get ready." The teenage boy left for his room while everyone else recuperated. They spent their time washing up and trying to prepare, but there was an overwhelming sense that the kids were in over their heads. They were just supposed to be a school club.

The time passed quickly. While everyone waited in suspense, they had all changed into spare clothes Ethan and Cato had. The sky was already beginning to darken. "Listen, guys, I have seen these creatures close up; we can't engage. We just have to find the hostages, rescue them and stay incognito." Austin stood at the front of the group.

"Last chance to back out," the boy stated, with an eyebrow raised. His dirty blonde hair now grown to just a bit untidy. He wore one of Cato's corn husk jumpers, which was surprisingly not itchy and well insulated. The unsure group all looked to one another, feeling the peer pressure. No one said a thing; they all stood up, and Ethan and Cato came out of the room.

"Sorry, I can't join you in your suicide mission but have places to be," the boy lied, showing zero guilt. "Goodluck." The boy raised both his hands so they stuck out vertically from him; he stood there for half a minute before anything happened. The air shifted and purple sparks flew from the mouth of the opening; it wasn't a clear image; it was blurred like one of those frosted glass pieces. A single droplet of sweat ran down the boy's face. "It will take you to wherever your teacher is."

"Thanks," Austin mouthed; he hugged Ethan and thanked him for saving them all. Then he stepped through the mist, his reality changing quickly all around him. The actual portal felt like it didn't exist; it was like just walking normally. He was back in the city, in a more or less deserted area, in a building filled with closed shops surrounding them. For rent and sale signs lined up in all the shopfronts. The light of day was no longer visible, only artificial, eery white glow. He was shortly joined by Jarred, Beatrice, Charlie, Lela, Ena and finally Fred in the back; the portal was abruptly closed right after Fred.

"So where is Mr T?" Fred asked. They all looked around, not moving too far from each other until Beatrice spotted the short blue teacher. He seemed frantic; he fumbled for his key card and got into an elevator that seemed like it hadn't passed any safety checks since 2012. Before anyone could catch up, the lift closed with a racket. Two rusted silver doors stared back at them instead of their teacher. They looked at the digital display, which started counting down the levels; apparently, they were on the fifth floor, but there was no view to prove it. The elevator went all the way down to something called the 'pb'. They called the lift back up again and entered the smaller area. It was tiled in a flower mosaic that looked very old, the colour draining from them; several tiles cracked when they stepped on them. Austin went to push the button where Mr Trolt had gone to; it didn't work.

"Fred, you want to have a look at this?"

"It seems to be exclusive access; you must need a key card to enter that level. Maybe I can override it if I get into the mainframe of the panel." The boy started at the screws with a screwdriver, which he just kept handy for some reason. *Was this a Westbrook trend?* It took a while; there were over 20 screws, but he got the metal covering plate off and started working at the wires. Everyone waited outside, saying they wanted to give the boy some space, but really everyone was scared the elevator would crash. Jarred and Beatrice left to look for an emergency exit from where they could possibly get into the 'pb' but to no avail; it was shut off from the inside. All hope was on Fred and his technical skills. Ena held a silver plate on her lap, trying to help the boy from outside the lift, handing him the different screws he had unscrewed and various wires he had pulled out.

"Trolt Industries." She held it above her head to show everyone. Austin caught Lela showing a worried face. Fred was the only one that seemed unfazed and still focused, his head practically inside the empty slot looking at the wires.

"Hey, Lela, can you pass the black wire?" He held out his hand, his head still in the slot.

"There are two, the short one or the long one?" She had a puzzled look on her face. The boy popped out his head and picked the short one up and reattached it.

"Okay, done; ready to go."

"What about this wire, though?" Ena asked, holding up the long black wire from the tip.

"Extra piece?" Fred shrugged. His tone did not fill everyone with confidence. But everyone entered, not having much of a choice. The plate was only held up by two screws unlike the original 20, but it stayed on strong enough. Fred placed his finger to the button, and they soon reached the 'pb' floor. They exited the lift and saw the sign 'private basement', but there were certainty no cars. The wall they faced was as new as the rest of the deserted shopping centre, but past the wall on either side, it just got older. Cement turned to bricks, turned to large stones holding up the shallow ceiling. The walls started closing in on either side until they were all in a single file line with Lela at the front and Charlie following up the rear. At one point, the ceiling got so low that Austin had to crouch down until it opened up to the familiar cavern.

"This is it; it's where they are being kept. Somewhere down in this cavern of mazes." A blue droplet landed on Austin's face; it was harmless to touch. "How does Mr Trolt know this place?" Austin asked the rhetorical question, hoping there could be any other answer.

"His name is on the plaque, what more proof do you want? How well did you really think you knew him!" Ena said. "Look, I'm sorry; I know you trusted this guy, but we have to move on with the mission. Do you know where the hostages are being held?"

Austin stepped into the crossroads, five paths in front of him. There was no way to tell which one was right; they were all identical. All dark soundless crevasses that could lead to a dead end or the hostages, no way to know. The floor was covered in moist dirt, but Austin saw hundreds of footprints leading in all directions.

"We need to split up," Austin said looking towards Lela.

"What if there are more crossroads? We will just get ourselves all lost and alone in a dangerous place," Ena countered, also looking at Lela to make a decision. The group leader seemed to weigh in both arguments before deciding.

"You are both right. Look, best way I see it is we split off into three groups. Austin and Fred. Jarred, Charlie and Beatrice. Finally, Ena and myself. We each choose a direction so that we will cover more ground. Be back after sundown and rendezvous on Grand Street." She handed each group a flashlight from her backpack. "It multiplies our chances of finding the hostages by three; we have to do it. If anything goes wrong, press this twice and speak into it. Only in an emergency though." Ena handed everyone walkie-talkies; they all were charged and were specifically designed for far charters in the ocean, so getting a signal underground shouldn't be too hard. Everyone said their temporary goodbyes, and each chose their own tunnel. Austin took the front, and Frederico covered the rear. Within minutes, it was completely dark and soundless; they used their flashlights, casting a dim glow that only reached a few feet in front of them. The tunnels shifted in sizes, but mostly, they could walk normally straight in one line. Although Austin lost count, the two of them tripped or hit their head on a low hanging rock. The mud below them began to sink to thigh deep; the muck making it that much harder.

"You think there are snakes in here, or something?" Frederico asked, clearly ignoring the bigger problem.

"Probably some sort of creatures, but I'd like to think that snakes prefer the surface, not this godless place," Austin said, mud still rising as they went further. "Hey, check this out, a Walkman, you think it still works?" Austin recognised the vintage item as something similar to his mum's own collection. It was just lying around in the mud in a small crevice, who knew when someone used it last. Austin pressed play, and a song began to make a metallic hum. To Austin's surprise, it worked, playing *Livin' on a Prayer* by Bon Jovi.

"Hell yeah! We needed a soundtrack to this. Also, I'm invoicing you my dry-cleaning fee, by the way," Frederico said trying to figure out if he could play any other songs. It was incredible that it still worked being kept in the moist environment. The song played two times over before Austin fumbled for it to switch off; there were lights ahead, not natural, artificial, which meant all kinds of nasty creatures, whose attention Austin did not want. The song stopped playing, and Fred complained till he heard them too. Low growls from something non-human; the room began to heat up the closer they got to them. Austin recalled many details from his dream about the Vorhëins, but it was different to be in their presence in person. Their voices trailed off with most of their sentences. They weren't the same ones he saw in his dream; they were a lot smaller and slightly varied: these had six limbs, rather than four and two sets of arms on either side. Similarly, they still had no eyes and had steaming hot magma surging under their skin. Austin and Frederico got closer; if there were guards here, it meant there was something worth guarding. The mud cave slowly rose on an incline to a mossy floor that covered some old tile, a mosaic of some kind. It was on the verge of crumbling with no one looking after it. The grey plaster walls gave the place a less earthy look, but the real supports of the structure were these massive pillars Austin had seen in his dream; they were also there back at the elevator and upstairs. The architecture lined up, so whoever made all these structures down here was also responsible for the abandoned shopping mall: Trolt Industries. Fred and Austin both crept behind a close pillar; the monsters had their backs to the pair, but Austin still didn't feel safe. Even without eyes, the monsters seem to be tracking them down. They started to stir, but the second seemed to calm the first monster. *They are always in pairs; guess, it's an efficiency thing,* Austin thought to himself. Austin felt something hit his shoulder, a piece of moss, not hard but enough to get his attention. Then he saw her, a mud-drenched girl, a little shorter than Austin, brown hair, all a wreck and moss still in hand. She aimed for Austin again, which hit his forehead, even though she had gotten his attention the first time. Without looking back, Austin grabbed Frederico's back and got him to turn around. He ran at her in a not so stealthy way; a couple was united again. Wendy had been missing for over a week, but more recently, she had escaped from her temporary prison. They kissed each other in a muddy dirty way, but it didn't seem like either cared.

"I tried looking for you forever," he said in a whisper, his hushed tone slowly getting louder with each word.

"It's okay; you found me. Do you have a wand for me? Mine got confiscated." The girl got straight to the point. Fred offered up his, a basic foot-long steel rod, seemingly useless unless you got a closer look at the words etched in tiny writing on the sides: 'Infused with River Cynex'. "Same fire used to make them perfect, you genius." She kissed him again enthusiastically. Before anyone could react, she ran up to the middle of the room. "Hey, you big hotheads, you kept me locked up for too long!"

"Look, we found her! The boss is going to be so pleased."

"We can't 'look'," the second one said more confused, then he focused on the sound of Wendy. Wendy said a spell from under her breath, and a huge gust of lava exited the first creature, surprising the second one.

"Get her!"

"Who gave her a wand?" the monster asked innocently, lava rushing from his body. Without an answer, the second monster slammed the ground with his both hands, shaking it. Lava started rising from pores in the ground. Austin, acting quickly, used a trick Lela taught him and levitated the girl in the air a few feet from the steaming liquid, which was still working at her skin. Her scream could've brought down the cavern itself, but it stayed. Austin flung the girl to the other side of the room in an attempt to get her out of the steam, leaving one standing Vorhëin between them. The lava bubbled over the mud entrance, which was now non-accessible. The girl seemed to be unconscious, and Fred tried running for her but was intercepted by the monster and shoved into a pillar; he crumbled to a sitting position. It then became a one-on-one. *Why couldn't this be a stealthy mission like planned?*

Austin didn't need his wand for this spell; he was about to do something crazy, even by his own status. He tried controlling the fire within the beast, just like he had done with the earth in Mr Davon's class. Except the earth was running at him at a surprisingly fast rate; he stayed still, not flinching and trying to focus on the *'entacio chatum'* spell. He was in deep thought, but there wasn't enough time. At the last second, he dodged it by jumping to the side and sending the monster into the wall, kind of comical. Austin tried once more, really trying to focus in on a memory, and he found one: a campfire, him and his parents roasting s'mores when he was just little, all of them together. Austin heard it before he felt it; the crackling of the fire within the beast made it hesitate then a burst, and lava spilled out the monster and onto the ground.

"We will regenerate once we get our heat back, you little punk. Then, we will come for you." The first monster groaned. Austin went to pick up his friend and got him to his feet, and together, they got to Wendy and poured their only cold water on her and brought her to her senses.

"We have to get you out of here. Do you know where any of the other hostages are, or an exit?"

"If I knew where an exit was, do you think I would be wandering around here in hiding? I came in with a black bag over my head as a hostage. I was hoping you would track the way you came," Wendy said back in her sarcastic tone.

"Well, about that." Austin peered back at the lava-covered mudhole they had entered from. "There has to be some other exit somewhere. Why don't we ask our new friend here?" Austin said, bending down to the lying down giant. Even with such little energy, it lurched a hand towards Austin's body, from which he just stepped back. It was very weak and slow now.

"Uh uh, amigo." Fred joined Austin in a crouching position. "We want to know the direction of the hostages. Do you think you could help us?" he asked in a condescending tone, his body stiff in its movement, with scrapes all over his body.

"What makes you think I would help you?" the monster said, still oozing out lava from its neck.

"Because if you do, you get to keep your nose, limbs and other body parts that might be missed." The boy was in full-on interrogation mode.

"That's illegal!"

"I think we left legalities on the surface, didn't we?" The Latin kid pointed at Wendy, a product of the kidnapping scheme that was set up in this dungeon.

"Okay, okay." The monster was breathing heavily. "Down that hall, a left, then a right. Stay straight till you see it, but they are guarded by the Western Wolf Pack, ents and plenty of other guards and every important personnel. The big sacrifice is in 30 minutes; everyone is going to be there."

"Thank you, friend," he said, patting the side of the monster's head almost affectionately.

The three left for that direction.

Chapter 16
Corruption

They followed the instruction of the ancient creature, and sure enough, the trio made it back to the main chamber. It was prepared for a festive party, gold banners hanging from the stalagmite-covered ceiling, red carpets covering the broken tiled mosaics, which were more kept in this room. They emerged from a side entrance behind the rows of seating, each guarded by armed waiters. All waiters were dressed for war, with gilded armour on top of a plain white button-down. Austin eyed one of the service people standing with her back to the small group, a long sword sheathed into the outfit on her side. In her hands was a serving platter with various goods, including champagne, caviar-filled pastries and oysters. All the plush seating on the tiered bleacher-like structure was filled out by guests, their identities concealed by identical metal-plated masks. All the guests looked like upper-class citizens; all modelling designer brands. The gathering was strange it looked like an Illuminati meeting. The setting seemed very formal and planned; the crowd of around 100 guests all talked in a low mumble. It gave Austin a very eerie feeling; the anonymity of all these people, just regular humans yet so evil. The tuxedos and gowns were so luxurious, it would almost be cool if they weren't all here to witness a massacre. 'A Birth to a New Era' Austin read a banner on the wall with some Latin writing underneath it, which Austin couldn't translate. After a few minutes, everyone had made their way to their assigned seats, not one person unaccounted for. They all sat looking towards the centre of the room, a golden-plated podium. It was the same room with the inground cell Austin saw in his dream. The people were visible in shackles from Austin's point of view. Like sheep to the slaughter, this was a lot bigger than Austin expected.

"If we can't prevent this…" Austin said in a hushed tone; the boy was very tense; sweat was dripping from his forehead. "I don't know if we can do this," he said to his two friends. Wendy and Fred gave each other a concerned look; they shared Austin's thoughts of doubts. The trio crouched on guard, waiting to make their move. Most of the audience had flown in from a much wider arched opening to a hall with emergency exit signs. The only thing blocking them was the countless security positioned between the exits. Also on guard were some malicious-looking ents, positioned strategically in three key locations. Two by the south exit, one on the furthest exit from Austin, the western gate and one in front of the eastern arch.

All the major exits were impossible to get through unnoticed. Much like the ent from the school, each creature stood around 20 feet tall, their heads almost reaching the jagged ceiling. Their tree bark was covered in a dark brown moss growing on their body; they all had shaggy beards with rose-gold leaves running down their humanly faces. Austin had seen the damage just one had done to the school when the sports wing was completely destroyed. They needed a distraction; there was no winning this fight, even if all of the group was here. Fred, Wendy and Austin peered at the scene from behind the bleachers, watching from high up, rows and rows of people, all anxious for the big event. The spokesperson one of the few without masks got onto the podium; he was an older white man whom Austin didn't recognise. The guy was more unkempt than most in the crowd; he was a larger man with a receding hairline and a deep scruffy voice. The man read a script through a thick set of rectangular glasses. He greeted the crowd formally, as if it were a completely normal event.

"We are aware that some of you are having concerns about the element bearer, but be reassured, we have the whole situation under control. We have a trusted member keeping an eye on him," the man addressed the crowd. Fred looked at Austin, his eyes wide, but Austin was just as confused. The man continued to speak. "The Other Side, or the OS as people are calling us now, are visionaries to set the world into an oasis of our own imagination. We are the revolutionists whom the world needs to enter a new stage. It's time for us to come out of the shadows and take over the democracies of the world, starting here at Hylenia and take the fight to the capital, Westbrook. We will not take no for an answer, and we will reign under our own laws, not having to be restricted by anyone. We will have complete control and power, and the wizarding world will not remain a secret anymore."

The man's speech was cut short, because at that point, a guard ran up to the spokesperson, informing him of something away from the microphone. The presenter looked shocked and concerned but assured the audience, "Looks like we had some stowaways. Would the crowd give a warm welcome to these two fine girls?"

Lela and Ena were shoved forward from the eastward exit in shackles, marks of a fight clearly apparent all over their skin and clothing. They were left defenceless, wands taken by a guard guiding them to the front. Their hands were in shackles behind their backs. Their clothes were burnt in various places, but Austin supposed he didn't look any better covered in mud everywhere from below the neck. They got pushed down to the floor in front of the podium; both girls were helpless in front of the big crowd, which started to laugh.

"We have to do something!" Austin was desperate; he wanted to run through the crowd and be by her side, but Fred held him back.

"Don't be stupid; she needs you alive," Wendy hissed after a slap to Austin's face; it made Austin refocus, but he still didn't like the friendly fire.

The man began to speak into the microphone again. Austin couldn't focus on him but only on his friends. Tears welled up in his eyes, his rage beginning to boil over. But a sudden glimpse of hope occurred; the spokesperson stopped his speech; his words begging to slur. He began to choke and a croak escaped his throat. The guests stood up, concerned, as purple froth emerged from the man's mouth. He started to convulse before finally passing out. Then three major things happened:

1. All hell broke loose, and people ran in all directions.
2. Guards started transferring the prisoners to a safe place, but arrows seemed to barrage them in an ambush. Austin couldn't tell where the archers came from, but it was from the opposite side of the cavern.
3. An ent ran after Ena and Lela, reaching for them.

It was all just the distraction that they needed. Austin prayed a silent thank you for whoever caused all the havoc. They jumped onto the seating area and were quickly overwhelmed by the waiters aiming the swords towards the trio: Austin, Fred and Wendy. Austin was growing impatient; he looked past the guards to the makeshift battlefield. He saw Ena stumble and Lela crouch beside her, trying to avoid the giant's grip. Austin aimed his wand to the ceiling and focused on a stalagmite, which began to shake. It made a noise so loud that everyone stopped what they were doing and looked. A big part of the ceiling came down and impaled the ent. The monster went limp, crushing a few of the distressed guests. The south exit was beginning to be overwhelmed with the amount of people trying to escape. The guards were all stunned and didn't know how to react and who to react to. The scene was hectic, the guards all charging at nothing in particular. Austin focused back on his current situation; six waiters all charged simultaneously, Austin ducked under the first strike triumphantly, but the victory was short-lived. A second waiter wasn't far behind; Austin attempted a sidestep against the waiter's onslaught. The silver blade caught Austin's right arm in the process. His hand gave, and Austin dropped his wand. He was now completely defenceless. He was running through the chances they had at winning this fight, and he didn't like his own odds. He watched as both Wendy and Fred were backing up against the railings; they were being surrounded. Austin's opponents were already orientating themselves after their first failed attempts. As a last resort, Austin ran towards his friends and rammed an unsuspecting guard from the back, his sword clanging to the floor. Wendy was battling two at once using Fred's wand; she was quite ferocious. There was a sense of fury in her eyes, bloodlust even. Her hair was wild, her body battered and bruised, but her spirits ever so high. She was using simple quick spells that only called for a flick of the wrist, sending powerful volcanic lava streams in every direction she pointed it at. *At least she is doing better than us.* Austin sighed and picked up the sword, unable to get to his wand behind three determined waiters. Austin held the sword in his left hand; it felt weird and uncoordinated, but he had a tight grip on it. The waiters charged again, and Austin sent his whole body into a full swing aimed at the leading guard. That was a crucial mistake; he countered the first guard's attack and went for a lethal swipe, and the first guard fell to the floor. He got a glimpse of Fred picking up their weapon. Austin had been so zoned in on that first guard that he had left his whole back exposed. He felt the cold metal slice at his already open wound. Austin howled in pain and fell to the ground; it was a quick jab, not too deep, but deep enough to put him on the bench for the rest of this fight. He had his head in the ground; he heard Fred fighting behind him, fending off the remaining guards. Then something he hadn't expected happened; he heard the familiar flap of wings hovering above him. Calypso! She was shielding Austin from an incoming waiter. He turned his head slightly; only one other waiter left fighting Wendy and Fred. Austin was blinded from a flash from Wendy's wand sending the last guards to the floor. He watched as Fred and Wendy, exhausted, just panted on the spot, watching everything, but then they came running for Austin; Wendy picked up his wand. Fred laid Austin down on a few chairs away from the fight, no one noticing them in the area yet. Everything around Austin began to blur, and dizziness started to settle in, the sound of the battle a far echo. Austin wondered how the other two had survived their onslaught, then he noticed each of their familiars. Fred had a fiery hawk that had been swooping guards; Austin looked towards the already defeated guards, which had many claw marks. Wendy had a wolf by her side, nothing like the Western Wolf Pack, hers had dark fur and intelligent eyes. Austin looked at his own familiar the Tachash. The opal coloured unicorn the neighed in distress for Austin.

"Make sure you keep him conscious, Fred!" Wendy screamed. Austin saw she was rummaging through a platter of one of the waiters and a pocket in one of the waiter's uniform. She hurried back to Austin. Fred was trying to talk to him, but Austin wasn't listening; the world was giving way and seemed to fade. Austin could feel his shirt being ripped off his back and a wet sticky substance applied to his wounds on his back and arm, which immediately reduced the pain. Wendy disappeared for another minute and returned with medical supplies, which Austin had no idea where she got it from, but he wasn't complaining. A bandage was wrapped around the major wound, and he was prompted up into a sitting position. He now saw the amount of rich red blood that had leaked into the cushions he had laid on. Wendy had a syringe and injected Austin in the chest and cast a spell, which all sounded like gibberish to Austin, his senses non-reactive. Fred gave Austin a few pills, which he swallowed. The pair were working and doing everything in their power to keep him alive. They placed a wet towel to his head and let him rest for a few minutes. Austin noticed that his wounds had stopped bleeding, and he began to feel almost normal. Austin saw the first aid cabinet that was broken into by Wendy on the wall.

"Wha…What did…What did you do?"

"Only stopped the bleeding with Mudcreek leaf, bandaged your major wounds, injected you with a heightened adrenaline inducing liquid and fed you a few powerful steroids. You should be able to walk in a bit, but don't push yourself just yet."

Austin ignored her statement and stood up and was quickly overcome with nausea and threw up over the side of the bleachers. He decided to sit for one more minute, but then he felt the rage fill his blood, and he was ready to join the fight that was still very active after ten minutes; most of the guests were still trapped in the area because the guards weren't letting anyone escape, in case the prisoners freed themselves. There was a full-frontal assault from the west gate, including some of his friends and a team of agents that had somehow made it to the fight. Lela and Ena were now nowhere to be seen. Austin took the armour off one of the fallen guards and put it over his bare chest. Austin began to move more easily, his movements very fluid. Although it was three sizes too big and he was still covered in dirt and blood, it was better than nothing. Austin was ready for the fight by some miracle with the magical medicine Wendy had given him. The trio made their way to the battlefield, already exhausted. At the edge of all the chaos was a passed-out guard with no visible wounds but still knocked out cold. Austin recognised him as the guard that had escorted Lela and Ena into the room. He had a set of keys, which Wendy had taken from him. Most of the crowd ahead of them was just the upper-class guest, who made no attempt to fight and created a lot of confusion, which played to Austin's benefit. From the crowd emerged a very bruised up Mr Bert, who came running at them; he had a wand in his hand and had blood spurted all over his clothes.

"Wendy, you came back! I told you to escape!" Mr Bert said. Instead of responding, she gave him a big hug. "We have to get back to the other prisoners; some of your other friends freed me, but they were quickly overwhelmed. We have to save everyone!"

"Show us the way," Fred proclaimed.

The trio followed the teacher through the crowd and back to the cell, which was guarded by over 10 guards. Calypso and the other familiars were not far behind, protecting their owners. Austin had nearly made his way to the cells, which had been locked again. He had been so focused on trying to get to the remaining prisoners that he had run his way right into the blast zone of a gun. Austin found himself staring down the blue, glowing, cone-shaped barrel. The gun was a new wizard model used primarily by prison guards and security personnel, but these looked modified. Ready for war, he felt himself freeze, everything slowing around him. He couldn't look away; he watched the transparent cannister glow with a slow buzz. Blue mist started to curl out of the blaster; he saw the gunman with his hand on the trigger. It caused the loudest sound Austin had ever heard, but he felt unharmed, besides the gaping hole in his back and hand, which now felt numb. Someone must've made the guards gun misfire and thrown off his aim. The guard started to take aim again, but Fred was quicker; he stuck out his wand and a high wall of fire separated the assailants from the group. He made a mental note to thank Fred for saving his life, now twice. He was tense in concentration while Wendy, Bert and himself rescued the rest of the cellmates using the keys Wendy had picked up. The bulk of the fighting was still at the west end of the hall, which left this area near defenceless. They had finally gotten everyone out, and now they needed an escape plan. The guards were making their way around the fire, and time was limited. The rest of the battlefield was complete chaos; another one of the ents had been taken down, but two were still fighting one on the main entrance and one on the western side so that left the eastern-most exit, the only safe option. Austin started guiding the captees the way Ena and Lela had come from. The crowd had mostly dispersed in hiding places, leaving them out in the open. They had to fight the stray soldiers, but most of the captees had picked up guns of their own or whatever was useful. They were finally given the chance to fight back, and they were certainly doing a good job. Even Wendy now wielded one of the blue mist guns and took the rear, shielding the group with a stolen shield in her free hand. She consistently shot the powerful energy balls efficiently, but not deadly. Mr Bert and Austin protected the group from the front and paved the way until they stood under the high arch. Lela and Ena apparently had the same idea and joined them along the way. Both had been released from their handcuffs, and each had wands that they had stolen off some unsuspecting victims. Austin gave Lela a short kiss and hugged her tightly being so grateful that they could be here in this moment.

"Does anyone know who is fighting on the far side of the hall?" Austin asked.

"Apparently, an undercover group of trained soldiers from the Council of Justice; that is what Charlie said, anyway. He was the one that got us free," Ena answered. Although completely irrelevant, Austin still felt jealous that it wasn't him who had freed and rescued them and then immediately felt stupid considering the current circumstances. Austin estimated that there were maybe 200 soldiers, all dressed in brown camo, fighting throughout the hall; they seemed to be winning for now.

Keeping track of all your surroundings and all the angles of the fight proved to be harder than expected, but everyone was still on their feet. Austin calculated the battlefield now that he was in a relatively safe space; he noticed several fights between his allies and the opposition. At the main entrance, a hooded figure was battling the ent; a sword plunged into his abdomen. The assassin clung to the oversized creature that was desperately trying to shake them off. The hooded figure wore a white blood-stained cloak with a hood and a metallic mask covering their face; it was the same as the rest of the guests, although Austin guessed that she was certainly not part of this organisation. On the other end, the allied forces were making some progress due to their element of surprise. Although Austin knew that there was certainly going to be more troops charging into the battle at any moment. This was their head base with thousands of the beasts and soldiers stationed all around. If they were to stay here, it was a losing fight; the opposition had a home advantage. Austin scanned the field, looking for his fellow friends, and that's when he noticed Jarred, Beatrice and Charlie, separated from the protection of the camo-wearing soldiers. Mr Bert followed Austin's line of sight and spotted Beatrice. He wasted no time and ran right back into the action. There was an unspoken agreement between the teens, and Austin ran after the teacher and so did Fred and Lela, leaving Ena and Wendy to stay and guard. They made their way through the crowd, mostly trying to avoid the fighting until they had met the others. Jarred and Beatrice had bows in their hands, and Charlie was using a baton fighting off the closer enemies. The fight was so chaotic, too many enemies surrounding them, all happening so quick. A guard aimed a gun at Beatrice; the blue mist rushed forward at her at an alarming pace; her back was turned, and she was defenceless. Austin's reaction time was too slow, but Mr Bert, who was a few seconds ahead of them, jumped into the line of fire. Austin looked with wide eyes as the blast hit Beatrice's father. The gunman went to fire again, but this time, Austin deflected the hit with a flick of his wand. The group made a small circle, standing guard from all angles. Beatrice put down her bow and got onto her knees and lay her head on her father's dying body. Although the blast was usually non-lethal, it hit the left side of his chest, his heart was singed. The pair was inside the circle, being defended by a crying Jarred, Charlie, Fred, Austin and Lela. Austin overheard their conversation.

"I am so proud of you and the woman you have become," the man croaked. "Your sister would be proud. I love you so much; be brave for me, and stay safe."

"No, you can't die!" she screamed from the bottom of her lungs, her defensive guard now put down. "Mariah and now you. No, no, no, no, no. Don't let it happen, Dad! I need you, please, we can make it out of here! You can't die, please," the girl pleaded, but the man had accepted his fate. Blood soaked into the ground.

"Beatrice Bert. You will carry on our name, and you will make me proud. I will be watching from above." His eyes went still as he breathed his last breath, but Beatrice didn't seem to take notice. The battle was still continuing all around them. Although all ents had now disappeared from the battlefield, more backup was flowing in from the southern entrance. Lela joined Beatrice and tried to pick her up.

"We have to get out of here and get to safety now," Lela said, but the girl was glued to her dad.

"Please, Dad, you can't do this to me. You promised me!" she said to the body.

More soldiers were surrounding the group, and everyone was fighting ferociously, but they were losing time and ground. Beatrice lost the fight in herself, her body going limp and allowing Lela to drag her away. The group started moving towards the eastern exit. Austin found himself in a personal confrontation, a tall, bulky guard who got the jump on Austin.

"You're Austin! Have you come to meet your end, boy?" he asked rhetorically and hit Austin's side with a dull baton, which caused the air to leave his lungs. "It's two birds with one stone. The boss needed to get rid of you anyway. We can lock you up with your daddy, huh?" The guard hit Austin in the leg, but Austin didn't fall; his willpower to stay up was too strong. He limped backward, trying to join the group again. No one had noticed yet; Austin was on his own and had strayed from the group. His back still ached, and his side was in agony; he was struggling to stay up. The pain was so intense, but he couldn't back down. The guard raised the weapon above his head with both hands and was about to bring it down hard on Austin's head. In that instance, the weapon was flung from his hands by what looked like a telekinetic force. The baton was suspended in the air; then a split second later, the weapon inverted its direction and hit the man with such force that he flew back and landed 10 metres in the opposite direction. Austin's eyes darted towards who had just saved him: Caleb Rhike. Rhike held his wand and had used it on the guard. They held eye contact for a moment, before he turned away to fight another guard. Austin limped back to the group. *Rhike? Why is he here?* Austin was frustrated; he couldn't figure anything out. It's like the puzzle pieces are all there in front of him, but he can't quite put them together. His dad was alive? Caleb Rhike is Phillip's brother, and somehow, they knew his mum. He is connected to past crimes at the school and is a known criminal who is linked to Wendy. Was he the one who was sent to spy on him? Then why would he save him?

The group helped Austin walk to the exit. The soldiers were now starting to get more organised and were closing in, with most of the guests having left now. The OS soldiers with wands took their stance at the main entrance, and other soldiers started coming at them from behind, more organised and prepared now.

"Time to go," Fred said. Wendy and Ena were holding off the few forces that dared block the exit. Charlie was swinging the baton out in front, getting them to the exit. He had naturally long arms, so he had the opportunity to hit anyone who came close to him while they were still out of reach. Frederico helped Austin walk, allowing Austin to put his weight onto him, and they walked with Lela and Beatrice taking up the rear all the way till they met the others. The hooded figure was nowhere to be seen as was Phillip Rhike. They had both disappeared once the guards were assembling. Ena and Wendy were both firing guns and holding shields, fending off anyone trying to block the archway.

"Where are the hostages?" Austin had to scream to be heard above all the loud noises.

Without looking back at him, Ena answered, "They took the second left which leads them up to the museum. This underground system goes everywhere in Westbrook; it's how they have been taking hostages. You guys go; we will meet you there. The authorities are on the surface. As soon as we get there, we will be safe. Apparently, there is also a fight happening at the council building." Austin took in all the information.

"I can't leave yet; my dad is down here somewhere. I have to find him!" Austin said.

It was Lela who spoke now. "Fred, you take Wendy and Beatrice out and Jarred, Charlie and Ena will cover your backs. I'm not leaving Austin alone. Ready? Go!" Everyone took off, the guards charging not 10 feet away. Right before they exited, Austin saw the Western Wolf Pack. The monsters from his dreams had leapt into action and were devouring the allies.

Once they passed the archway that exited the hall, Ena collapsed; the ceiling blocking the guards gave them time to leave before the guards found another route. The four of them left for the second exit, no time for goodbyes. Austin ran with Lela by his side, each leap sending jolts of pain throughout his body. His body was filled with so much adrenaline and whatever medicine Wendy had given him that he could continue. They ran until they saw the tunnel split into four exits. They had no idea where they were going, but they had no other choice. Hand in hand, they judged their options. The ceiling started giving in; Austin saw the strain on the ceiling, cracks starting to appear. The small circular room lit by torches hung on the walls illuminated the dirt room.

"Austin, I'm so glad you made it out alive. I saw what happened in there." The blue troll appeared out of one of the exits.

"Stay back! You are behind it all! These are your tunnels; it all connects back to you." Austin pointed the baton he had lent from Charlie at the empty-handed professor.

"Let me explain," the troll said, his hands up in defence. Austin didn't strike, letting the troll explain and still holding the weapon against him. "These tunnels aren't mine. Well, they are, but originally, they belonged to the elders before Hylenia was established, a sacred ground, and many years ago, I had organised the restoration project for these tunnels. They deserved it. It was simply a preservation attempt. I soon figured it was hopeless; the place can't structurally support itself. It's amazing it's still standing, really. This place has been destabilising for decades, so I gave up, even though it's in my name. The project was abandoned halfway, and whoever it is that is doing this is hiding behind my name. Why would I have helped you so much if I wanted you dead?" The troll made a good point, but Austin was still suspicious.

"Why are you here today?" Lela asked, her hand still interlaced with Austin's.

"When I got word of what was happening, I needed to shut it down; it's my responsibility. It finally clicked on our tour today when your vice principal came up to me questioning me about the cavern and details about the project. She has been using this place together with her fellow council members to spread corruption."

"He is lying!" Caleb appeared from another entrance. "I have been studying these disappearances with the council; he is responsible for all of it. The night Wendy was kidnapped, she was supposed to meet with me and tell me all she knew about you and your twisted mission with Tony. But she conveniently went missing before that, right?"

With her free hand, Lela held her wand at his throat. "Not a step closer, and why are you here, and what is your relationship with Austin's mother?"

"Natalie sent me here to look after you; we have been suspecting the prophecy for a while, ever since you were born. When Natalie and Tony met, they connected all the wizard bloodlines from all four siblings. It's rare seeing as the bloodlines usually don't mix with each other, let alone two partners from two each. Knowing this and the events leading up to your arrival here at Westbrook, your mother sent me here to look after you and protect you," the man explained.

"You didn't answer each question," Austin stated bluntly, the pain now starting to curl up his spine and to his back injury.

"I'm here to protect you, Austin; isn't it obvious? I needed to remain undercover and so has my brother. That is why we had enrolled him," Caleb pleaded. "I just find it too big a coincidence that you enrolled as a substitute teacher at some school for Troleze. Was no one else capable of this besides a businessman and the mayor of Troll Village? You have been spying on Austin and planning his demise," Caleb targeted Trolt.

"Your relationship with my mother, and why has she been so secretive about it?" Austin was getting agitated that Caleb kept on avoiding the question.

"Back years ago, the year when you were born, we knew we had to protect you from evil spirits and monsters that would be attracted to your power. So myself, my brother and your mother planned a mission to steal a scripture that would mask your power to predators. We couldn't tell anyone about the real reason; we planned the mission because it would lead to much controversy in the council, like there is today. It's always been about you, Austin. Don't you get that?"

"Not so fast, pretty boy." The hooded figure emerged behind Rhike, a blade to his throat. "I wouldn't move if I were you." During the fight, Austin almost thought their features were masculine, but up close, he finally noticed her. His eyes welled up, and his hand slipped from Lela's. His girlfriend looked at him, his face white, sweat building up. Lela knew who it was: the first disappearance; they had worked endless nights on it, even though Austin knew that Lela got jealous with how much time he spent on finding her. Irora Winter removed her hood, revealing her new haircut, no longer the girl Austin remembered. Her head was shaved on the sides, abrasions from the battle clearly apparent.

"My business isn't with you guys, so I would leave before the explosives I have set up bring this cavern down in about 30 minutes."

"Irora," he said the name in a weak voice.

"How do you know my name?" Her tone of voice shifted to shock, but her grip was still on the blade to Rhike's throat.

"I thought you were dead. I stopped looking. I never should have stopped; I'm sorry." The boy stuttered his way through the sentence. This was never how he imagined reuniting with her; he wanted to be her knight in shining armour, but she was her own hero.

The girl paused for a second; her platinum-blond hair flicked to the side, her fair, almost white skin glowing in the fiery light. "Who are you?"

It hurt more than a bullet for Austin; it struck his heart, confusion racing through his mind.

"She won't remember you, Austin; she is a failed experiment, a prototype for a trained assassin. She was the first recruit with enough electroshock therapy, and over a year's training and an untold amount of drugs, you forget who you are." The detective made for a dramatic entry. Lela shifted her wand to the detective.

"And how long have you known about this?" Trolt is now the accuser.

"Since I logged into his computer network; everything traces back to you, Caleb," Weatherson stated calmly. "Ever since Austin gave me enough evidence to start looking into you and your brother Phillip. You got sloppy we saw the books, you kidnapped Wendy."

"This is being pinned on me." Caleb now addressed Irora whose blade still was at his throat. "Listen, I had no idea about this. These people fed you my face the same people that drugged you. Your brain is playing tricks on you. I am here for Austin, not you." Irora released the dagger and kicked him forward, taking a step back, her blade at the ready and alternating its position at everyone in the room, not sure who to believe.

"Look, I know these tunnels better than anyone down here. I can bring you to your dad before crazy decides to blow the place to a crisp," Mr Trolt said. "My best guess is that they are being held in the storage containment section; you will need my pass. Assuming it still has clearance and no one changed the locks." He put his hand into his pocket and dug out the card he used to get into the elevator. He passed it to Austin as a sign of good faith, but Austin still had his doubts about everyone in the room.

"Take me to him, and then we can confirm everyone's stories. Irora and Lela, you take the rear, followed by Weatherson, Rhike and Trolt. I will stay upfront; no one tries anything." After a life with his dad barely present and his recent disappearance, Austin didn't know what to make about seeing his dad again. Nerves filled his body, doubt entering his mind, but with Trolt's directions, they led out of a tunnel, which soon became very modern, with steel walls, cold, hard floors and electric lights illuminating the corridor. Void of any feeling, just building. They soon got to a restricted area with frosted glass at least two inches thick. Austin waved the card in front of the reader, and a little LED light changed its colour from red to green, and the doors slid open on either side. They all walked through the room, no one speaking. The hall was lined with five doors on each side with glass windows seeing through to cement rooms and emergency alarms sounding from their infiltrations, with a red light flashing. Nothing in the first room; the second room was something like an armoury with weapons of all kinds, but Austin moved on. Austin peered into the next room through the glass, just containers and files. The fourth room looked oddly familiar to Austin, but he couldn't pinpoint where he knew it from. It just looked like a regular office room. The fifth room looked like a prison cell, with a crib, an exposed toilet and a bare set of a table and chair. The same cell layout for the next two rooms. In the seventh cell was a man; he looked dirty. He had an unkept beard and stained white top and trousers. He could've been mistaken for a homeless man; the conditions here were shocking. The man looked frightened, but Austin moved to the next room's window and another prisoner, and the next room with a nasty-looking futuristic torture device of a chair. He noticed Irora's reaction to that room, like she had been there; she shuddered. He finally got to the final door, and he recognised the man, his father, The man quickly got up and went to the glass, not a word spoken; everything else on his mind didn't matter in that one moment. He then had a sudden thought.

"Trolt, how did you know we were looking for my father?" He let the danger out of his vision. He heard a grunt. Weatherson, maybe Rhike. His senses started to turn on again, the feeling returning back to his body; his guard back up. He swung around to dodge the projectile that was flung at him. Weatherson aimed his flail, which he must've picked up from one of the storage rooms. The weapon: a spiky metallic ball connected to a link chain to a wooden staff. The first hit damaged the glass behind Austin's head but did not break the glass. Austin's father watched helplessly through the cracked screen. The crooked cop, Austin always had his suspicions; the man always had it out for him. Rhike had already passed out, so maybe he was telling the truth. Trolt was facing the girls, a chilling grin entering his face. One of the doors of the empty cells was opened by Lela; she had her wand at the ready and Irora with her dagger. Austin guessed they were trying to trap their old teacher. The troll clapped his hands, and everything seemed to shift. Lela took her shot, aimed her wand and sent a blast towards the troll, but it seemed to fade halfway, like it just disintegrated into thin air. The troll had created some sort of forcefield. Blue mist curled around everyone's feet and transported them like they were in some other dimension.

Chapter 17
The Prophecy Complete

The concrete hallway was now no longer blared with the red flashing alarm. The blue mist spread throughout the whole room, and Austin felt a change in himself, almost like he was lighter, more fluid; it felt like he was in a dream-like state, except he wasn't in control, but his path was set. Fortunately, Weatherson must've felt exactly the same confused look shown on his face. Lela tried firing her wand again, but it wasn't working. The moment of confusion and hesitation from Weatherson was quickly dismissed, and he fired his flail in almost slow motion. Austin found himself also slowed down; the only one that seemed unaffected was Trolt, who was now laughing, his back towards Austin. In a dodge, Austin leapt from the spot where Weatherson aimed and landed on the troll's back, breaking his concentration and momentarily bringing them back to reality, which was enough time for Irora to send herself towards Weatherson and combat him. Lela stayed focused on Trolt, the bigger threat here; no one knew exactly what he was capable of. Austin wrestled Trolt to the ground, holding the troll's hands behind his back and trying to prevent him from creating the forcefield again. Austin realised too late that the troll wasn't even fighting back; instead, he was focused and began to glow. In a split-second, Austin was pushed off in an energy blast radiating from the troll himself. It was so unusual that a magical creature didn't use a wand to control magic. Magic was often unpredictable without a medium like a wand is controlling it; Austin thought back to one of Mr Davon's first classes of the semester. Nonetheless, Mr Trolt seemed to have mastered the art of magic, only relying on himself. Austin landed against one of the glass windows; his will had just about given up. He landed on his still open wound and was no match for the troll. The troll clapped again and made no mistake of being arrogant and making sure he saw each of his opponents. They were warped back into this twisted reality. Austin felt hopeless as he watched as Lela was lifted like a ragdoll by some imaginary force and locked into the open cell. Weatherson looked pretty battered up and bruised after Irora was done with him, but she was plucked away from him before she could finish the kill. The troll simply tossed her into the cell with Lela then took to Weatherson himself, levitating him to the ceiling and then forcibly dropping him, which caused a loud thud. The middle-aged man laid still, not even a twitch. Austin wondered if he was dead or just unconscious.

"Now, Austin, I thought you would've put up more of a fight, seeing as you had both of your girlfriends at stake. I will enjoy torturing them right in front of you." The troll's face contorted into a twisted smile. Austin was fighting back tears; the pain searing through his body was beginning to be unimaginable, and most of all, they had lost. His euphoric sentimental moment of reunification was gone. Austin's vision started to blur; the blue filter was straining his eyes; it felt as if it was weakening his whole body.

"Oh, I have been waiting to see that look on your face. You are so much less than you were made out to be. And to think that I was originally scared of you." He began to laugh. "You were so easily manipulated, just like your father."

"I don't understand why are you doing this? Why help us with the ritual and slowly point us in the right direction? Why didn't you just kill me before when you found me in the forest?"

"Poor, poor Austin; what you can't seem to understand is that there are greater forces at play than you and me. Fate and the sacred timeline. I have been playing to the rules of the game, letting the prophecy unravel as best as I could, manipulating it all under my own vision. I can't change the prophecy. Even if I killed you, some other all-powerful wizard would rise to power. I just had to let it pan out. You actually surprised me a bit; you were supposed to be the one doing the ritual. You weren't meant to survive the dreamcatcher ritual. See, if you had died in that dream realm, the prophecy would've died with you. As long as nothing intervened on Earth with the prophecy, the rest is free game. But Hurt insisted on being the one that entered that tub."

Everything was adding up. Austin hated himself for trusting Trolt so much that he felt stupid. "How are you doing all this? Why now!"

"Austin, I am a troll of nature and organic powers. I wouldn't want to upset the spirits by pre-emptively breaking fate or the prophecy. So I waited until the timing is right, I waited for the blood moon. I have studied the prophecy longer than you have been alive, and I have seen to it that all the necessary events have occurred, and now it's time that I take over. As for this…" He motioned to his makeshift world. "A gift of my ancestors. You wizards are so naive thinking that your magic outpowers the ones of nature. I have been practising for years in these tunnels before anyone even knew my name. Before I met Tony or became the mayor. This is my birth right to practise this magic and keep it alive, and I can't do that when the wizards want to eradicate all ancient forms of magic because it has been deemed too powerful and is now forbidden. I can't even practise in the real world at sites that would make my magic more powerful. I am restricted to Hylenia. Treated like a second-class citizen. No control; my heritage is taken from me. Well, I say it's my turn to have power, and there will no longer be a separation of worlds. The countries of the world will all turn to me as their leader as soon as they see what I can do. They are all destroying my planet, burning it to the crisp, all for money. PHHH. Deforestation, coal mining, POLLUTION! Humans are careless and expendable. If they aren't going to do anything about saving the environment and neither is Hylenia because they want to keep the peace between the two races, then it's up to me. When your father finally figured it out, he actually wanted to stop it. Betray his own partner? Isn't that right?" He turned to the glass. He opened the door, and the man attempted to charge but was flung right next to Austin and held in place.

"Because peace is more important. Wizards never truly understand the repercussions of dissing Mother Nature. In some ways, they are as good as the humans. So it is time to reinvent the world in my image, a place where humans and wizards don't have so much power. Where the world is in a stable balance."

"Well, what about all the people in that gathering of yours? Most of them are wizards?" targeted Austin.

"Ohhh please, half of them don't even know why they are attending; they are just pawns for me. Their resources are very valuable, and I promised them money and power, much like my deal with Weatherson. I needed intel, and they were all so quick to give it up and sacrifice everything, turning on themselves, and when the time is right, they are expendable." He pointed his wand at the collapsed officer.

"You are willing to sacrifice so many precious lives! You are evil!" Tony blurted out.

"It's all for the greater good."

"Why the kidnappings?" Austin asked.

"The spell book is really just a sacrifice to fate; it will allow me to do whatever I want as long as I have Mother Nature on my side. Twist things to my own design just enough. It would've given me everything I needed to break down the barriers of Hylenia and start on my rampage; it's pure power, that is why I needed to sacrifice only the most powerful wizards of the generation. Now let's play through the events of the prophecy, shall we?" He didn't give Austin time to answer.

"'Two angel-blooded being separated in thunder.' Check." He pointed at Irora and Austin.

"'The new world will yield to the one who holds the power.' Contrary to most beliefs, it isn't the chosen one but little old me."

"'The big war arose full of plunder.'" He went on as this was self-explanatory.

"'The chosen one goes forth to scower.' Well, here you are"—he hesitated—"scowering."

"'Ancient ones arising from the dawn of the first era.' The ents, the Vorhiëns and the Western Wolf Pack; it actually wasn't so hard to convince them. All I did was say it was their time to shine. They had always been so scared of the council since they had been abolished and sent away, but the council has grown weak, no longer able to control them."

"'The shadowed ones will come and bring terror.' The Western Wolf Pack doing my bidding."

"'It begins with the creation of the first chimera.' When Westbrook was first founded by the siblings, they created Rhicon, the first chimera. I'm sure you both know the story."

"'When it comes into contact with the element bearer.' And I believe that has all occurred."

"You know, it has been so easy dodging the blame for these past years. Framing your dad and many others and now the vice principal. I can just see the headline: 'Chosen one killed at the hands of his vice principal.'" The cruel smile surfaced again. "With the connections I have made, it has all been too easy; all I needed to do was fight a few teenagers. Sorry for this next part." The troll aimed with Lela's wand, which he had picked up. The tip began to spark, and it turned a deep blue. Austin couldn't watch; he turned his head and waited for the strike. The powerful attack was very loud, but Austin didn't feel it hit him. *This has got to stop happening.* He opened his eyes and smelled the smouldering flesh; the beam had hit his father. Finally, Austin had reunited with his father, and now he was is going to die anyway, and he will never get the chance to reconnect. The troll re-aimed the wand, this time directly at Austin. He watched Lela and Irora helplessly bang against the glass, but they were trapped, probably sealed to a worse fate than him. The tip began the spark again and build up power. He held onto his dad's body and stared right at Trolt; he had accepted defeat. Who was he to fight an army with 20 years of planning whilst he had only three months of training? He thought he could change the world because the council had inflated his ego by giving him a formal title, but he was a novice. The power exited the wand; Austin saw it happen in slow motion, the energy shooting towards him at a fast pace, thrusting forward, and right before it hit his face, it burst away an invisible shield, taking the brunt of the blast. The heat singing in Austin's face, but it was over after a second. Mr Trolt saw what Austin didn't, re-aimed his wand at the far side of the corridor and struck three times. The three short blasts were deflected just as easily. Mrs Rimesdome appeared, dressed in her councilwoman outfit, having changed since the excursion. She wore a runic charm around her neck on a necklace. Austin recognised the symbol, and it was a defensive charm voiding any natural spells on the environment. She was unaffected by the blue field that was wearing down Austin's senses.

"I have been preparing for you!" the woman shouted as she marched forward. The rune glowed an orange colour; she seemed to have a yellow bubble around her. She started into a sprint, her wand at the ready and deflecting more strikes until she got within a metre of Mr Trolt, when he pulled his biggest move yet. He tossed the wand to the ground and pushed his hands, outstretched palms, facing Mrs Rimesdome, eyes closed. The air escaped Austin's lungs. Trolt had control over the whole field besides Mrs Rimesdome. Austin's body began to pulse the pressure building up on his body without any air. He was suffocating. Trolt then created a weapon out of thin air; a blue mist whip curled between his two hands and struck Mrs Rimesdome's chest and struck the rune, breaking it in half. Her yellow bubble depleted, and Austin saw the fear in her eyes, panic setting in and the air escaping her. She let out one final blow: an orange blast, almost a fireball-like, and she leapt with it and landed in a wrestling match with the troll. The blue field faded without Trolt's concentration, Austin gasped for air. The two wrestled for power, although Mrs Rimesdome was far superior in height and weight. Trolt's powers rose to its full potential, and they glowed within a white field. He blinked from existence teleporting away, whilst Mrs

Rimesdome was left covered in white energy, a look of confusion on her face. The white power began circling uncontrollably and began moving faster around her, more and more unstable. The glow was beginning to be too bright. Austin looked away, knowing what was about to happen. Mr Trolt had placed some sort of curse on her. Mrs Rimesdome looked at Austin and the everyone else. "Austin, I'm sorry I couldn't protect you enough." Her eyes were holding back tears. "You get out of here with Caleb and those girls and release that poor man" She hesitated. "I will stay here with your father," Austin could read the impression on her face she didn't think she could withstand this curse. "I promise you I will be fine. I will find a way out with your father." She tried to comfort Austin. "Now go there isn't the time!" Austin followed her instructions letting the other hostage go and he ran away not one word. Then he felt the shock of the blast it was very sudden. It must've been one of the explosives that Irora rigged up. Austin thought she was bluffing. She really wasn't the old Irora Austin finally came to the conclusion, she was someone unrecognisable. Cracks and fissures appeared on the ceiling. Austin acted on instincts and released the lock on the door and left with Irora and Lela, one on either side of him. Austin knew that Irora's bombs would bring the place to a rubble any minute now if she wasn't lying. They had to get out of there fast, but they couldn't leave Caleb, who had been passed out the whole fight, waiting for death. Irora picked him up and lay most of his weight on her, and Austin did the same, even though he could barely hold his own weight, but he didn't complain. Austin's eyes welled with tears. They backtracked their steps at a running pace. Austin looked back at his dad for one last time next to Weatherson. Mrs Rimesdome standing over the top of them, the curse seeming to grow more powerful there was clear strain on her face. He wept as he ran. Bits of the ceiling were already falling in chunks. Austin then heard another bomb, but he had no idea from what direction, but they had to stay on their path. It was their only choice. Another moment later, a third bomb went off and then another. A massive boulder of dirt collapsed from the ceiling, blocking their path. Lela, who had retrieved her wand from the corridor, raised the piece high enough for all of them to crawl underneath it. Austin couldn't even guess how heavy and difficult that must've been, but it was no time to compliment, just run. They had to jump over a few crevices and dodge the collapse of the tunnel system as they heard more and more bombs going off. All these timed detonations were a low rumble and strategically placed. It was terrifying, but surely, they made it to the exit and ran up and collapsed into the museum where their tour had begun. First responders were quick to rescue them. Someone took Caleb on a stretcher away from Austin and Irora, and Austin just knew he would be in good hands and survive. Austin noticed all his friends safe; all in the back of some emergency vehicle. Ena had not left Beatrice's side. All the hostages were also being attended to. Austin couldn't keep his eyes open any longer and collapsed and let the chaos sort itself out. It was no longer his problem.

Chapter 18
Resolutions

Austin woke up in a doctor's room; this time not in Peggy's room but a hospital in the heart of the capital. Several other beds lined out with patients all from various battles. Some were in police uniforms, some in casual clothes; the only thing everyone had in common was that everyone had some sort of serious injury. Austin saw broken limbs not yet attended to, burn marks and one man had an arrow in his shoulder. A TV blared in the background on a news channel broadcasting the distress of the capital at major fighting junctions. The TV flicked through a few images of buildings completely collapsed, the ground thick with ash and many victims with multiple wounds limping around. Everywhere was chaos, although the underground tunnel network was just ground zero. Many of the photos showed deep potholes and crevices in major roads, some cars fallen through many car accidents, apparent little fires rampaging everywhere with no one tending to them. Another patient, a gruff man in the army uniform, was awake next to him. "What battle were you in, kid, caught at one of the intersection car pileups?" the man said smugly, then continued about his story. "I was in the biggest surface battle, defending the capitol building and all the council members. A battle we won."

"Actually, I was fighting in the tunnel systems, defending and freeing the hostages and preventing the Other Side from gaining too much power and personally fought their leader, Mr Trolt."

"Damn, son, that is pretty badass," the guy said, bewildered. "I saw you come in here with a lot of injuries; those are some battle scars. You were a top priority; you're lucky you didn't succumb to your wounds."

Nurses filtered through patients and buzzed around; they were all clearly very tired and working overtime. From what Austin could see on the screen, the battle had been mostly won and was very sudden and quick. The fighting was done after a day. The Other Side was vastly outnumbered on the surface but still managed to tally a large number of casualties on Hylenias's side. Austin thought about his dad and everyone else who sacrificed their lives for the greater good and how they all just became a number to the news. The concept of death had never really resonated with Austin, but now, it was so close to him, he felt a hollowness and felt shallow, even though he was still in bed. He wasn't too bothered by his injuries, although they were still painful. A nurse named Jeff came in and checked all of Austin's vitals and offered Austin some painkillers, which Austin took promptly.

"Some news from the doctor, we were unable to seal the wound on your back for over 12 hours since the original injury, and we are afraid that there will be a scar left after it's fully healed. We did our best, but we can't leave it scarless after so long after the injury," the nurse said, his head down, writing a few things on a notepad. "One more thing. We will move you to a recovery room since you have had all your operations, and now all you need to do is heal. Is there anyone I can contact? Mother? Father?"

"Yes. Mother, Natalie Bolden." He gave Jeff his mother's contact details. "And can you check the system for Lela Bishop and a Caleb Rhike? I want to know if they are okay?"

The nurse went away for a minute and returned with answers. "I have contacted your mum; she is on the way, and Lela will be in your new room as a visitor, which is Room 113. There is no record of Caleb Rhike in the system. After 30 minutes, Austin was moved to a private room, and shortly after that, he was joined by Lela, whose right arm was in a cast, and she had stitches on her forehead, but she was just as beautiful as ever. She joined him on his bed; they sat there in silence for a minute, just embracing each other, before Lela broke the silence. "I'm sorry about your dad."

"I am too; I always dreamt of rescuing him and spending time with him, but I never thought our time would be cut so short. It's not fair; I only just found him." Austin sighed; he needed a distraction. "Do you know what happened to Rhike?"

"He is at Westbury Hospital with most of the others; we were split up, taken to one of the two hospitals. They said that he should be okay."

"Nurses said I will be able to go tomorrow morning; they just want to monitor me overnight to see if there are any fluctuations."

"I will arrange for the school bus to pick everyone up then," she said with a smile; even now she was still acting like the responsible leader. They spent the rest of the night watching crappy reality TV. It was a false sense of happiness, and it entertained them, and for a moment, they almost felt like normal teens on a normal day. They ignored their current problems, just laughing at the corny jokes on the TV.

****

They left the hospital at 7:30 in the morning in clothes bought from the hospital giftshop.

Lela wore a simple pink tee with a print of a stuffed brown bear and love heart balloons. Austin wore a blue tee with a print of seven different types of sports balls. Charlie was also at their hospital with them and joined them as the bus pulled in. He was mostly cleaned up; he didn't have too many abrasions in sight, but he still walked on a bit of a limp. Regardless, he still had a smile and was just happy to be there. The three of them walked onto the bus and got a cheer from the whole grade and pats on the backs, in Austin's case, on the shoulder, as they walked past the aisle all the way to the back of the bus with their friends. Beatrice sat in a foetus position, her legs pushed up to her chest as she looked out the window, and Ena was beside her, with a concerned look. Lela sat in between Ena and Wendy, who sat next to Jarred. Charlie sat in the next row with Unity, and Austin sat next to Frederico. Carter, Jack and Riona led the cheer for Austin and his friends and said a little speech each about the loss of Mr Bert, Mrs Rimesdome and Mr Bolden. The bus was silent most of the way back, not as filled with life like on the way to the city centre. As they neared the school, Lela got a message, and she shot right up. "Mr Hurt has been released on all charges!" The school bus cheered again. The school bus chatter started again, and everything seemed to go back to normal. They entered the school through the front gate, and everyone filed out; the whole school cheered them on as everyone went into their buildings. Many parents were waiting for their kids' arrival. Austin's mum was no exception. She was joined by Irora, who was awfully quiet; maybe her amnesia was irreversible. Austin ran up to his mum and gave her a big hug; it had been a bit since they had seen each other last, and Austin had not left on good terms. He was just glad to be with her again.

"Mum, I'm so sorry about Dad."

"It's okay; it will be okay," Natalie said, not sure if she was convincing herself or her son. Lela and Beatrice came by and stood beside Austin. "Mum, this is Lela and Beatrice." Austin made the introductions through weepy eyes. Lela kissed him on the cheek and made eye contact before leaving Austin with his mum and Irora to have time to make a decision. He saw the look in Lela's eyes; he had to make a decision tonight about the Irora thing. It must've been tearing her apart. Beatrice gave Natalie the tour of the school to the other two girls it must've changed quite bit since his mom went here. It was all so confusing to Austin; he was just thankful that Lela was so patient with him. While Irora and Natalie were browsing the school and talking, Beatrice came up to Austin.

"I'm sorry about your dad."

"I'm sorry about your dad." She held Austin's hand; she was quite small for her age. The height difference was almost comical, but she made up for that with ferocity. Now though, she let her guard down and hugged Austin. "I have to get back to Ena's room. I will leave you guys. Bye."

Austin started walking to his mum and his ex and overheard a bit of their conversation.

"You can stay at my house as long as you need. I know you don't know who I am, but I want to help you in any way possible," Natalie said to Irora.

"Where are my parents?"

"They spent ages searching for you, but ultimately, they moved to the regular world. I believe they are living in London. I have tried contacting them, but it is a bit difficult between the two realms. We will find them together," Natalie finished up as Austin approached.

"You know, maybe you could even enrol here. I know you don't really know what this place is, but your past self really loved this school and always wanted to enrol." Austin struck a nerve. His ex's face was strained with concentration, but she just shrugged. Austin couldn't imagine not knowing anything about your past. It would make trusting everyone ten times harder. They all approached and entered Austin's simple wooden room. Irora went to take a shower, leaving Austin and his mum to talk.

"Something I still don't get is how Mrs Rimesdome found us?" Austin asked.

"Austin give me your wand." He did as she said.

She fiddled around a bit and finally found what she was looking for at the bottom end of the wand; a detachable part came undone, and a little chip fell out. A tracker.

"Austin, I'm so sorry I never told you about anything, but everything I ever did was to protect you; that is why we lived in a small town away from prying eyes. You are so special, Austin, because you are a descendant of all four houses. The houses all hate each other, and it's so rare for them to intermingle. Your father was a Terra-Killian-born wizard and me, a Venus-Destiny-born wizard. It is said that those with genetics from all four siblings retain some of the gifts of the original siblings. The dreams you have been telling me about are something philosophers have hypothesised as a gift of Destiny. You are 100% pure wizard, Austin. A true-born wizard, which is rare enough, but like Terra, you are also an elemental bearer. You will grow to be such a strong wizard. But for now, please stick within these walls, continue with your friendships, no more quests or anything dangerous because I couldn't bear to lose another one of my boys. That is why I have had the Rhikes keep close contact with you and made sure Rimesdome has been very protective. Me and her used to go to school together, as well as your dad and the Rhikes. The original five."

They continued to talk until Irora came out, and then they got her dressed in some of Austin's clothes, which were all way too oversized, but they needed to make it to the emergency assembly; there were rumours about a new vice principal. Austin made a note to drop by Ena's to get some spare clothes; he didn't want to ask Lela. His mind was still skewed, and his emotions were all very strong. If you had asked Austin the question: "If you found Irora, would you date her again?", six months ago, he would've said yes in a heartbeat, but now, everything is so much more complicated. He still had feelings for her that never went away, but there was something that didn't seem right. All three made their way into the assembly room, where they were serving breakfast.

Principal Dark, dressed in black, a mourner's outfit, addressed the students and gave a simple recap of the loss of the past vice principal. "We will have a memorial for the late vice principal, but for now, regular classes will be postponed until tomorrow, considering exams are next week. We understand that this may be a challenge for some students, so we will have exemptions for the sophomore class. We will have a new vice principal, which some of you may already know: Kiara Clark." As the new vice principal, Clark entered the stage; there was some weeping and some cheering. Many mixed emotions, but Austin just knew Mrs Clark from his one meeting with her, in which she had accused him of betraying the trust of the council. The previous school counsellor talked about how she was excited about the new position and formally went about her condolences. A bitter-sweet day.

"One more thing, everyone. We have recovered the spell book, and we have upped security and security profiling on all staff and students, so nothing like this can ever happen again. Please note that there is nothing to be afraid of, and that the Other Side is dormant for now. Even though this is the harshest attack in 100 years, we believe that we can keep our students safe within these walls, so more restrictions will be placed for safety reasons in these tough times, and we will slowly ease when the council deems everything safe." Mrs Clark excused the assembly, and everyone broke up.

Austin noticed Phillip Rhike approach him and his mum. "Hi, Austin. Hi, Natalie." The man hugged his mum, then extended his hand to Austin's for a handshake. "I just want to say thank you for helping my brother; we have been keeping an eye on you, and I know we haven't always seen eye to eye, but I am forever grateful. We were the ones supposed to be watching over you, and you were really protecting us, funny. We see that you are perfectly fit to protect yourself. I am resigning after this semester; it's up. Best of luck, kiddo." He walked away. The rest of the day, Austin spent catching up with his mum and showing her around and introducing her to people, and Austin also met a fair share of parents himself. Parents day came early this year.

****

Austin had finished his final midyear exam yesterday; he could have never passed without Leslie's help. His semester was eventful, and he made a vow to keep studying more next semester. He thanked Leslie with a coffee and talk sit down session to just talk after all that she had done for him. Austin had heard that Charlie had rejected her, not for any reason but just not wanting to be in a relationship. He had felt bad telling her to go for it just so she could get her heart broken. "Hey, I know you really liked Charlie; anyone would be lucky to have you."

"Thanks, but a gal's got to get her heart broken a few times before she can figure out what she really wants. It's fine." She was so calm about it when Austin had still been figuring out what to do about his situation. He had already told Lela that he was only in love with the old Irora and had no interest in the new and improved Irora 2.0, but something still felt wrong, and Austin knew Lela felt it too. He had been procrastinating having the conversation; the jitters had been eating him up from the inside. They finished up their coffee, and Austin went looking for Lela. He was walking through the hallways when he bumped into someone familiar, Mr Hurt.

"Thank you, Austin. Thank you. Some part of me felt I deserved it for not looking after her well enough, but I heard a voice talk to me; it was her, and she told me to fight, and I couldn't have fought my way out of the system without yours and the Pacifist Club's help, so thank you," the man said with a smile on his face. He sure was one weird teacher, very spiritual, but he will always be a teacher at Westbrook, no matter how wacky or misunderstood. Two minutes later, he had reached Lela's door. He stood outside for a few minutes; people passed by him, giving him weird looks. To them, it would look like Austin was frozen in time, but he was building up the courage to knock. Somehow, with all the fighting and the events of the past six months, this was the scariest part yet. He was about to knock; he had his hand in the fist position, and right before it hit, the door swung inwards. Ena opened the door, giving Austin a knowing half-smile and walked out. Austin walked in, and Lela was sitting in a cross-legged position, facing away from him by her desk, a light drawn over her as she drew on a canvas. Art supplies sprawled over the whole table, anything Austin could think of.

"I didn't know you could draw, and you're good at it too," Austin said, slowly walking up to her. There was something calming about her room; it was cosy. Austin had been here a handful of times, but now, it felt different; something was missing.

"Yeah, I mostly keep it to myself, but Ena sometimes keeps me company while I draw; it's a boring and a long process to anyone around me while I do it."

She didn't look back but continued on her work. "I don't know how to begin this." He walked up to her and massaged her shoulders.

"I don't know either."

"You are an amazing person and the best girlfriend. I have grown to love the little things about you. The way your hair bounces when you move, your fierce attitude, leading the Pacifist Club, the cute pendant earrings that you always wear, showing you aren't afraid to show yourself. I fell in love the first day I met you. You have always been so sure of yourself, and you let me into your friend's group like you had known me forever. We have been through so much together;

there is now real history, and it feels wrong ending it, but it also feels wrong continuing. I still love you, but something is different."

She turned around, and Austin now understood why she hadn't faced him; she was crying. "I love you too. This will never truly end; the chemistry is there, but the circumstances have changed, and that isn't anyone's fault. I think we just need time to rethink what we need in a relationship and take a step back and look at everything without a bias."

"So that's it. We are taking a break," Austin said. Lela stood up and hugged him, her head on his shoulder. She pulled away and went back to her drawing; she drew a horizon. "But still friends." Austin was familiar with it; it was the lake view from the Mertamic Port, drawn to eerie details. "What are you drawing?"

"Just a view I had in mind; it's sort of calming; it's the perfect combination of storm and calm."

"Are you sure you have never seen this before?"

"What are you going on about?"

"That is the Mertamic Port," Austin said dully. Although he hadn't been there since that night, he still remembers every detail, and Lela just drew it out. Austin thought about it, but it was too great a coincidence. They looked at each other concerningly, but Austin gave up on the strangeness of it all, for today, at least. He walked out of the room and to his room. It was the last day of this semester before the break; there was a weird calm anxiety to it all. He had made plans to go out and see Ethan for a few days and then go back to Mertamic for a bit, the rest left to his choice when the time came. He was going to do some serious catching up with Irora. Austin's body was still caffeinated, and he was not feeling sleepy at all, yet so many things were running on his mind, but he finally gave way to his sleep. He had spent the previous nights with barely any sleep, just studying last minute. So today, he was going to have the biggest sleep. Another dream flooded his mind. He was in a seemingly never-ending room, an electric current running through the water on the floor, which extended as far as the eye could see. The water was only ankle-height, but it stung his whole body in a dreamlike way. The floor was a cold, exposed concrete with grey columns every four metres. The room was the same in every direction he ran in. The same room, the same water, the same harsh white lighting. The longer he ran, the more pointless it became. Austin knew he was in a dream, but he felt like he needed to find something; something was tugging at him. Until he finally saw an outlier to the pattern: an exposed wire, just two wires extending out of a column, harmless little things, one red and one black. Austin went and grabbed one in each hand and was immediately shocked to the ground and fried in the water. Austin woke startled; sweat covered his bed; he was actually wet. His dreams were becoming stronger. He looked at his suitcases, still packed everything the way he left it before he went to sleep. His mind was playing tricks on him.